MW00801064

The Haunting of Destiny Dove

KELLY ABELL

This is a work of fiction. Names, characters, places, and incidents are products of the author's imagination or are used fictitiously and are not to be construed as real. Any resemblance to actual events, locations, organizations, or persons, living or dead, is entirely coincidental.

World Castle Publishing, LLC
Pensacola, Florida
Copyright © Kelly Abell 2022
Hardback ISBN: 9798839358898
Paperback ISBN: 9781958336434
eBook ISBN: 9781958336441
First Edition World Castle Publishing, LLC, July 18, 2022
http://www.worldcastlepublishing.com
Formerly Titled Haunted Destiny
Licensing Notes
All rights reserved. No part of this book may be used or reproduced in any manner whatsoever without written permission, except in the case of brief quotations embodied in articles and reviews.
Cover: Karen Fuller
Editor: Erik Johnston

PROLOGUE

Frosthaven, Connecticut 1815

Enya awoke gasping and coughing. The moonlight streaming through the window created an eerie haze in the cloud of thick smoke in her room. Confused, she slipped from her bed and yelped when the hot floor burned her bare feet. She squinted, trying to see through the smoke, but tears blurred her vision.

"Enya! Open the door," her father yelled.

Oh dear Lord, what has he done? "I can't get to the door, Father. The floor is too hot." She coughed again, choking on the thick smoke. She had to find a way out. "Where are Mother and Shane?"

Her father pounded on the door again. "Let me in, you wench. I can't get to you through a locked door."

Her father slammed his body into the door, and Enya jumped, but the latch held firm. Her thoughts rushed at her all at once, fear chilling her despite the heat. He had not said, "get you out." He'd said, "get to you." Her heart hammered. His folly with drink had caught up with him again. It didn't matter that her father, the Honorable Judge Frost, was one of the most prominent men in town. When the drink took over, he became as mean and low as any of the criminals he'd put behind bars. She had to get to Shane and her mother.

Enya moved into action. Bracing for the burning pain, she dropped to the floor on her hands and knees and scrambled to the door. Her long, wool nightgown protected her knees from the hot, sticky varnish coating on the floorboards, but not her hands. Pieces of skin tore from her palms on her fast trek to the door. Without thinking, she reached up and grabbed the copper knob. Her flesh seared, and a scream ripped from her parched throat, drawing even more smoke into her lungs. Cradling her hand, she crumpled to the floor.

"I can't open it," she cried. "It's too hot."

A spasm of coughing shook her body. She couldn't open the door from inside, and her father couldn't break it in. Relief warred with terror. Was burning to death better than facing her drunken father? Sweat broke out on her forehead and trickled down her back. All she could hear was the roaring of her own blood rushing through her ears. If it weren't for her mother and brother, Enya would jump out the window. A broken leg would be far better than being on fire and far better still than facing her father's wrath. How many times had she borne the bruises from his unjustified abuse?

She had to find her brother and mother. How long could they last in this smoke and heat? As if summoned by her thoughts, an angry storm of the thick, black smoke rolled under the door.

Time had run out.

"Get Shane and Mother," she shouted above the roar of the flames. "I'll try to get out the window and jump down."

"I've already taken care of them. Open the damn door. The smoke is choking me to death."

His angry voice struck fresh terror in Enya's heart. What did he mean, taken care of them?

She glanced around, hunting for another way out. Smoke swirled about the room, thinning just long enough for her to see the little angels carved in the French Rococo mirror on her dresser.

"Oh little angels, spare our souls," she offered up in prayer.

Wrapping her nightgown around her burned hand, she yanked back the bolt and turned the scorching knob.

The door burst inward along with an enormous back draft fed by the oxygen that remained in the room. Her father, engulfed in flames, stumbled across the threshold. She screamed at the sight of her father on fire and scrambled to pass him, but he grabbed the edge of her nightgown. She peered over her shoulder, gasping and frozen in place as shock rippled through her. Her father didn't scream, even as flames ate away at his body. He yanked her close, singeing her hair with the blaze that licked his clothes.

She screamed again, fighting with all her strength. "Let me go!"

The hem of her gown caught fire, burning her legs. She kicked and scratched, but still, he held her.

"Finally, I have you, you Irish witch. You were always trouble. I should have drowned you the day you were born." He leaned in, arms tightening around her, searing her skin. His raspy whisper chilled her blood. "Now you're going to pay. With your mother and brother gone, you have no one left to save."

Enya shrieked. She yanked to free herself from his death grip. The scorching pain seared through to her very soul. He only held her tighter to him and swiveled them both to face the mirror. A blast of hot air stirred the smoke enough for her to see their ghastly reflection.

"Look at yourself, Enya. Are you proud now? You've killed your mother and brother, and now you and I will spend eternity together in a fiery grave."

The mirror revealed her smoky bedroom with her and her father being swallowed by the crimson and orange blaze.

"NO!" Enya jerked her head from the horrifying sight.

He yanked her hair, twisting her head until she faced the mirror. Despair overwhelmed her. All the years of fighting this horrible man to protect what she loved had ended. Her prayers to the angels would go unanswered tonight.

"You know, it's ironic that you'd die from the very element you were named after. So watch, you witch," he growled. "Watch while we burn."

She did watch, and what she saw in that mirror was more terrifying than the flames scorching her skin. Her father changed. Boney protrusions pierced the skin on his forehead and the hands that held her formed into talons which pierced her arms, keeping her anchored against his morphing body. His face, oh dear sweet Lord, his face formed into a twisted combination of goat and bull with jagged teeth. The last thing she experienced in her short, innocent life was the sulfurous stench of his breath and his demonic laugh.

CHAPTER ONE

Arcadia, Florida
Present Day

Destiny Dove and her family left Naples for Orlando that night, the rain pelting the car with big, fat drops. They'd gotten a late start because her mother had a headache and her father had worked too late. Excitement about reaching Disney World consumed her. What a wonderful, magical place. She'd only been one other time, and now they had eighteen-month-old Elijah, probably too little to remember the trip, but he would have fun anyway. She tugged a mirror from her purse, snapped on the overhead light and checked her hair. Rain always frizzed the dark locks, but it appeared that maybe this time, the straightener's work was holding. Her hair hung past her shoulders, held back from her face with one sparkling clip. She'd had trouble with her eyeliner that morning, but now it ringed her green eyes with slate gray precision. Digging out the lip-gloss, she swiped it across lips she thought were too thin. Her mom always told her she was pretty, but Destiny still didn't quite see it. The make-up helped a lot, but at fifteen, what girl really thought she was all that pretty? She snapped the mirror closed and shut off the light.

Her mother started a round of "Ninety-Nine Bottles of Beer On the Wall," and Destiny glanced at Elijah and laughed. He didn't know the words, but he sang anyway in his sweet baby voice. Without warning, her mother's song morphed into a scream. Cursing, Destiny's father yanked the wheel as the car skidded sideways. He fought to wrestle the van under control. The back end slid, and he overcorrected.

Flipping, the van rolled over and over, rattling Destiny's brain in her skull. She fought the battle with nausea and lost. When the van came to a stop on its roof, the abrupt silence startled her.

She hung upside down from her seat belt in the dark. Swiping a hand across her dirty mouth, she called, "Mom? Dad?" They didn't answer.

Elijah screamed. Destiny blinked, trying to adjust her eyes to the darkness. She peered over at her brother and spied something wet covering his head. *Oh God, he's bleeding.*

Disoriented, Destiny struggled to find the seat belt latch.

Elijah screamed, "De-ne-ne!"

She struggled harder with the belt buckle and eventually found the button. The strap flew back, dropping her onto the roof of the car. Ignoring the pain, she scrambled to her baby brother.

She yanked at the buckle. "It's going to be okay, Baby Bro," she soothed. "Sissy's going to get you out. Just hang on."

She tugged until pain radiated through her shoulder blades. Panic led to desperation as she couldn't see through the dark smoke. She yanked harder as thick smoke filled the cabin. Elijah kept screaming, and finally, it occurred to Destiny to just release the entire seat. She wrapped both arms around the plastic safety seat, searching for the buckle that held it in place.

Then, a pair of large hands closed around her ankles and yanked her away from him. *No! No! No! I almost have him.* "Wait!" Destiny screamed. She fought back, kicking out, her foot connecting with what must have been a nose. "I can't leave without my baby brother," she yelled again.

The person continued to jerk at her legs, finally pulling Destiny through the window. "Let me get you out first, and then I'll come back for him," he replied, half-carrying, half-dragging her to a safe distance.

Outside the car, Destiny glared at the police officer.

Glancing down, Destiny observed her new white jacket covered with soot, dirt and oil. Her mother would be so mad. Thinking of her mother sent her into a panic. Her parents…where were they? Rain poured into her eyes as she searched frantically for her parents but didn't see them anywhere.

The cop yanked her to her feet, and together they stumbled away from the car. Behind them, a boom resounded through the night. The blast propelled them both into the air, and they crashed to the ground about fifteen feet away. The van lit up in flames, and the acrid odor of burning oil and rubber filled her nostrils.

She ignored her bleeding limbs, scrambled to her feet and shouted, "Elijah!"

Oh God, he was still in there! She took off running back to the inferno that used to be her family's car, but the cop was faster. He tackled her from behind. Again, the pain of bones meeting asphalt rattled through her. *Crap!*

"Elijah!"

"Stop," the cop yelled. "There's nothing you can do. He's gone."

Keeping a tight grip in Destiny's shoulders, the policeman held her until the magnitude of his words sank in. This was his fault. She'd almost had Elijah free, and that creep had pulled her out of the car. Destiny turned and pounded away at the guy with her fists, not caring how hard she hit him or how much it hurt. He was going to pay.

He let her do it. He just let her beat on him until she ran out of strength. Energy spent, Destiny sobbed. Her throat, raw from the smoke she'd inhaled, couldn't compare to the pain in her heart. The big sister was supposed to protect her baby brother at all costs. She had failed. Her parents were going to be furious. She'd had Elijah right there in her hands yet failed to save him.

Gently, the officer steered her over to a waiting ambulance. "Where are my parents?" she sobbed, sitting robotically on the tailgate.

"Let me go take a look," he said. "My name is Paul, by the way. I'll be right back." He gestured to a nearby paramedic. "Let these men here check you over."

Destiny waited at the back of the ambulance, watching the rain sizzle on the burning car that still held her brother inside. *Oh, God.* Grabbing her stomach, she threw up down the side of the ambulance.

A sound that reminded her of a basketball rolling across concrete reached her ears. She lifted her head, curious about the source. Her blood froze, and a scream clogged her throat as a bodiless head tumbled toward the vehicle, wobbling from ear to ear and coming to rest facing Destiny. *Mom!* The eyes were closed, the face covered in blood. She wanted to look away but couldn't.

All of a sudden, the eyes popped open, eyebrows drawn together, skin flushed red.

"You didn't get the baby! You didn't save your brother! Why didn't you get him out of the car? What kind of a sister are you? What kind of daughter are you?"

"I tried!" Destiny yelled back. "The seat belt was stuck, and that cop…he pulled me out before I could get to him."

"That's no excuse," her mother's head accused.

"I tried," Destiny yelled, sobbing. "I tried…."

***

Destiny woke with a scream and kicked at the sheets like a wild animal fighting to free itself from a trap. Sitting up, she banged her elbow on something hard and pointed. Pain radiated down her arm, sending tingles through to her fingertips. She cradled her sore elbow and waited for the nightmare to fade. *Where am I?* The room didn't feel familiar, and she blinked to help her eyes adjust to the darkness.

A beam of moonlight shone through the small window directly on her right and gave her just enough light to see the tiny room. Her bed was flush against the wall, and the nightstand was directly to her right in the cramped space. That explained the banged elbow. She recognized the quilt on the floor that in the light of day was a pale lavender and white, but now in the moonlight, reflected only shades of gray. She pulled it off the floor, straightened the tangled sheets and flopped back onto her pillow. Gradually her upper body relaxed as she took deep breaths and focused on a few water-stained ceiling tiles. She was safe and in her grandmother's mobile home.

"Destiny?" Her grandmother, Rose, rushed into the tiny bedroom and plopped on the edge of the bed. She pulled the teenager's trembling body into her arms. "You were screaming. Was it the nightmare again, honey?"

Destiny stiffened in the arms of the one woman she'd been taught her entire life to fear. She wanted comfort, but everything was still too fresh, still too terrifying. But this old woman was all Destiny had left for a family. Trust was a difficult thing to give, but she was going to have to try.

"I just keep seeing it over and over, Grams. It's like a horror movie that just won't end. I can't get Elijah out of the burning car, and then Mom's head just screams at me…it's just horrible."

Tears rolled down the old lady's wrinkled cheeks. Destiny knew her grandmother felt grief and pain too, but at least she hadn't been in the car when it happened. At least she wasn't an orphan.

"Quiet now, Destiny. It was just a dream. Dreams can be so real, can't they?" She lifted the sobbing teen's face to her own. "There was nothing you could've done to save your mother, father, or Elijah. They barely got you out of the car before it caught fire. I can't begin to tell you how grateful I am that they did!"

Destiny blinked her tears away and gazed up at her grandmother with wet emerald eyes. "I just can't believe they're gone. I miss them so much."

Rose pressed Destiny's head to her breast and held on tighter. "I know you do, sweetheart, so do I. We'll just need to find a way to move through each day one step at a time. It's not easy, but if you let me, I can help you through this. Do you think you can rest now?"

Destiny knew she'd never go back to sleep. She hadn't slept a full night since the accident. When Rose picked her up at the hospital that dreadful night, Destiny hadn't known the woman was her grandmother. When she found out, Destiny was more than wary. Rose and Destiny's mother, Teresa, had parted ways many years ago over the way Rose chose to earn her living. Rose felt that Teresa denied her own destiny, and Teresa thought Rose was crazy. It created a chasm between them that not even the birth of grandchildren could bridge. The day after the accident was the first time Rose and Destiny had seen each other. All Destiny could remember was the portrait her mother painted of Rose, and it was nothing like a sweet little old lady sitting in her rocker with her knitting. It more closely resembled the Wicked Witch in the *Wizard of Oz*.

Not wanting to worry her, Destiny nodded and pushed away from her grandmother's arms. She lay back down on the small bed as Rose tucked the damp sheets and quilt tighter around her body.

Destiny caught the wistful look in her grandmother's faded blue eyes. "You look so much like my Teresa, raven hair and eyes the color of the ocean. We may not've agreed on many things, but I'm glad she left such a wonderful piece of her behind. You get some rest now." Smiling, she backed out of the room and softly closed the door behind her.

Destiny rolled onto her side and tucked her pillow under her head. Her elbow still ached from where she'd slammed it into the nightstand, not surprising since her room was the size of a closet. She couldn't think of it as her room yet. A far cry from what she was used to…the adjustment was just one more thing to cope with.

Here she was, stuck with the woman that her mother referred to as the old crone, the biddy, the bat, and many other unflattering witch names. Destiny never really understood the feud between her mother and grandmother, but it must have been serious for them to have stayed separated for over fifteen years.

To Destiny, Grams Rose didn't seem all that bad. Oh sure, she was a little strange, and she couldn't think of anyone else whose grandmother was the town palm reader or ran a new age book store, but she felt the old woman meant well. She certainly had smothered Destiny with affection since her arrival. She didn't want to seem ungrateful for her Gram Rose's charity, but nothing was the same anymore.

She squeezed her eyes shut and clutched the pillow closer. She had to start over with a new school and new friends. Her stomach clenched. She didn't belong in some backwater town. She belonged in Naples with the finer things in life, like high-end malls and Starbucks.

All that was gone now. Grief poured from her eyes until the first rays of dawn slipped into the room.

CHAPTER TWO

Destiny rested one sneaker-clad foot on the bottom railing of the paddock and watched the five horses graze. A beautiful bay gelding, two appaloosa mares, and two of the biggest Belgians she had ever seen captivated her attention. Sighing, she wished they'd come closer. She loved horses but lacked experience with them. Maybe there were a few perks to living at the back end of a horse farm.

The hot sun blazed down on her bare shoulders, a drop of sweat trickling beneath the rim of her pink tank top. Her white and pink striped shorts stuck uncomfortably to her butt, and she'd pulled her hair into a high ponytail to stay cool. She picked at a splinter of wood. Here she stood…just styling it with the horses, hot pink Converse shoes and all.

Two riders approached on horseback. Not able to identify the breed, she marveled at the way the sun glistened off their shiny black coats. A teen about Destiny's age sat confidently astride one of the horses. She had on jeans, a red tank top, and brown riding boots. The wind caught the girl's long hair, and it streamed out behind her in golden strands.

She gasped as she caught sight of the guy on the other horse. Even at a distance, Destiny could tell he was a hottie. Brown, wavy hair touched his shoulders. A black t-shirt hugged a broad chest and strong biceps, and black jeans strained around powerful thighs as he directed the horse. No hat for this cowboy, but he did have the worn black boots angled into silver stirrups. As they approached, he waved. She raised her eyebrows and glanced over her shoulder, certain someone was behind her, but no…he was waving at her. She waved back.

"Hi," he said.

Oh God, he's even better looking up close. His arms rippled with muscle while he tried to hold the prancing horse still. He had the body of a Greek god.

"Hi," Destiny replied. Little butterflies fluttered in her belly, and all the spit dried up in her mouth. Licking her lips, she caught a hostile glance from the boy's companion.

"I'm Jake Turner, and this is Amy Morgan." He dismounted and came closer.

Amy got off her horse too. When she reached the fence, she made a point of slipping her arm through Jake's, announcing, "I'm his girlfriend."

Destiny sensed the stake that Amy had just driven into the ground. Jake was hers and hers alone. Destiny held her gaze and said, "I'm Destiny Dove. I just moved in." She indicated the mobile home with a jerk of her head.

"Oh, so you're her," Amy said, curling her lip and sniffing. "My mother said someone our age had moved in down here. This is my parents' farm. I live up in the big, white house."

Jake gaped at Amy's rudeness.

Destiny's cheeks flamed. *Great...things are getting off to a great start.* "Yep, that would be me," she said.

"Will you be going to Blake High this fall?" Jake asked, his lips curving.

God, what a great smile. Those dimples, that luscious face. Those perfectly straight teeth. And those eyes! Bluer than the sky.

Amy sized Destiny up with narrowed eyes while shifting from foot to foot, slapping the reins on the fence. Built like a model, Amy was all boobs and no waist, with long slender legs. Destiny could definitely see what kept Jake's attention. Amy thrust her chest out, emphasizing her assets. Destiny struggled not to roll her eyes.

Destiny's gaze shifted back to Jake. "Is that the local high school?"

"Yep. Amy and I will introduce you to some of our friends this summer so you don't feel so alone when you start school."

Amy glared daggers. Becoming annoyed, the normally non-confrontational Destiny often let things slide, but Amy's possessiveness irked her. She couldn't resist needling her a little. She thrust her own chest out, although it was considerably smaller than Amy's, and didn't miss the dip in Jake's gaze. Amy didn't either.

"That would be really sweet," Destiny said, giving him a most charming smile.

Amy's violet eyes—definitely made that color with contacts—actually grew darker, reminding Destiny of a cat ready to pounce on a toy.

"Do you play any sports?" Amy asked.

"I cheered back in my school in Naples," Destiny replied. "Then played a little volleyball. Didn't make the varsity team, though."

"That's cool. Amy, here's a cheerleader. Hey," he jabbed Amy in the ribs with his elbow.

"Ow, Jake," she whined.

"Sorry." He faced Destiny, eyes wide, brows lifted. "Listen, I bet you can still try out for our squad if you want to cheer. The coaches haven't left the school for the summer yet."

"No, Jake," Amy said. "We've picked our squad for next year. We don't need any outsiders coming in and messing everything up."

"Good God, Amy," Jake said, completely missing her anger cues.

Destiny wondered if he was really patient or just really stupid. "No problem," she said. "I'm sure there's no way I can try out to make the cheer squad. I'll try out for something else. But thanks for the suggestion."

Amy smiled, relief flooding her face.

Jake, on the other hand, wouldn't let it go. Rubbing the neck of his horse, he said, "No, I mean it. If you want to cheer, I bet Ms. Ramsey would give you a tryout. They haven't even gone to camp yet. You should call and then go up to the school."

Amy glared at Jake.

Destiny choked back a laugh. "No, that's okay. I don't have a way to get to the school, anyway."

"Oh, well…I could take you."

As soon as the words left Jake's mouth, Destiny's glance flicked to Amy. About to explode, Amy's face reddened, and Destiny expected steam to start rolling out of her ears. If she didn't stop, this Jake would get killed. He seemed like a really nice guy too.

"Thanks, but that's okay. I'll worry about it next year." Destiny rubbed the horse's nose again.

"Well, that would suck, wouldn't it? To miss a whole year of cheering? Let me pick you up in the morning, and I'll introduce you to the coach. We can see if she's willing to give you a tryout. No harm, no foul if she says no. Whaddya say?"

Boy, he's cute, but he sure is thick, Destiny thought but had to admire his persistence. She gave in. "Okay, how about nine?"

"Jake, we were supposed to work out the horses at ten. There's no way you'll be back in time," Amy said with a pout.

"Sure I will. You've got that doctor's appointment anyway, right?"

Amy huffed out a sigh and stomped her booted foot.

Destiny smiled. Busted. She and Jake had a date. Not normally a boyfriend-nabber, she just couldn't resist putting Amy in her place. She offered Amy a smug smile.

"Well, we need to go." Amy mounted her horse, backing him away from the fence.

Jake gave her an annoyed look, then grinned. His mouth was just a little crooked, and Destiny found that immensely charming. "I'll see you in the morning, okay?" He mounted his horse.

"Okay." Destiny returned the smile. "See you then."

They rode back toward the barn, and Destiny headed back up to the trailer, still not thinking of it as home. She bet Amy wouldn't be so high and mighty if she could see could her old home. *Man, what a snob.* It had been hard enough to leave all her stuff behind, but she'd had to leave her friends too. And Amy was the first teen she'd met? Life didn't look too promising. She fought back the tears that stung her eyes.

When she reached the porch, Butch, Grams's golden retriever, lumbered over to her. He bumped her arm with his head, so she scratched his ears. He smelled like a dog, but that was comforting in a way. He didn't care where Destiny came from as long as he got his kibble. Dogs were never judgmental.

"There's a good dog," she said, rubbing his soft golden head. A tear plopped squarely between his eyes, but Butch only whined and licked her.

"I'm glad you're here, boy. From the looks of things, it's going to be a long lonely summer."

"What's the trouble, young 'un? You seem awful sad for such a pretty girl."

Destiny's head snapped up in surprise. A man, as old as or older than her grandmother, stood in front of her. He was wearing a stained white t-shirt, bib overalls and had one dark brown hand in his pocket. He looked like a farmhand. Where had he come from?

"Who are you?" she asked, feeling just a little uneasy.

"They used to call me Patch."

Used to call you? That's strange. "What do you want?"

"I just seen you over here crying and wondered what all the fuss was about."

She watched the dog approach the dark-skinned man. He wagged his tail and barked out a soft woof.

Satisfied, Destiny asked, "Do you work on the horse farm?"

"Yep. Was a trainer. Old man that owned the place used to raise thoroughbreds and race 'em up in Tampa. Don't see too many of 'em around no more, though. Morgan is too busy doctoring to worry much about the horses. He just mostly keeps a few saddle ponies around for his daughter and wife to ride."

It was weird how this man kept referring to himself in the past. "That must have been fun to train racehorses."

"Hard work, Missy. They can be right stubborn at times, but most of 'em are born to run. It's in their blood. I had me a few winners in my day." He remained standing but looked steadily at her. "What's with all the tears?"

"Oh, nothing. I just moved here, and it's been a little tough getting adjusted."

"Ah. That your mom, dad, and brother that died in that car wreck a week or so ago?"

"Yes, how did you know about it?" she asked, surprised.

"Oh, I knows things. I'm real sorry about that. I know that must be hard, losing them and having to move here. Where you from?"

"Naples," wiped a tear away. "I had a nice house there and friends. I was popular, and people liked me. Now I'm here, and I don't know a soul. I don't make friends very easily."

Patch picked up a stray piece of straw and stuck it in his mouth. "Well, now, it looked to me like you was having a right nice chat with those two. I bet you've made two new friends already."

Her glance drifted to the Morgan's barn, where Jake and Amy laughed at something Jake had said. "Who, the football king and his cheerleader girlfriend? Nah. She doesn't seem to want to have anything to do with me. I think she's afraid I'll get my hands on that boyfriend of hers."

The old man chuckled. "I've known Jake Turner's dad a long time, and they're good people. You'll have a friend in Jake. Now, Amy Morgan, on the other hand, might be another story. She's a might spoiled, but she'll probably warm up to you. Don't judge the whole batch on just a few apples." Patch took a few steps, then twisted around to face her again. "Listen, child, I know things seem rough right now, but you give it some time, and I have a feeling you'll have smooth sailing before too long. Just takes time, that's all. Time's a great healer."

Eyes down, Destiny mumbled, "Yeah, I guess." She rubbed the dog's head some more. Butch stood up, forcing her arm to drop to her side. "Where do you live?" Destiny raised her head, and he was gone. Her jaw dropped, and she stepped down off the porch. "Where did he go, Butch?"

He just simply wasn't there. She turned and looked back toward the house, and he wasn't there either. Where did he go? People sure did move fast around here.

CHAPTER THREE

Rose came home from the Mystic Cat, the book and novelty shop she owned, around six that evening. Destiny, having nothing else to do, found the ingredients in the kitchen to make a taco salad. She had the small table for two set with her grandmother's pink plastic dishes and worn out silverware.

"Well now, isn't this nice?" Rose placed her handbag on the chair by the door and walked to the kitchen table. She surveyed Destiny's work with an appreciative smile. "You must have been really bored to have done all of this. Don't get me wrong, it's much appreciated, but it can't be much fun for you stuck out here all summer with no friends to play with."

Destiny rolled her eyes. "I'm too old to play, Grams. It's been okay today. I met two new kids my age."

"Who?" Rose sat at the chair and took a long drink of the cool iced tea Destiny handed her.

"I was standing out by the paddock this morning, and Jake Turner and Amy Morgan rode up on two of the most beautiful horses I've ever seen. They looked like twins, Grams, and black as onyx."

"Samson and Goliath," her grandmother interrupted. "Yes, I'm familiar with those two spitfires. I'm not sure Mr. Morgan should be letting teenagers handle them. They have quite a bit of spirit. I'm afraid Amy might get hurt. I don't worry too much about Jake. He can handle a horse. By cracky, he can. One of the best riders in the county. He's also a pretty good football player. Bright future, that one." She slipped a look at Destiny. "Right, cute too."

Destiny sat down with the bowl of ground beef for the taco salad. She spooned some onto her grandmother's plate, then added some to her own, crumbled tortilla chips on top, and then added cheese, lettuce and tomato. "Yeah, I noticed that, but his girlfriend has a pretty tight hold on him. She made it perfectly clear that he was her man."

Rose laughed a crackly laugh, one that belonged to someone who had smoked all her life. "I bet she does. He's quite a catch. His daddy owns his own horse farm just south of here and owns the town hardware store. Been in his family for years. I think he hoped Jake would grow up to run it one day, but I think he's in for a disappointment. Jake's destined for bigger things. He'll be a good friend to you, though."

That was the same thing the old farmer had said. Destiny hoped so. Jake was really hot. She wouldn't mind getting to know him better at all.

They both chewed in silence for a few minutes before Destiny said, "He offered to take me to the school tomorrow to talk to the cheerleading coach before she leaves for the summer. He thinks they may let me try out and be on the squad. I'm not sure Amy was so thrilled with that idea. I think I might just go to needle her. She's so snooty."

Rose forked more food into her mouth. When she finished chewing, she said, "Destiny, this is really tasty. I wouldn't have thought of putting these ingredients together for a salad." She forked in another mouthful, waggled the utensil in the air, then stopped. Her eyebrows shot up above the frame of her glasses. "Well, crap."

Destiny covered her mouth with her hand, hiding her smile. "What?"

"I never even thought about your schooling and what we needed to do there." She reached out and grasped Destiny's hand. "I'm sorry, honey. We'll take a ride over to the school tomorrow before the store opens. I reckon we need to get you registered and all that."

"It's okay," Destiny said quickly. She was not about to let her grandmother spoil her "date" with Jake. "I can ask about registration when I talk to the cheerleading coach. I'll take care of it."

Rose held Destiny's gaze, and then she laughed. "I wasn't born yesterday. Okay. You go with Jake. Let me know if you need me to sign anything." She returned to her food.

"Oh, and about Amy…she's just spoiled. She gets everything she wants from that doctor father of hers and her mother's an antiques buyer who travels all over the world. They dote on her because they feel guilty about leaving her alone so much. I think it's a little sad, really. I feel sorry for her. With no one there to raise her, I think she just does the best she can and comes off sounding like a snotty rich kid. Wouldn't hurt her to know there is some new competition in town, though." Rose swiped her mouth with a napkin. "You like that cheerleading stuff?"

"Yeah. I'm not the best on the squad, but I make a pretty good base and catcher. I'm strong and dependable. I haven't dropped anyone yet."

Rose chuckled. "Well, that's good news, I guess." She leaned forward on her elbows, still waving her fork. "Then you have fun with Jake. I don't have anyone to mind the store anyway, plus there's a tour group coming in tomorrow from Ocala, and they'll want to have readings. I'll be exhausted by tomorrow night. I hate tour groups."

Destiny watched her grandmother enjoying the meal she'd made. Interactions between them were still a little awkward, but Destiny just didn't see what her mother had complained about all those years. Grams was pretty cool, actually. She spooned more taco meat on her plate and stuffed more salad into her mouth.

"That reminds me, Destiny," Rose said. "I've been meaning to ask you how you would feel about coming to the store a few days a week and helping me out. I just need someone to watch the register while I do my readings. It's a wonder no one has robbed me blind while I'm upstairs. I had a college girl that worked for me, and she transferred at the end of this semester. I could really use the help."

Destiny stopped chewing and looked at her grandmother, her eyes wide. She swallowed and said, "Uh, I don't know, Grams. I'm not really…um… sure about what you sell. I wouldn't be able to answer anybody's questions." The last thing Destiny needed was to get caught working at her grandmother's shop. Cool or not, what Grams did was weird, and Destiny would die before she'd have her friends think she was as weird as her grandmother.

Destiny squirmed under Rose's gaze.

"I see. You're afraid of what your friends might think. I know." Rose stood, picked up her dishes, and took the two steps it took to reach the kitchen sink.

Destiny stood quickly and met her with her own dishes. How did she do that? It's like she always knew her thoughts. "I'll do this, Grams." She gently took the plate from her grandmother's arthritic fingers. "I cooked, and I'll do the dishes." She put the plates on the counter and began to run water in the sink.

While she waited for the sink to fill, Destiny put away the leftover food and cleared the rest of the table. Guilt tugged at her conscience as she realized she'd hurt her grandmother's feelings. She watched as the old woman wandered into the living room—a whole five steps to the left— and sat, small and doll-like, in her big black wooden rocker. Leaning back, she closed her eyes, so Destiny took a minute to study her. Rose's gray hair rivaled her own in length, but she kept it wound up in a bun most of the time. Sometimes she wore her thin locks down her back in braids. Destiny liked it in braids and thought it helped her look younger. Her blue eyes sparkled when she laughed and added beauty to an already pretty, if somewhat wrinkled, face.

Destiny stood in the kitchen watching her rock, and love stirred in her heart. It struck her that Rose was her only family, and she barely knew her.

Finished with the dishes, Destiny joined Rose by plopping on the couch. Not being much of a TV watcher, she picked up a book and resumed reading. After a while, Destiny thought Rose had fallen asleep, so she jumped when the old woman said, "Have you given my suggestion any more thought?"

"Grams," Destiny rested the book on her lap. "I don't want to seem rude, but what you do is really…" she searched for the word, "different. I mean, I appreciate all you've done for me, and I know I should help you, but is there another way I can do it? I'll keep the trailer clean, cook your meals, and wash your clothes, that kind of stuff."

Rose smiled. "Destiny, what did your mother tell you about me while you were growing up?"

Destiny opened her mouth and then closed it.

Rose shook her finger. "I want the truth and nothing but the truth. I'm a big girl. I can take it."

Destiny sighed. "She said you were a witch. That the stuff you sold in your bookstore was what witches used. She said you were a bit of…."

Destiny winced, "a freak."

She had asked for the truth.

To Destiny's relief, she smiled. "I see. And what do you think now that you've lived with me for almost three weeks?"

"I don't think you're a freak if that's what you're asking. I guess you're not really a witch either. Maybe Mom meant witch as in mean and not an actual candle burning, spell-casting witch." She shifted on the couch. "Um…at least I haven't seen you *do* anything like that. You're not a witch, are you?" Destiny's stomach flipped. What would she do if her grandmother said yes?

"No, honey, I'm not."

Destiny let out a breath. "Oh, good. I'm glad about that. Mom always said that stuff you sell in your store is creepy."

Rose spared her an expression of tolerance and sighed. "Just because people don't believe in the same things you believe in doesn't make them creepy. Teresa never seemed to embrace the fact that the world is full of all kinds of people. Good people who just happen to find their religious center in different ways. None of them evil, mind you." She stopped rocking and locked Destiny in her gaze.

"I do carry lots of odds and ends that people who practice in alternative religions are looking for. I'll tell you there's nothing evil about what I do, nor do I let anyone into my store that practices on the dark side. Light and goodness are all that enters my store." Rose smiled and resumed her back and forth motion, the wood of the chair softly creaking. "I offer a service for those in need. They seek out my help, and I do what I can to bring peace to their world. What people choose to believe about me and what I do is their own business."

"About that…."

"What?"

"What is a reading?" Destiny knew what her mother said, but she wanted to hear it from Rose.

"What did your mother say about that?"

Again, Destiny found it somewhat disturbing how Rose could get into her head the way she did. "Mom said you claimed you could talk to the dead. That you would take people whose relatives had died and tell them things, messages or something, from whoever it was that had died.

That's just not possible, is it?"

Rose sighed. "My dear girl, I have what I consider to be a gift given to me by God." She leaned forward in her chair, her elbows on her knees. "Hand me that Bible over there," she said, reaching out a hand. Destiny uncurled her legs and grabbed the worn leather book from the table. The pages were crinkled from frequent flipping, and bookmarks stuck out from different sections. Rose removed it from her hand, grabbed the tail of one of the braided pieces of yarn and tugged the book open.

"Let me read you something," she said, adjusting her glasses on her nose. "This is from I Corinthians, chapter twelve. Verse four says, 'There are different kinds of gifts, but the same Spirit distributes them.'" She glanced up.

Destiny stared, captivated. "Go on," she said. Her mother had never mentioned this.

"Verses seven through eleven say, 'Now to each one the manifestation of the Spirit is given for the common good. To one there is given through the Spirit a message of wisdom, to another a message of knowledge by means of the same Spirit, to another faith by the same Spirit, to another gifts of healing by that one Spirit, to another miraculous powers, to another prophecy, to another distinguishing between spirits, to another speaking in different kinds of tongues, and to still another the interpretation of tongues. All these are the work of one and the same Spirit, and he distributes them to each one, just as he determines.'" Rose stopped and laid the Bible in her lap.

"Wow," Destiny said. "That's pretty cool."

Her grandmother nodded, petting Butch, who'd plodded over to her side. He snorted and settled down beside her chair. "The gift I have is called The Shade Sight and has been passed down through the females in my family for generations. We have what you might call a sixth sense. We can sense Shades."

"What's a Shade?" The only shade Destiny knew of sat on top of a lamp.

Rose chuckled. Heat burned Destiny's cheeks.

"A Shade is what you might think of as a ghost, someone who hasn't ended up where they are supposed to for their eternal rest. They are but a shade of their former selves because they can't let go of the mortal

world and move on to the Great Beyond, or Heaven as some refer to it."
She stood and crossed the room to return the Bible to the table.

"This could be for various reasons," Rose continued, joining
Destiny on the couch. "Maybe they aren't done with whatever mission
they wanted to accomplish in life, maybe they wanted to tell someone
something, and they died too soon, or maybe they just don't want to let
go. Either way, my job as a Shade Seeker is to help them in any way I
can. I can also talk to spirits."

"Aren't ghosts, or Shades, whatever you call them, and spirits the
same thing?" Destiny scooted back against the arm of the couch, grabbing
the pillow and hugging it to her chest. A tiny shiver crawled down her
spine. Curiosity tugged at her mind, yet she remained uncomfortable
with this conversation. Her mother certainly wouldn't have approved.

"Oh no, there's a vast difference between the two. Shades are
trapped, unable to move on. Spirits have already crossed over and come
back to visit. My clients come to me to contact their loved ones who
have moved on. It gives them peace of mind to know that the person
they loved is safe and happy on the other side. For the ones who have
yet to cross over, many times I can help them see the Light and move
from the grayness to where they are meant to spend eternity."

Destiny stared at her grandmother. Maybe she still had her mother
in her head, but this was just beyond her understanding. "Okay, Grams.
You're really starting to make me crazy here."

"I understand. That's exactly how your mother felt. It embarrassed
her. She didn't want any of her friends to think she was weird."

"Do you blame her? I mean, it's not like you could be invited to
speak at career day." Destiny held up her hands and then slapped them
on her thighs.

Rose pursed her lips and shook her head. "No, I never blamed my
Teresa for the way she felt about me. I just hope you can be more open-
minded than she was. It's a big universe our God has created, Destiny,
and we are a tiny speck in the vastness of it. Never forget that. No matter
how a human chooses to worship whatever divine entity they believe
in, there is a life beyond what we now know." She remained quiet for a
while.

Destiny had gone back to her book when she said, "So...what do you say about the bookstore? Why don't you try it, and we can see how it goes? If it creeps you out, as you call it, you can stay home. I wouldn't push the issue, but I really need the help."

Now she'd done it, gone and played the guilt card. Crap. Destiny could just picture herself working there and a group of girls, like Amy and her friends, coming by the bookstore, and there she'd be. Just great…she sighed. "I'll try it."

"Wonderful," Rose patted her granddaughter's leg.

Destiny started to go back to her book, but then she remembered Patch. "Oh, Grams, by the way, I met someone else today. He's an old farm hand." She got up and strode to the kitchen for a drink. "His name is Patch. Do you know him?"

She turned around with the glass in her hand, and Rose was just staring, her eyebrows popping up over her glasses.

"You saw Patch today?"

"Yeah. Old guy, dark skin, bib overalls, white hair. He was really nice. I was feeling kind of bummed after I talked to Amy and Jake, and he made me feel better. He kept referring to himself in the past, though, which I thought was really weird. Maybe he has Alzheimer's or something."

Rose stood and approached Destiny. She placed both hands on the girl's shoulders, her mouth quirking up on both ends.

"What?" Destiny said, peering into her grandmother's eyes.

"Honey, Patch has been dead for over forty years."

The glass slipped from her hand and broke on the tile floor. Destiny staggered against the counter, her head spinning.

"Whoa there," Rose said, though Destiny barely heard her for the blood rushing through her ears. Rose helped Destiny to the couch, where she sat just before her knees gave out.

CHAPTER FOUR

Amy hummed to the tune she was listening to on her iPod while she brushed her hair. Jake was going to be there any minute. She was looking forward to going to the club with him and her other friends. They'd planned the end of the school year party months ago, and it was going to be a blast. Her best friend Jessie had hired a D.J., and they were going to dance the night away. She almost didn't hear the phone ringing on her bedside table. She danced her way over to the small twin bed and plopped down on the worn Winnie the Pooh coverlet.

She scooped up her cell and mashed the talk button. "Hello?"

"Hi, Ames, it's Jake. You almost ready?"

"Yep. You can come over any time. We're gonna have so much fun at this party, Jake. I can't wait."

"Yeah, I know. It's going to be a blast. Listen, why don't we ask that new girl, Destiny, to come with us? It'd be a great way for her to meet some new friends, and when she starts school, she'll already know some people. What do you say?"

Amy couldn't believe it. She dropped her brush, and it clattered on top of the dresser. "Jake, who are you, the local cruise director? She is perfectly capable of making her own friends. Isn't it enough that you took her over to the school and got her a cheerleading tryout? She's probably going to throw the whole squad out of rhythm. It has taken us a full year to get our routine down. She's probably going to screw everything up."

Jake's patience came through in his voice. "Amy, you know she's lonely. She just lost her mom, dad and brother. How do you think that would feel? I'd be crushed if I lost my family like that. The least you can do is give her a chance. I watched her audition, and she was actually very good. She's a great dancer, and she knows some of the same cheers you use. I think she's going to fit in great."

Amy rolled her eyes and sighed. "Jake, what is your fascination with her? It's beginning to get on my nerves. You are not her babysitter. She can find and make friends on her own." She became sullen. "I really wanted this party to be fun, and now you want to invite her. I just wanted it to be you and me and our friends tonight. You're going to ruin it."

"Okay, okay," Jake relented. "I just thought it would be the nice thing to do. Maybe we can invite her to go out with us another time, you know, like with Jessie and her boyfriend, and we could ask Steve to come along so she won't feel like a fifth wheel."

Amy kicked the stuffed pig lying on her floor into her closet. He just wouldn't give up on this girl. *What is it about her?* Jealousy boiled in her veins. She would just have to distract him at the party tonight. "We'll see. Now hurry up. We're going to be late."

Amy placed her cell phone back in its beaded hammock and rushed to finish putting on her makeup. She wanted to look extra special for Jake. She was going to make sure he thought of no one but her. This Destiny girl was going to be a pain in her butt. She could just feel it. She had worked too hard to get Jake's attention, and she was not going to let some granddaughter of that freak Madam Rose take him away from her. She wasn't stupid. She saw the way Destiny had admired Jake. She couldn't take her eyes off him that day down at the paddock.

Amy had to admit that as far as eye candy went, Jake was Ghirardelli. That brown wavy hair and those blue eyes; what a combo. She loved to run her fingers through all that hair, and she liked it better during the summer when he let it get a little long. The coach made them shave their heads when football practice started, so she only had about another month and a half to enjoy those luscious locks. Destiny wasn't going to get anywhere near him if she could help it. Amy smacked her lips together, smoothing out the strawberry lip gloss. Jake loved the strawberry flavor. She was going to make sure he got a mouthful of it. She smiled to herself as the doorbell rang. Grabbing her beach bag, she headed downstairs.

Amy's mother was just answering the door as she stepped off the bottom step.

"Hi, Jake," Sarah Morgan smiled and opened the door.

"Hi, Mrs. Morgan, how's the antique business going?"

Sarah smiled. "It's going fine, Jake. Actually, I just got a delivery today that I want the two of you to look at. It's out in the garage. Do you have time?"

"Sure," Jake said.

"No," Amy said simultaneously.

Jake smiled at Sarah. Amy didn't miss the bold admiration plastered all over his face. She elbowed him in the stomach.

"Ow," Jake said, rubbing his mid-section. "What was that for?"

Sarah, oblivious to the exchange, said, "Now, Amy, don't be a party pooper. Come out and see this. I think you'll be pleased."

Amy sighed and rolled her eyes. The young couple followed Sarah through the front hall, the kitchen, and out the mud room door. Scattered about the concrete floor where Sarah Morgan's Jaguar was usually parked stood a suite of bedroom furniture. Intricate carvings covered the dark wood of the headboard, footboard and bedposts. Tiny wooden-eyed cherubs emerged out of the wood within the carving, staring into nothingness. Amy shivered. Creepy. What had possessed her mother to buy such ghastly looking furniture? A nightstand and a dresser with a large mirror carved with the same hollow-eyed cherubs stood nearby.

Amy wrinkled her nose. The furniture smelled of smoke and wore a thick coat of soot. Sarah walked over to it and spread her arms wide.

"Surprise!"

Amy looked startled. "Surprise? What do you mean, surprise?" This was positively the ugliest furniture she had ever seen.

"This is yours, Amy. Don't you love it? It's going to look so much better in your room than all that little girl Winnie the Pooh furniture you've got now."

Amy's face flushed pink. "Wha—" She shrugged her shoulders so high that when she dropped them, her hands slapped to her sides. "Mom, this is hideous. I can't put this crap in my room. Where did you get this? A bonfire pit?"

"Amy, it's not that bad," Jake chimed in.

She glared at him.

"My dad and I have some stuff down at the hardware store that will strip the soot right off of it. Then all you'll need to do is sand it down and re-varnish it." He studied the piece. "The hard part will be those angels and all the nooks and crannies. I like it. I think it has character."

He had lost his mind. Amy crossed her arms over her chest. "Well, then you take it home with you. I hate it."

Sarah's face fell. "You really don't like it?"

"Mom, those angels are creepy. Who could sleep with those things staring down at you? This isn't going to work."

"Well, let's get started on it, and then you can decide when we're done. There are some rags over there. Let's see how much of the soot we can wipe off before we go down to Jake's dad's store and get that solvent he was talking about."

"Mom," Amy interrupted. "Jake and I are going to Jessica's party. Remember? I told you about it last week."

Sarah blinked and refocused on her daughter. "A party?"

Oh great, she'd not paid attention again. "Yes, the after school bash at the country club. You said it was a great place to have a party." She stomped her foot in frustration. Her mother was famous for pretending to pay attention.

Sarah huffed out a breath and said, "But Amy, we need to start on this furniture if we want to get it in your room before school starts. I canceled appointments with my clients for today, so you and I could work on it."

"Well, don't you think you should have checked with me before you did that?"

Amy watched Jake walk around the mirror attached to the dresser, trying to ignore the altercation. All of a sudden, the mirror wobbled and tipped forward, falling right on top of him.

"Jake!"

He turned, catching the frame inches before it bashed him in the head. Muscles rippling, he pushed it back against the brace.

"Whoa," he said. "That's weird." He peered around at the back of the mirror. "It must have come loose from its bolts during shipping.

Want me to tighten that up for you, Mrs. M?"

Sarah, her face pale, replied, "No. That's okay. Are you all right? That thing nearly cracked your skull open."

Jake smiled his killer smile. "No, I'm fine. It's very heavy, though. I think I should really fix it before it falls again."

"No," Sarah said, much to Amy's relief. "Just prop it up against the brace. It should stay that way until Amy's father gets home." She frowned at Amy and sighed. "Okay. You two run on, and I'll just wipe the pieces down and get it ready for us to work on tomorrow. But no plans tomorrow, young lady. I want to start working on this project."

Amy knew when she'd won. Anxious to escape, she rushed toward Jake's jeep. "Okay," she yelled over her shoulder.

Jake watched her go and then turned back to Sarah. "You sure you don't want me to tighten up that mirror for you? It wouldn't take a minute."

Sarah smiled. "No, you go on. Amy will be screaming for you any minute." She turned around and picked up a white cloth. "Have fun at the party. Have her home by eleven."

"I will, Mrs. M. See you later." Jake walked down the driveway and opened the door of his Jeep Wrangler. Amy was already buckled in and waiting for him. He climbed in and held her gaze.

"What?" Amy said. "Start this thing up, and let's get out of here."

"Amy, you were kinda rude to your mom, don't you think?"

Her jaw dropped. He thought *she* was rude? "She goes out and buys that crap without even asking me. Now, I have to spend most of my weekends this summer working in the heat of the garage on that ugly bedroom furniture that I don't even want. Why couldn't she have just taken me down to the furniture store like a *normal* parent would have done and bought me some brand new furniture?"

"Because she wants to spend time with you. Don't you get that?" Jake smacked his hands on the steering wheel.

"Oh, so now, all of a sudden, I'm important enough to spend time with? What about all those other times when I sat at home with a nanny while she traveled all over the country and Dad was at the hospital?" Her throat grew tight, tears pricking her eyes. Sore subject.

"Maybe she feels bad about that, Amy. Did you ever think of that?"

Amy stared out the window and didn't say anything. They passed Destiny's trailer, and she spotted her on the porch. Jake waved at her. Destiny returned the wave, smiling brightly. Amy seethed. Just her luck to have someone like *her* move in right in her back door. She really hated that girl.

"I still say we should have invited her. I feel kinda bad." Jake glanced in the rearview mirror.

Amy twisted to face him. "God, Jake. You fall for every sad story you hear. She'll be fine. She'll make her own set of friends and hopefully leave us alone."

Jake's eyes shifted from the mirror to Amy, an expression of disdain covering his handsome features. Amy knew she sounded crabby, and from that look she'd just received, figured she'd best make amends. "I'm sorry, babe. I'm just in a rotten mood."

He nodded and focused on driving.

***

Sarah watched as the couple drove off, then turned back to the dresser. "Teenagers," she sputtered as she slapped the white cloth against the mirror. The soft cotton snagged on a raised splinter of wood, and Sarah had to tug it loose. The force of her yank caused her to lose her grip on the cloth. She watched it flutter to the floor. She knew that having a teenager would be a challenge, but since Amy turned sixteen, she'd become increasingly difficult. Maybe they indulged her too much. She was certain she gave in to her daughter more than she should. Guilt was a powerful weapon, and Amy used it well.

Both she and her husband, Jeff, were extremely busy. Ever since she started Antiquities of Morgan, her antique store and consulting business, it seemed Amy grew more defiant and sullen every day. Maybe it would be a good idea to have Amy work in the store with her. That way, she could keep a watchful eye and spend more time with her. She would also cut down on the number of private clients she was working with. Now that Jeff was head of the trauma department at the hospital, she didn't need the extra money. Spending quality time with Amy was more important.

Feeling better, she bent down to retrieve the cloth. Without warning, the top right dresser drawer shot out and struck her hard against the left temple. She dropped like a stone to the cement floor.

CHAPTER FIVE

Jake and Amy arrived at the country club just as a van load of their friends pulled into the parking lot. They exchanged hugs, high fives, and knuckle punches in greeting and meandered their way into the clubhouse. Amy, impressed by what her BFF Jessica had done to the place, admired the wide banner that read, "Welcome Summer 2011! We're Juniors!" stretching from one end of the long wall to the other. Purple and black balloons floated above the room, and streamers of the same colors swooped from corner to corner. No one could say this wasn't a Spartan get together.

Amy searched the room for her friend and found her giving last minute instructions to the D.J.

"Hey, Jess!" Amy shouted above the noise.

Jessica swung around, her mahogany French braid flipping over her shoulder. She waved to Amy, her pearl bedazzled cover-up raising slightly to expose the turquoise bikini beneath. Jealousy pricked Amy as she wove through the bodies in the room to reach her friend. They'd shopped for bathing suits together for the party, and Amy had found that bikini first. Jessica had grabbed it from her, squealing all the way to the dressing room. Amy lost out because not only did the suit look fantastic on Jessica's bronzed body, but it also enhanced the blue-green of her eyes. She'd been forced to settle for the red and white striped version of the same style.

"Where have you been? I thought you weren't coming," Jessica said, wrapping her arms around Amy's neck.

"My mom held us up. You aren't going to believe what she did, Jess." Amy pulled Jessica's arm, and they sat in two nearby chairs.

"What?" Jessica leaned in conspiratorially.

"You know I wanted some new bedroom furniture, right?"

"Yeah?" Jessica's brow furrowed, confusion clouding her expression. Clearly, that was not what she'd expected Amy to say.

"Well, she ordered this crap from her antiques catalogue, and it arrived today. She wants us to refinish it together. It is the most god-awful-looking stuff you've ever seen. It's been in some kind of fire and is covered with soot. Then it has these creepy little angels on top that stare at you. It just sucks. I wanted new furniture, not that crap."

"Is that all? The way your face looked, I thought your parents were getting a divorce or something."

Amy rolled her eyes. Obviously, Jess didn't get it. "Aw, hon, I'm sorry. Maybe it will, like, be really nice once you get it finished."

"Ugh, do you honestly think I want to spend my entire summer working with my mom on that junk?"

"It won't take you all summer." She took Amy's hand. "Besides, you've been saying you want to spend some more time with her."

"Well yeah, at the spa or going shopping. Not this."

Jessica laughed. "You're so funny, Ames. Come on, forget about it for now. Let's go to the pool and get a look at those gorgeous boy bods."

Amy followed her friend, frustrated. Didn't anyone understand what living with her parents was like? They were never home. And when she did have a chance to do something with her mother, she'd come up with refinishing furniture? How lame was that?

Joining their friends Diana, Lyndsay, and Becca by the pool, the girls caught up on the latest gossip. After all, it had been three days since they'd last seen each other.

Amy had the juiciest news, so she spoke first. "Okay, here's the thing. There's a new girl in town. She lives at the back of my property in that skanky old trailer where Madam Rose lives. Her name is Destiny Dove, and she's Madam Rose's granddaughter." A collective gasp followed that revelation.

"I'd heard there was someone new in town," Becca said.

Amy scrunched her nose at the petite blonde. The girl was a goody-two-shoes, but her dad owned the local bar and grill in town, so Amy tolerated her. It was a great place to hang out, and Becca's friends got to eat free.

"My dad was telling your dad about it," Becca continued, pointing to Lindsay.

Amy wasn't surprised by this statement at all. In her opinion, Lindsay's dad hung out at that bar just a little too much. Anyway, they digressed. Amy said, "Hey, focus back on me…I'm having a crisis here."

"Sorry, Ames," Becca said, and all four girls waited expectantly.

"Jake and I were riding yesterday, and she was standing down by the paddock. Jake decides it would be the *polite* thing to do to ride over and introduce ourselves." She tossed her hair. "Ladies, she could not take her eyes off my man. I'm surprised she didn't start drooling down the front of her shirt. Then, if that wasn't bad enough, my stupid boyfriend offers to take her over to the school to meet Coach Windham and try out for cheerleading."

"Well, surely Coach didn't let her try out," Lindsay said, her blue eyes widening. "We've already chosen the roster this year."

"Oh, not only did Coach let her try out, but she made the team." Amy reveled in the shocked faces around her, pleased that her friends understood.

"No way," they chorused.

"Yep. And I'm sure she's happy that Jake was the one to help her. You should have seen the way she looked at him. He's not the smartest egg in the crate when it comes to girls, but I knew exactly what she was doing." Amy had her audience, and she milked it to the max, determined to protect her turf. If she had her way, Destiny would remain friendless.

Jessica said, "Hey, Amy, don't worry about it. We'll take care of this at practice in August. We'll do a basket toss and just forget to catch her. She'll break her arm and be out the rest of the season. We got your back, girlfriend."

The girls giggled at Jessica's brilliant plan when Jake suddenly stepped up behind them. "Boy, I'm glad I'm not the new girl in town."

Jessica missed his sarcasm, but Amy knew that look. He was angry.

Jessica said cheerily, "I know, right?"

"No, not right. I can't believe you all. Destiny is a nice girl, and she doesn't deserve to be talked about like this when you don't even know her. I saw her try out. She's a good cheerleader, and she might just add some spice to your squad. I'm getting a little tired of the same old crap." He frowned, crossing his arms.

Mortified, Amy couldn't believe what Jake had just said.

"Jake, I'm beginning to think Amy's right," Jessica said. "Maybe you do have a crush on this chick."

Okay, that was enough. Amy marched off to the refreshment table to get a drink, leaving Jake standing with her friends. Tears stung her eyes. How could he humiliate her like that? She was his girlfriend, for God's sake. Amy sensed him come up behind her but refused to turn around.

"Amy, I can't believe you did that." His tone was harsh. "Why did you throw Destiny under the bus?"

Amy whirled around. "Why do you care so much about *her*, Jake? Huh? I'm your girlfriend, not Destiny. Why did you defend her like that?"

"I shouldn't have needed to defend her." His blue eyes flashed, his lips drawn into a thin line. "You were plotting her assassination, and you barely know her. Amy, you carry a lot of weight around here. Now she's going to start school with everyone hating her. She doesn't stand a chance. I would think you could be a little more compassionate."

"Good," Amy said stubbornly. "She's weird, and you just can't see through it. She's not been here a month yet, and she's already got her claws in you. I can't believe—"

Amy's cell phone rang. She blinked away tears and noticed her father's number flashing on the iPhone screen.

"Hello?"

"Amy? It's Dad."

"I know. I can see your name on the caller ID. What's up?"

"I need you to come over to the hospital. Your mom's had an accident."

"What?" Amy stepped away from the people so she could hear. "What happened?"

"I'm not sure exactly. When I got home, she was lying on the floor of the garage, out cold. I called 911 and had them bring her in. I've run some CAT scans and taken a few X-rays. I think it would be good if you come on over."

"Okay, I'm on my way. Is she going to be okay?"

Worry raced up her spine when he said, "Just get on over here, okay?"

"Okay, I'm coming." She pressed the END button and stared at her phone.

Jake put his hands on her shoulders. "What's wrong, Amy?"

Fresh tears trickled down her cheeks, and she dug in her purse for a tissue.

Jake's eyes widened in alarm, and he pulled her into a hug. "Is everything okay at home?"

Amy shook her head and managed to explain to him what her father had just told her.

He waved down Jessica. She came rushing over when she saw the state of her best friend. "What's wrong, Amy?" Her eyes went accusingly to him. "Did you break up with her?" She placed her arm protectively around Amy's shoulders.

He rolled his eyes. "No, I didn't break up with her. Her mother's in the hospital. I've got to take her over there. I just wanted you to know why we were leaving. I'll call you when I know more."

"What? What happened? Is she going to be okay?"

"I'll explain it later. We need to go."

Jessica nodded as Jake gently took Amy's elbow and guided her away from her friends toward the car. He helped her in and then jumped in on the driver's side. Gravel flew from the tires as he peeled out of the parking lot.

CHAPTER SIX

Destiny swam back to consciousness at the sound of her grandmother's raspy voice calling her name. Something cool laid on her forehead. Opening her eyes, Destiny found herself on the couch with Rose on her knees next to her. The soft, paper-thin skin of her hand warmed Destiny's cheek as the old woman stroked each side of her face.

"Destiny? Are you back with me?"

Destiny nodded. "What happened? Did I faint?"

"You did, dead away. If I hadn't been right there, you'd have cracked your skull on the floor. As it was, you took me down with you. Took all my strength just to get you over here onto the couch."

"I'm sorry, Grams," Destiny whispered.

"I know what a shock that must have been for you, Destiny. To find you'd spent an hour or so this afternoon talking to a Shade."

Destiny stared at her. It was more than any human mind could comprehend or believe. Even after her grandmother had spent all that time blathering on about the Shade Sight, it was hard for Destiny to believe Patch was a ghost.

"Grams, he was as real as you and me. There is no way he could be a ghost or a Shade, or whatever. He wasn't transparent or anything. He stood in front of me just like you are now."

Rose struggled to her feet, and Destiny pulled in her legs to give her grandmother room to sit on the couch. Once settled, Rose said, "Give me your hand."

Destiny drew her brows together but obeyed.

"Tell me when you start to feel the heat." Rose held Destiny's hand tightly between her palms. For a few seconds, she experienced nothing, but then it started to get hot. Then it burned. Destiny jerked her hand away. "What the—"

Rose smiled. "That's energy, Destiny. We are all made of it, and some of us can manipulate it better than others. You know those magicians you see on TV, like David Blane and that Mind Freak guy, what's his name?"

"Kris Angel," Destiny said.

"Yes, Kris Angel. Well, you've seen what they do with throwing cards through windows and such, right?" Rose mocked, throwing a Frisbee.

Destiny nodded, still skeptical.

"Well, I believe they are manipulating the energy fields around them. Causing those fields to shift and warp. Shades can do the same thing. Some do it better than others, but it takes a great deal of energy for a Shade to manifest." She shifted on the couch, easing one leg straight. "That's why you often feel a temperature change when one is around. It gets really cold as they draw the energy from what's around them. The longer they've been a Shade, the better they seem to be at it. Patch has been dead nearly forty years. He's learned to manifest quite well. That's why he looks so solid to you."

Not sure she bought into that theory, Destiny said, "Tell me more about Patch."

"He worked on the Morgan's farm back in the forties. He died of a heart attack and just never left. I'm not sure why he's hung around so long, but once a person rejects the Light once, they have a more difficult time finding it a second time. Patch just doesn't want to cross over anymore. I guess he likes being on this farm and staying with his horses. He's never told me why he chose to become a Shade."

"You've seen him too?"

Grams nodded. "I see him quite often. Sometimes it can be quite amusing on a Sunday afternoon to sit on the porch and watch the grooms come running out of the barn claiming they've seen a ghost. Patch has quite a sense of humor." She placed a hand in Destiny's. "You know, honey, I was waiting for a sign from you to see if you had The Gift of

Shade Sight. Now I know."

"I still don't get it. He wasn't real?"

"Honey, he was real, just dead. You'll need to recognize the difference. Sometimes it will be very obvious, but other times you'll need to seek more subtle signs."

Destiny shivered, and her skin crawled. This was just too weird for words. "Grams, I was having a hard enough time believing that you could do all this. Now you're telling me that I can too? I can see ghosts."

Rose nodded. "And talk to them too, apparently."

This was just freaking great. Destiny stood up and paced the small living room. How was she going to explain this? She could imagine the introduction to her new friends now: "Hi, I'm Destiny, and I can talk to ghosts." Yeah, that would go over real well. Jake and Amy were going to think she was a super freak.

Destiny faced Rose. "Okay," she said. "How do I stop it? There's got to be a way to turn it off. This just isn't normal. I don't want this 'gift' as you call it." She drew imaginary quotes in the air.

Rose sat back on the couch and sighed. The sadness of her expression pricked Destiny's conscience. She patted the couch. "Destiny, come here. Sit down and let me explain something to you."

For a moment, Destiny just stood there staring at her. She patted the cushion again. Huffing out a sigh, Destiny plopped down on the couch, arms crossed over her chest.

"You aren't normal, Cookie. You've been blessed with a gift that allows you to help all kinds of spirits, both living and dead."

"I don't want to help spirits. I want to be a normal teenager with friends and go to the prom and go on to college. I don't need a bunch of Shades, as you call them, dragging me down. No wonder Mom ran from this gift like her butt was on fire."

"Honey, listen to me. You come from a long line of mediums. I beg you not to reject this like your mother did. Let me help you learn to control it, to block it when necessary. If you learn to manage it, you can live a very normal life and still help others." Destiny winced. Why did she have to be the weirdo? Why couldn't this be someone else?

Rose continued, "I can't count the families I've brought to peace because I can deliver messages from their relatives that have passed on. I've also helped solve a few murders here and there. It's a blessing, honey, not a curse, and I can teach you to make the most of it."

"This is scary, Grams," Destiny said. "I don't want to see Patch again. I mean, he was nice and all, but he's dead. Living people shouldn't talk to dead people. It's not right."

"I know it's scary, Destiny, but the work we do is really more important to the dead than it is to the living. When a human body dies, and the soul doesn't pass on to the Great Beyond, it causes an unbalance."

"You sound like Obi-Wan from *Star Wars*," Destiny said and lowered her voice. "Luke, I sense a disturbance in the force." She imitated the heavy breathing of Darth Vader.

Rose laughed. "Sort of like that, yes. The disturbance must be corrected. The unbalanced must be balanced. It's important work, or we wouldn't have been given the ability to do it."

Destiny pondered that for a few minutes. She could see her point, but why in the crap had this happened to her? Her life was screwed up enough with the loss of her parents and her baby brother. Now, this? She glanced at her grandmother. Rose's watery blue eyes were so serious, and in that moment, it occurred to Destiny how hard it must have been on her not to see her own daughter all those years.

"Destiny, I'm not saying this will be easy, and at times you'll feel like the life force has been drained out of you, but you'll be able to put restless souls at peace. I can teach you and help you cope. We'll find a way for you to be able to deal with it, so it doesn't embarrass you in front of your friends."

Destiny wasn't so sure about that. If these Shades could just pop in all of a sudden, how could that be controlled? "Can I think about it for a while?" That much she could promise.

Rose smiled and appeared relieved. "Sure, honey. You think on it. Help me in the bookstore, and do your own research. When you're ready, we'll work on it together. Just don't run away from it like your mother did. She refused the training she needed to build the proper shields. It can keep you from going crazy."

"Well, I suppose that would be helpful," Destiny said and curved her lips.

"You go get some rest now," Rose said. "You've had a hard day."

"I'll say." Rising, Destiny stepped to the sink to get a glass of water. Out the window, a bunch of red lights flashed up at the Morgan's house.

"Hey, Grams, come here."

Rose joined Destiny at the sink. They watched paramedics remove someone from the house on a stretcher. It wasn't Amy because Destiny had seen her leave earlier with Jake. It had to be one of Amy's parents. Having just been through the loss of her own parents, Destiny sympathized. "I hope everything is okay. Should we go up there?"

"I'll call the hospital later on," Rose said. "You go on to bed. You've had your own shock for today."

No kidding. "Okay. Maybe I won't have any bad dreams tonight," Destiny said. Hope sprang eternal.

"I hope not, sweetie," Rose replied, wrapping her granddaughter in a tight hug.

The embrace was warm. Even though she hadn't known her grandmother long, the love the old woman had for her was overwhelming. And she was grateful.

CHAPTER SEVEN

Amy tapped softly on the hospital room door. She pushed the heavy door open and peered in. "Mom?"

"Come in," her father called from inside the room.

Amy slowly entered the room, towing Jake behind her. The walls were pale green, the floor black tile. IV poles and monitors surrounded the bed. The antiseptic smell made Amy wrinkle her nose as she stepped all the way in. Two uncomfortable-looking brown vinyl chairs, like the one her father sat in, stood next to the window. The ceiling-mounted TV was on, but the sound was muted.

Her father motioned her into the room. "Hi, Jake. Thanks for bringing Amy down."

"No problem, Dr. M. How is she?"

"Yeah, Dad, is she okay?" Amy approached the bed. Her mother's eyes were closed, and she looked terribly pale. The dark bruise running from her temple to her lower left jaw was clear evidence of her accident. "She looks terrible."

"I know she does, honey, but she's going to be fine. We did the X-rays, and I had them do a CT scan just for good measure. She has a slight concussion, as I suspected, but nothing more serious. She's going to have one whale of a headache when she wakes up, but other than that, she's going to be okay."

Jake wrapped an arm around Amy's shoulders and hugged her tight. "That's great news. What happened? She was fine when Amy and I left to go to the party. Hey, did that mirror fall on her? It fell over when she was showing us the furniture, and I caught it just in time. I asked if she wanted me to tighten it, but she said no."

"To be honest, Jake, I'm not sure what happened. I'll have to wait for her to wake up to ask her. I got home and found her on the garage floor. It looked like she fell up against one of the drawers. If you look closely at the bruise, you can see a faint outline of the drawer handle. I'm not sure how she could have hit it that hard...very strange."

Amy's eyes welled up with tears as she moved from Jake's embrace and hugged her father tightly around the neck. "I was really scared when you called, Dad. She looks so bad. Are you sure she's going to wake up?"

Jeff stood and squeezed her tight. "She'll be okay. There was no swelling in her brain, and I don't see any sign of permanent damage. I'm just a little surprised she hasn't come around yet, but I think all is well. I must admit I was scared too."

A muffled groan from the bed drew their attention. Sarah lifted her hand up to her head. "What happened?" Her speech was slurred from the painkillers, and Amy thought she sounded drunk.

"Hey there, Sleeping Beauty." Jeff stepped over to the bed and shined a small flashlight into Sarah's eyes.

She jerked her head away, groaning again at the sudden movement. "Get that bright light out of my eyes. Are you crazy?"

Jeff laughed softly. "Yep, Amy, I think your mom is going to be just fine. Sarah, stop fidgeting and let me look at you. You took a bad spill in the garage, and I want to check your pupils."

"Well, that certainly explains the headache." Sarah gave in as Jeff shined the flashlight in her eyes and gently pressed on the knot at her temple. She winced. "Ow, Jeff, that hurts."

"I bet. Do you know you even have the imprint of the drawer handle on the side of your face? It looks like you took a running start and slammed the side of your head into the dresser. Do you remember what happened?"

Sarah slowly nodded. "It was very strange, really. I remember Amy and Jake leaving for the party, and I reached down to pick up the cloth I was using to clean the mirror, and I swear that drawer flew out and hit me. I know that sounds crazy, but that's the way it seemed. I don't remember anything after that. Oh, wow, my head really hurts." She reached up again, pressing both hands to her temples. She noticed the IV hanging from her right hand. "Am I in the hospital?"

Jeff smiled and ran his big hand over her forehead, pushing her light brown hair to the side. "You are. I had them bring you in. You were out cold when I found you. I could tell you had a concussion, but I wanted to make sure nothing else was wrong. We did some tests. You've been out for several hours." He reached for her hand. "You scared me, Sarah."

She sighed and tried to smile but winced instead. "Sorry," she said softly. Her eyelids drooped, and she relaxed her head into the pillow.

"Mom?" Amy walked to the other side of the bed and took her mother's other hand. "I'm sorry we went to the party. If I'd been there helping you, this might not have happened."

Jake stepped up to the bed beside Amy. "Yeah, Mrs. M. You should have let me tighten that mirror."

With effort, Sarah opened her eyes again and turned her head to look at Jake and then Amy. "Hi, Jake. I'm glad you're here with Amy." She took a deep breath and let it out. "Listen, Amy, it's okay. This isn't your fault. I love you."

She leaned down and hugged Sarah gently, tears sliding down her cheeks. "I love you too, Mom. I'm so sorry you got hurt."

Sarah weakly patted her daughter on the back before her hand slipped down to the sheet. She sighed deeply again and fell back to sleep.

Amy was concerned. "Is she okay, Dad? Why can't she stay awake? Are you sure you looked at everything?"

"She's fine, Amy. The painkillers are making her very sleepy, and that's just what she needs right now, rest. Let's go home and come back later. She'll probably sleep the night and the better half of the day tomorrow. I'll come back in the morning before rounds and check on her. I'll come home at lunch and bring you back over to visit."

"I could bring her over if you like, Mr. Morgan. We were going to exercise the horses in the morning. I could bring her over after that and save you the trip."

"That would be great, Jake. That okay with you, Amy?" When she nodded, Jeff gathered his stethoscope, flashlight, and the medical journal he'd been reading. He put his arm around Amy and ushered her toward the door. Jake followed close behind.

She looked back over her shoulder, worry evident in her expression. "Dad, Mom said the drawer flew out and hit her. That's just not possible, right? She's not losing her mind, is she?"

"No, your mother is not losing her mind. Maybe she just tripped and thought that's what happened. I'm surprised she even remembers anything at all. Don't worry about her. She'll be able to talk to us more clearly once we take her off the pain killers." He pressed the button on the elevator. "I'm on the fourth floor of the parking garage. Jake, where are you parked?"

"We're on the second floor. I'll bring Amy straight home. See you soon." Jake steered Amy out the door while her father got on the elevator.

"You okay, Amy?" Jake asked as they entered the parking garage.

"Yeah, I guess." Her tone was cool.

Jake's eyebrows rose. She knew she should feel more thankful to him for bringing her to the hospital, but his betrayal at the party still stung.

"Just take me home, please," she said.

CHAPTER EIGHT

Destiny sat on the front porch in a pair of shorts and a tank top. The warm air stirred just enough to keep the mosquitoes away. Naples had mosquitoes too, but out here in the country, they were large enough to carry someone away.

She gazed at the main house, thinking about all the wild events of the day. First, she'd found out that she'd talked to a ghost, and then Grams told her that it would be a regular occurrence. The Shade Sight, she called it. If working at the Mystic Cat wasn't bad enough, now all the kids here would learn Destiny took after her grandmother and could see and talk to spirits. What a way to win friends and influence people. She planned on keeping that little parlor trick to herself and hoped no one would find out.

In a way, she looked forward to working at the bookstore the next day. She wanted to find some books about her new gift. The way Destiny figured it, information was power. The more she knew, the less it would intimidate her. Her mother never supported such theories. Whenever the subject arose, Destiny's mother would claim a headache and go hide in the bedroom. Destiny wanted to do what Grams said and stay open-minded, but that meant taking a risk. Patch was friendly for a dead guy. Maybe they would all be similar, and this wouldn't be so bad...yeah, right.

Jake's Jeep pulled into the driveway. Amy got out and slammed the door, and marched up to the front porch. *Uh oh, must be trouble in paradise.*

Immediately Dr. Morgan's car lined up in the driveway beside Jake's. They exchanged words then Dr. Morgan went inside. Jake backed out of the driveway and started down the road. Destiny expected him to drive on by when he surprised her and turned into her small gravel driveway.

"Hey," he said, coming up on the porch.

"Hey," Destiny mimicked him, thankful she'd taken the time to put on some shorts and a tank instead of sitting outside in her pajamas.

"I drove by and saw you, so I thought I'd stop. It's late, though. Is it okay?"

"I don't see why not. Come on up and have a seat."

Destiny admired Jake's Hawaiian swim trunks and white tank top. His muscles positively bulged. *Wow, what I wouldn't give to have him for a boyfriend.* She hoped Amy knew how lucky she was. He plopped down in the vacant white plastic chair. Her face grew warm. These chairs sure couldn't compare to the wicker rockers the Morgans had on their front porch. She hoped Jake hadn't chosen the chair with the crack that pinched someone's butt when they sat in it.

"Did you hear about what happened to Amy's mom?" he asked, scooting his feet out of flip-flops and propping them on the banister.

"I saw the ambulance and wondered what was going on. What happened?"

"Mrs. M. fell and knocked herself out. She has a concussion. And what's really weird is she has this bruise on the side of her face in the shape of a drawer handle."

She drew her brows together. "Okay…now that's just weird. How did that happen?" No one fell hard enough to do that. There was more to this story, and she was eager to hear it.

"I've no clue. I've had marks similar to that in football, but they were usually the result of some giant guy plowing into me at breakneck speed. I can't figure out how she hit the drawer that hard unless she took a running start and slammed her face into it."

Destiny snorted at the mental picture of Amy's classy mother charging at a dresser like a bull at a red cape. "Nope, I can't see that at all," she said. "Maybe she fell off a stool or tripped and fell into the drawer. Any idea what she was doing when it happened?"

Jake leaned back in the chair and stretched his long muscular legs, flexing his toes. A girl had to admire that body. Even in the white tank, Destiny could see the line of his six-pack. Man, he radiated hotness. She fought the jealousy that stabbed her heart. She certainly hoped Amy treated him well. He was a decent guy, and he deserved to be treated with respect. He caught her gazing at him, and she dropped her eyes.

"Yeah. She bought Amy this furniture for her room."

"Well, that was nice," she said, thinking about all the stuff she'd had to sell when she'd moved. No chance of getting anything new here. Her grandmother could barely afford the light bill, from the looks of things. She'd bet owning a book store didn't bring in much money.

"I don't think Amy thought so. She hated it." He grinned and shook his head.

"Why? I would love to get new furniture."

"This wasn't exactly what you'd call new. You know Mrs. Morgan is an antiques dealer, right?"

Destiny nodded.

"She ordered this furniture from a catalogue. It's really old and appeared to have been in some kind of fire. It's covered in soot, but I think that can all be sanded off. Mrs. M. got it in her head that she and Amy could work on it this summer. Sort of a mother-daughter project."

Destiny thought about her own mother and how she'd never get to do anything similar with her ever again. Her chest burned, and she blinked away tears. Never had she been so thankful for the darkness.

"Anyway," he went on, seeming not to notice her reaction, "Amy hated it. She said it was the ugliest furniture she'd ever seen. She was pretty harsh about it." He dropped his feet to the porch and leaned toward Destiny, resting his elbows on his knees. "I'm like, dude...your mom wants to spend some time with you this summer. You complain about her not being around all the time, and then when she does something that brings you together, you complain. I don't get her sometimes. It's like she wants everything her way."

Surprised that Jake would diss his own girlfriend, Destiny said, "Some girls are that way, I guess."

"She can be. I mean, she can be really sweet too, don't get me wrong, but I think she was really harsh with her mom about this furniture."

"What does the furniture look like?" she asked, pulling her feet up into the chair, a move that caught Jake's attention. He eyed her legs, and his gaze traveled to her face. His blue eyes sparkled in the dim, washed-out glow of the porch light.

"Amy's mom called it French Rococko or something."

"Rococo," Destiny corrected, grinning.

"Yeah, that's it. Pretty fancy stuff. It has all these angels carved on the headboard and the frame of the mirror. I went around the dresser to get a better look, and the mirror nearly conked me on the head."

"What?"

"It fell. Right when I came around the dresser. It's a good thing I caught it, or it would have crashed to the floor. It was heavy too."

"Wow," Destiny commented.

"Yeah, I thought the mirror might have fallen on her, but Dr. Morgan said it wasn't on the floor when he found her. I offered to tighten it for her, but she said no."

"I bet it will be really pretty once they refinish it." It had to be better than the sardine can Destiny slept in.

"If they even work on it now. I don't know. I'll be surprised if they do."

"Well, that would suck if they didn't. I think it would be fun to work with my mom that way." She cleared her throat and stared into the night.

Jake's eyes went wide. "Oh crap, Destiny. I'm sorry. I wasn't thinking."

She raised her eyebrows at his sensitivity to the loss of her parents. He knew about it, and he cared. She liked him even more at that moment. "Well, I hope Mrs. Morgan will be okay," she said.

"I think she will. She may have one hell…I mean heck of a headache for a while, though." He actually blushed. His brown hair, longer than what Destiny thought would be respectable in this town, was tucked behind his reddening ears. He scuffed his feet back into his flip-flops.

She grinned again. Jake really was the best.

The screen door squeaked, and Rose stepped out on the porch. "It's late," she said in her matter-of-fact tone. "What are you two doing out here? Giving the neighbors something to wag their tongues about?"

Destiny waved her arms around. "What neighbors?"

"Sarcasm doesn't become you, young lady," Rose said, giving Destiny what she'd come to refer to as the stink eye. She hadn't gotten that look very much since she'd moved in, but she preferred to avoid it.

"Sorry, Grams. We were just talking about what happened up at the Morgan's today."

"What did happen? Is everything all right?"

Jake repeated his story. Rose's eyes grew dark, and one brow lifted. She glanced from Jake up to the house and shuffled over to the porch railing. That only took about two steps on the tiny porch, plus she had to scoot behind Jake's chair to get there. Destiny found that slightly embarrassing, sure that Jake was used to much nicer accommodations than where she currently found herself.

Rose eyed the house for several seconds, then turned and said, "Well, you best be headed home, Mr. Turner. And next time you come calling, make it earlier."

Heat flooded Destiny's cheeks. Could she have been any ruder? Jake didn't seem to mind, though. He just said, "Yes, ma'am, Madame Rose. I was just leaving anyway. Bye, Destiny."

Destiny smiled and gave him a little wave. He went to his Jeep and saluted as he backed out into the road. Destiny faced Rose. She was staring at the Morgan house again.

"What is it, Grams?" she asked, joining her at the porch railing.

"Something's not quite right up there. Do you see that?"

"What?"

"There at the garage. That pale greenish glow?"

Tingles started at the base of Destiny's spine and slithered up into her scalp. She shivered. A pale green light, the color of mint, glowed in the garage window.

"That's weird," she commented. "What is it?"

"I'm too far away to get a good reading, but I can tell there is something up there that is not of this world."

"What do you mean? A ghost or something?" Oh boy, not this again. The neighborhood appeared to be infested with spirits.

"Or something," Grams said. Then abruptly, she turned and said, "Time for bed." The screen door slapped against its frame behind her.

"Oohkaay," Destiny said, drawing out the word. She turned, viewed the Morgan's garage again and gasped. There in the window stood the shadowy figure of a girl with long hair. Behind her swirled that greenish haze. She watched in horror as the girl disappeared right before her eyes. Destiny ran into the house and locked the door. Butter and biscuits, that was scary. If this was what she was in for, she needed to look for a way to get rid of this gift of hers, and fast.

CHAPTER NINE

Amy leaned one shoulder on the door jamb that led from the kitchen to the garage. Spooning Cheerios into her mouth, she stared at the offending furniture that her mother was so fond of. She just didn't see the attraction. Why her mother wanted to refinish this disaster that others called bedroom furniture was beyond her comprehension. At times Amy thought her mother was stupid. Why, all of a sudden, would she want to take on refinishing furniture as a mother-daughter project? It was as if her parents really didn't know her at all.

Her mother was crazy. It was going to take weeks to completely re-finish this crap. The dresser alone presented an impossible challenge. All those creepy angels. Amy shivered. She walked closer and set her bowl down on the charred surface. She touched the wood where her mother had wiped away some of the soot.

"*Amy*...." A voice whispered her name. She spun around, hair raising on the back of her neck. What the...?

Crash! Amy yelped, jumping back against the wall. What was that? The sound had come from just behind her. The cereal bowl lay scattered on the concrete in a thousand pieces, milk and Cheerios everywhere. How did that happen? She remembered putting the bowl in the center of the dresser. No way could it have fallen off on its own. And who had said her name?

Prickles of fear crawled from the base of her neck all the way down her back. Something caused the bowl to fly off onto the floor, but she could see no evidence of anything that could make that happen.

No science genius, she knew enough to know that bowls didn't fly off dressers by themselves. Amy approached the garage door and peered out the window. Maybe one of her friends had come by and thought it'd be funny to scare her. Nothing. The driveway was empty. Could she have imagined it?

She walked back to the dresser and stepped on something wet. Ew! Milk and soggy Cheerios. Hopping over to the workbench, she grabbed the roll of paper towels, wiped off her foot and then cleaned up the mess. She threw the shards of ceramic, the milk-soaked paper towels and her socks into the garbage can.

Amy shivered again and pushed the button raising the garage door. Rays of sunlight flooded the freezing space. She soaked in the sun's warm rays, chasing away whatever boogie man had called her name.

Amy turned back to the furniture, thoughts of her mother lying in that hospital bed drifting through her mind. She hated arguing, but it just seemed like they couldn't agree on anything anymore. It was like aliens had taken over her parents' brains, and they had no clue about what she liked, disliked, or wanted in her life. Not only were her parents clueless, but Jake seemed to have taken a stupid pill where she was concerned. He'd tried to play peacemaker with her mother yesterday. He'd even said the furniture wasn't that bad. Was he blind? He had even offered to help. He could easily tell how upset she was, so why had he sided with her mother? He should be taking her side. Just like at the party yesterday.

Maybe she was the one going crazy. Ever since that girl moved into Madame Rose's trailer, Amy's life had started falling apart. Maybe she'd put a hex on Amy's family or something. After all, her grandmother was a witch, so it would be natural for it to run in the family. Amy definitely hadn't missed the way she'd been staring at Jake down at the paddock. It was like she was trying to hypnotize him or something. Amy resolved then and there to make Destiny regret the day she moved to Arcadia.

Having nothing better to do to fill her time until her dad brought her mother home, she faced the offensive furniture. Her mother had started sanding the top of the dresser, and the blonde wood peered out from beneath the soot. It didn't look all that bad. Maybe she could surprise her mother when she returned from the hospital. She went to the built-in workbench and selected a piece of sandpaper, and attached it to the hand sander. She stuffed the earbuds of her iPod into her ears and pressed the button. No reason to hear any more strange voices.

She sanded the dresser's surface with short strokes as she had seen her father do when he worked on wood. Soon she fell into a rhythm, her muscles warming with the exercise. Her mother was right. Hard work was soothing to the soul. Wouldn't she be shocked when she returned home?

Fueled by the rock music and thoughts of pleasing her mother, Amy worked until she noticed she'd nearly completed the top of the dresser. She sighed with satisfaction, striding to the workbench to replace the worn sandpaper. Returning to the dresser, she froze. In the center, a sooty handprint soiled the smooth sanded surface. The tiny hairs at the nape of Amy's neck stood on end and her arms prickled with goose flesh. She glanced at her clean hands, her brows drawing down in confusion. How had that gotten there?

Carefully and cautiously, she approached the dresser and timidly placed her hand over the handprint matching it finger to finger. The moment her fingers made contact with the surface, a thrust of icy cold pain shot up her arm, increasing in intensity as it climbed. She snatched her hand away, her fingers burned by the cold.

Amy snorted out a nervous laugh. What was the matter with her? She'd just placed her own dirty hand on the dresser's surface before getting the sandpaper, that was all. She had no reason to be afraid of a piece of furniture. No…she couldn't explain the shock of icy cold that still tingled up her arm, but it was just a stupid piece of wood.

She would just sand it away and be more careful where she placed her dirty hands. With unbridled determination, Amy attacked the sooty spot. She rubbed and rubbed, applying more force with each stroke. When she lifted the sander, the handprint was still there. She rubbed again with increased intensity. She panted in time with her strokes. The muscles in her arms ached from the effort, but the handprint remained stubbornly in place. Amy kicked the front of the dresser with her foot.

"All right, handprint. I don't know how you got there, but you're going to come off if it's the last thing I do."

She pressed down hard and gave the sander a shove. Pain erupted in the palm of her hand so suddenly that she dropped the tool, and it clattered on the cement floor.

"Ow, Ow, Ow," she shouted, shaking her right hand and jumping up and down.

Turning her hand over, she discovered a splinter the size of a toothpick lodged in her palm. It was so deep that she couldn't even get a fingernail under the edge to try and work it out. Instantly, the soft flesh of her palm began to redden and swell.

"This is just great," she grumbled aloud, cradling the injured hand with her good one. "Now, what am I going to do?" Her dad was at the hospital and wouldn't be home for hours. The wound was swelling, and she knew she couldn't get the splinter out by herself. She examined the dresser where the stubborn handprint still remained and next to it, a deep gouge in the wood.

"Stupid piece of crap," she muttered, kicking the dresser a second time.

Tossing the sander, she walked into the house and went to the kitchen sink. She turned on the faucet and placed her hand under the flow, watching the water, tinged lightly pink with her blood, swirl down the drain. The sink was directly beneath the kitchen window that looked out onto the back yard and the acreage beyond. She noticed Madame Rose's trailer.

Amy looked at the clock. It was almost four o'clock. Madame Rose's shop didn't close until six, but her car was in the gravel driveway. Maybe she'd come home early today. She started toward the kitchen door and stopped. What was she thinking? She couldn't let that witch treat her hand. She might go all voodoo on her.

Amy pulled her cell phone out of her purse that was sitting on the kitchen table. She dialed her father's number and waited for him to answer. He didn't. Her hand throbbed, and she knew if she didn't get that splinter out, she might face an infection. Walking back into the hall, she went to the half-bathroom on the first floor. She opened the medicine cabinet and took out some alcohol and a pair of tweezers. Wincing at the sting, she poured the alcohol on the wound and pried at the splinter. She got a grip on the edge and tried to draw it backward out of her hand and yelped. It was no use. She couldn't do it alone. Her hand throbbed as she reached for her cell phone to try her father again; still no answer. "Crap," she said to herself.

Amy walked back into the kitchen and stood, looking out the window again at Madame Rose's trailer. She thought about calling Jake and having him take her to the hospital but then remembered he was helping his dad bale hay today. He probably didn't even have his cell phone with him. She definitely needed help, and it seemed the only one who could help her was Madame Rose.

Slipping her feet into her sandals, she pulled the back door shut behind her. Walking across the yard, sweat ran down her palms, the saltiness stinging the wound. What would she say? She'd only seen Madame Rose up close once, which was when she was six years old. The woman scared her to death. All that long, gray hair that she just let hang down her back. Her hands were all twisted with arthritis, and she was hunched over with a slight hump on her back. Her frosty blue eyes seemed to look right through her. No wonder her friends thought she was a witch.

Amy swallowed hard as she walked up the porch steps. The door swung open as she raised her hand to knock. She braced herself for the sight of the old woman, but Destiny peered through the screen.

"Amy? What are you doing here?"

"I've got a really large splinter in my hand, and my parents aren't home. I thought maybe Madame Rose could take a look at it for me."

"Ow. That looks pretty wicked," Destiny said, pushing open the screen door. Amy followed her into the tiny kitchen as Destiny turned and called over her shoulder. "Grams, can you come here for a minute?"

She gestured Amy into the small kitchen. "She's just changing clothes. How did you hurt your hand?"

Amy glanced around the place and was surprised by how small it was. From where she sat in the kitchen, she could see all the other rooms. To the right of the kitchen was the family room with a doorway that led into a bedroom. It was so small it looked more like her closet. To the left of the kitchen was a short hallway, which led to the bathroom and another bedroom. The place was clean but worn. The wood veneered cabinets were sagging on their hinges, and the vinyl floor needed replacing. Amy couldn't imagine living this way. There was barely enough room for one person to be comfortable, much less two.

Madame Rose came out of the bedroom on the left, surprising Amy with her appearance. She was not the hag in witches' robes that she had expected. Her gray hair was twisted into a tight bun at the back of her neck, and she wore orange Capri pants with a red and orange striped shirt. She shuffled a little when she walked, but she definitely wasn't the hunchbacked arthritic person that Amy remembered. Maybe at six years old, things looked a little different.

"Amy, isn't it?" she said, her raspy voice like the sound of dried leaves blown about in a soft breeze. She did have blue eyes, but they were softer than Amy remembered, like a blue sky on a summer day, not frosty and cold.

Amy swallowed. "Yes, ma'am." She held out her injured hand. "I have a splinter in my hand, and it's very deep. My parents aren't home, and I thought maybe you could take a look at it for me."

"Oh dear," Madame Rose said as she took Amy's red, swollen hand into her cool, dry one. "Let me have a closer look." She sat in the chair next to Amy at the kitchen table. "Destiny, go to the bathroom and get my first aid kit. I'll also need my magnifying glass from my bedside table."

Destiny returned to the table with the requested items. She placed them in front of her grandmother. "Here you go, Grams."

"Thank you, now look under the sink there and hand me my mortar and pestle and the herb bag."

Destiny did as directed and joined them at the table. Amy watched as Rose shook some dried green herbs out of a black leather pouch into the mortar. Pouring a little water into the bowl, she ground the herbs with the pestle until they formed a thick paste. Taking a small spatula out of the black leather bag, she scooped some of the paste out and started to smooth it over Amy's hand.

Amy jerked her hand from the old woman's grasp. "What is that for?"

Rose gently reached for her hand and held it. "It's a paste made with some herbs from my garden. It will help the swelling go down and relieve some of the pain. Once the swelling has gone down, then I can get the splinter out."

Amy looked dubious. "I've already tried pulling it out. It's stuck in there pretty tight, you know? Um…do you know what you're doing?"

Rose smiled. "As a matter of fact, I was a nurse for fifteen years, long before you were born. That was before I became a witch, you know."

Both Amy and Destiny gasped. Rose started laughing. "Close your mouths before a bug flies in." They snapped their jaws shut. "You two look like a couple of bass from the pond. I've never seen such a look. Isn't that what you and your friends think…that I'm a witch?"

Amy swallowed, cheeks flaming. It certainly was, but how did Madame Rose know that?

"The funny thing is…" Rose said as she swathed the paste on Amy's hand, "people are always willing to believe just about anything as long as they hear it from enough people. Let me remind you that just because you hear a rumor doesn't make it true. It just so happens that ancient people used natural remedies, many of which grow right in your own back yard."

Amy marveled as the pain in her palm eased.

"The reason you had no luck getting the splinter out is because your hand is swollen. Your flesh is mashing in around the splinter and trapping it. Once this paste does its job, I'll be able to see what I'm doing."

Amy pushed on her palm, her eyes wide. "Wow, that stuff really works."

Rose just nodded and smiled. While she waited for the poultice to do its work, she pulled a small pair of scissors, some Iodine, and some butterfly bandages out of the first aid kit. She poked at Amy's palm with a fingernail. "Does that hurt?"

Amy looked down at her hand. "No. It's numb. I can't even feel you pushing on it."

"Good. Now we can get the splinter out. You might want to look away as I do this."

Amy glanced toward the sink, squinting her eyes. She jumped when Destiny said, "How did you get a splinter this size in your hand?"

"I was sanding an old dresser my mother bought for me, and I guess my hand was too far to the side of the sander."

"So you did decide to work on it? Jake said you didn't like it."

Amy's head snapped up, and she looked pointedly at Destiny. "When did Jake tell you that?"

"Last night, when he stopped by on his way home. He wanted to let us know about your mom. I'm really sorry, by the way."

Amy's eyes narrowed as she contemplated Destiny's words. "Jake stopped by here last night?"

Destiny smiled, eyes sparkling. "Yeah, but he didn't stay long. How's your mom doing this morning? Jake said she had a nasty fall and hit her head on that furniture she bought for you."

"Well," Amy said. "Jake is just a regular George Stephanopolis, isn't he?"

Rose took the sterilized scissors and finished cutting through the thin top layer of Amy's skin. She went down the entire length of the splinter, and when she was finished, she laid the two flaps of skin open. After blotting away the blood, she reached in with tweezers, lifting out the splinter. She laid it on the table beside the bottle of alcohol. She then poured a generous amount of alcohol on the open wound. Amy didn't even flinch. Once she patted the wound dry, she closed the two flaps of skin together with the butterfly strips. "There," Rose said, examining her work. "All done."

Amy turned her head and stared at the wound. "Wow, I didn't even feel that. Those herbs really do the trick. How did you learn about all that herb stuff? They don't teach that in nursing school."

Rose smiled. "My mother was a Native American. She taught me all the old ways of healing. It's not so hard once you know where to find all the plants. It's easier today, as I can order them from the Internet instead of searching for them in the woods." She laughed at Amy's expression. "What, you think I don't know how to use a computer?"

Amy closed her mouth, knowing she was being rude, but it surprised her that this woman knew her way around modern technology. "I just...I mean, I didn't know you could order plants on eBay." She laughed lamely.

"As I said before, Amy, don't believe everything you hear. People make judgments about people because they're afraid of something unknown to them. Just because something is foreign doesn't make it dangerous." Rose gathered the items and carried them to the sink. "I've found in my life that the things I'm afraid of are generally the things I don't know anything about. Knowledge is power, Amy. The more you know, the more you're able to understand. You never did answer Destiny's question. Is your mother going to be okay?"

Amy glanced at Destiny and then back at Rose. "Yes, she is going to be okay. It's weird, you know?"

"What?" Destiny said.

"That we both got hurt working on that stupid furniture. It's like it's cursed or something." Amy laughed nervously. "Isn't that crazy?"

"Mmmm. Maybe not so crazy," Rose commented.

"What do you mean?" Amy asked, curiosity filling her expression.

"Well, have you noticed anything strange happening with the furniture other than you and your mother getting hurt?"

"Like what exactly?"

"Is it extremely cold in the area, for example? Have you heard anything odd? Smelled anything strange?"

Amy pondered the question. "You know, it was cold in the garage this morning. I thought the air conditioner was broken, but what would that have to do with the furniture?" She omitted hearing her name spoken, certain the old woman would think she was nuts.

Destiny shifted in her chair. "Grams, I think Amy better get back to her house. Her dad may have tried to call or something and wonder where she is." She grabbed Amy's wrist and pulled her up out of the chair. "I'll walk you back."

"Wait, I wanted to hear what Madame Rose was going to say about the cold. How did you know about that?"

Amy caught Destiny mouthing the word "No" to her grandmother.

"What?" Amy said.

"Nothing," Destiny said. "Come on, let's go."

"Wait," Amy protested.

Rose must have caught on because she said, "Destiny's right. Your father might be wondering where you are. You show him that hand as soon as you see him and make sure it doesn't need some real stitches. I tried not to cut too deep, and I think the butterfly bandages should hold it, but you want to be sure."

Amy glared at Destiny as she dragged her out the front door of the trailer. "Thanks, Madame Rose," she shouted over her shoulder.

Once they were outside, Amy jerked her wrist loose from Destiny's grip. "What's the rush? I wanted to hear what she had to say about the cold. Don't you think it's weird that she would know about that?"

Destiny started across the yard toward Amy's house. "She's just guessing, that's all. I mean, you and I both know that it's just furniture."

"I know, but it really was cold in the garage this morning."

"I'm sure you're right. I bet something is wrong with your air conditioner." Destiny switched the subject quickly to get Amy distracted from her grandmother's words. "Are you and Jake going riding later today?"

At the mention of Jake, Amy stopped walking.

"He's my boyfriend, Destiny. I want you to stay away from him."

Destiny cocked her head, appearing confused. Amy bet she'd be a great actress, but she wasn't fooled. She'd known plenty of girls just like Destiny.

"What are you talking about?" Destiny asked and then answered her own question. "Oh, you mean him stopping by here last night." She resumed walking, and Amy scuttled to catch up. "Amy, it's not like I stood out in the middle of the road and flagged him down. He saw me sitting on the porch and stopped to tell us about what happened at your house. Jake was obviously concerned about your mom, and he wanted to let us know what was going on. I thought it was really sweet."

Amy wasn't buying the innocent act. "He's mine, Destiny. Stay away from him."

"Look, Amy, if you're insecure about your relationship with Jake, that's not my problem. He's trying to be a good friend, and I really appreciate it."

"That's the thing about Jake," Amy said. "He is really sweet, and he doesn't see it when a girl is trying to put the moves on him, but I'm not that stupid. I know what you're doing."

Destiny rolled her eyes and shrugged. "Whatever. I'm not trying to steal your boyfriend, Amy. I'm new in town and just need to make friends. I'm not trying to make trouble."

The girls reached the garage. Amy pushed the buttons on the

keypad, and the door rolled up. "Just so we have an understanding."

Destiny peered into the garage and nodded. "Okay, okay. Can I see the furniture?"

Amy led Destiny over to examine the bedroom suite. She glanced at the bed frame and then wandered over to the dresser. She appraised the hand-carved cherubs and agreed with Amy. "Those really are creepy," Destiny said, pointing at the angels.

"I know. Isn't it horrible? I can't imagine why my mother thought I'd like it in my room."

Destiny said, "Oh, it's not so bad. It has a certain personality. The angels are a little creepy. Look at the way they all stare at the center of the mirror."

"I know, right?" Amy said. "If you think those are creepy, come here and look at this."

Destiny wandered over and glanced at the handprint on the top of the dresser.

"How'd that get there? It looks like it was burned into the wood." Destiny leaned down to peer at the black sooty print.

"I know. It just showed up after I finished sanding. I went to change the pad on the sander, turned around and there it was."

Destiny raised one eyebrow.

"I know, you think I'm crazy. There's something else weird about it. Touch it."

"Why?" Destiny asked, her expression doubtful.

"What? You chicken? Go on…touch it."

**

Destiny stared at the dresser. What was Amy trying to pull? Tentatively, Destiny placed her hand over the burned print. A shock of cold and pain shot up her arm. Energy sizzled through every nerve ending. She tried to pull away but couldn't. For a minute, she wondered if Amy had tried to trick her with super glue or something.

The mirror glass filled with a silvery fog, drawing Destiny's attention. It swirled to a point in the very center where a figure formed in the mist. The wooden angels watched, their cherub lips forming strange grins. Was she hallucinating?

A girl's figure approached. Her stringy brown hair hung in her face, her thin charred arms by her sides. Destiny's heart pounded, and she tried again to jerk away, but her hand held fast. The ghostly girl came closer. She raised her head, and at the sight of her face, Destiny's breath caught in her throat. The poor girl's completely charred skin fell off in clumps. Both eyes were gone from their sockets. Destiny could only see dark holes where the eyeballs should be. The apparition's teeth were exposed to the jawline where her face had been burned to the bone. Destiny heard screaming…the girl's or her own, she wasn't sure.

Behind the ghost, the shadow of a taller figure approached. The girl turned, and her sightless eye sockets widened. Her disfigured face turned back to Destiny, her blackened arms reaching out for help. The black shadow completely engulfed her, dragging her backward until they disappeared. The maniacal laugh that followed chilled Destiny's blood.

A powerful yank released the hold, and Destiny fell backwards on her butt. She scooted backward, crablike, away from the dresser.

"Destiny, what is wrong with you?" Amy came up behind her, halting her backward scuttle. "I was yelling at you, and you acted like you didn't even hear me. What were you looking at in that mirror?"

"If I were you, Amy, I'd get rid of that as fast as you can." Destiny scrambled to her feet.

"What? Why? What the heck did you see?"

Through her fear-fogged brain, Amy's words registered. Destiny couldn't let Amy know what she could do. Destiny forced her brain cells to think, trying to come up with a plausible explanation for her behavior. "Um…I didn't see anything. I…." Destiny backed toward the opening of the garage.

"You must have seen something. I tried to pull you away, but your arms were locked stiff. Your body wouldn't move. Did you have a seizure or something?"

Okay! A seizure. Destiny grasped at the lifeline Amy had just thrown her. "I guess." She reached the driveway. "I've gotta go home." Destiny dashed around the corner of the house. If this was what her gift had in store for her, she needed to find a way to get rid of it. Fast.

CHAPTER TEN

Destiny reached her front porch in record time, heart hammering. She sat down hard in one of the two chairs that crowded the small space. What she'd witnessed in Amy's garage was the most frightening thing she'd ever seen. That girl in the mirror, with the burned face, and what was with the shadowy figure behind her? What did it mean? Obviously, the girl was dead, and that was why Destiny could see her, but what was up with Shadow Man? She could sense the terror in the girl, so she knew the presence of that weirdo wasn't good.

This so-called "gift" of hers had to go. She needed to do some research and find out if it was something she could turn off. This was so not cool. Patch was one thing, and that was scary enough, but what she saw in Amy's garage totally terrified her. Her eyes welled up with tears. She missed her family and her old life. Before the accident, she had been a normal teenager, living the high life in Naples, never having to worry about anything. Now she lived with her weirdo grandmother in a neighborhood where she had no friends and probably never would once Amy ran her mouth. They were all going to think she was as crazy as her grandmother.

The screen door squeaked, and Rose stepped out on the porch. "Amy get home okay?" She glanced at Amy's house, then turned her gaze to Destiny's pale, sweaty face. "What's wrong? You look like you've seen a ghost." She chuckled at her own joke.

"That's not funny, Grams," Destiny snapped.

"Whoa, easy now. Watch your tone. What has you all riled up?

Something happen up there?" She indicated Amy's house with a twist of her head.

"As a matter of fact, something did happen. Something very terrifying. I'm not sure I ever want to go back up there again." Destiny pulled her feet up into the chair and hugged her knees.

Rose sat down facing Destiny. "What was it, honey?"

Destiny put her face down on her knees. "I really don't want to talk about it. It was horrible."

Rose laid a hand on Destiny's head and stroked her hair. "I think it will help you to talk about it. I can help, baby. Did it have anything to do with that odd light we saw up there last night?"

"I don't know, Grams. Maybe."

"Why don't you start at the beginning and tell me everything. Don't leave out a single detail."

Destiny looked up and shook her long hair back away from her face. She recounted her experience up to the point where the Shadow Man appeared. Rose listened intently, her expression grave.

Destiny began to shake. Reliving the event brought back the same adrenaline rush she experienced in the garage. She stood, but Rose stopped her. She put her hands on Destiny's shoulders and gently pushed her back into the chair. "You sit here. I'll be right back."

Rose went into the house and returned a short time later with a small shot glass. She handed it to Destiny. "Here, drink this. It's good for what ails you."

Destiny accepted the glass and held it up to her nose. Shocked, she sputtered, "Grams, this is whiskey!"

"I think I know what it is since I poured it. Go on now, drink it. Swallow it down in one gulp. It'll burn a little bit going down, but it will give you courage to face what's next."

Destiny crinkled her nose and drank. The amber liquid burned its way down her throat, and she coughed. It tasted horrible, but once it hit her stomach, a warming sensation spread through her frozen muscles. After a second or two, she did feel a little stronger.

Rose watched her and smiled. "Better?"

Destiny nodded and coughed again. "Wow, that stuff's strong."

"Yes, it is and not for everyday consumption, but after what you've been through, I thought you could use it. Want to finish telling me what happened because I've a feeling you're not done."

Destiny took a deep breath. "Well, as I was watching this horrible girl, this shadowy figure began to form behind her. It never had a face, but it loomed up over her. She looked back at it, and I could tell she was scared because she opened her mouth to scream. I heard screaming, but honestly, Grams, I don't know if it was me or her. Then Amy pulled my hand away from the dresser, and I fell on the floor."

Rose was quiet for a moment, then she said, "Did you ever feel threatened by this shadow man? Were you as afraid of him as the girl?"

"Well, duh. I was afraid of both of them."

"I know that, honey, but think back a minute. Did the shadow figure seem more threatening than the girl?"

Destiny thought about that. "Yeah, I guess so. It all happened so fast that I'm not really sure. Amy started to quiz me about what I saw, and I just couldn't tell her. She'd think I was insane. It was obvious that she hadn't seen it."

"Hmm. This is very interesting. First, Amy's mother gets hurt, then Amy, now you experience this apparition. What'd you tell Amy?"

"She asked me if I'd had a seizure, and I just went with it. Then I ran. I know she didn't believe me, Grams, but I just can't let her know what I can see. I'll never live it down. She'll spread it all over school. She's already mad at me because Jake wants to be my friend. How am I ever going to learn to live with this? It's horrible. I can see why Mom chose to ignore it. How can I turn it off like she did?"

"She didn't. She just ran from it. Destiny, honey, it's not something you can turn off like a switch. But, I can teach you how to shield yourself from it. It won't stop you from being contacted, but it will put you in better control of how you receive the images and sounds. Your mother would never let me help her. Did she ever suffer from headaches?"

"Yeah. Really bad ones. She would stay in bed for two or three days. Dad said they were migraines, but they weren't, were they?"

"No, they weren't. My guess is she tried to ignore messages from the spirit world without the proper shields. That would certainly give you one whale of a headache."

Destiny nodded. After a quiet moment, she said, "Grams, do you see these visions all the time? Do the dead always look like they did when they died? You know, all bloody and messed up and stuff?"

"Sometimes. In my experience, the more violent the death, the more horrible the image I see." Rose settled back into the white plastic lawn chair. "Now take Patch, for instance. You saw him, and he didn't look ugly and nasty, did he?"

"No."

"Well, he died a non-violent death, right here on this very farm. That is why you see him as he lived. People who die violent deaths are ripped from their bodies so quickly that the transformation doesn't have time to take place."

"This is all so weird, Grams. No one is going to believe me if I tell them what I saw. Anyone I meet is going to think I'm a freak." Her eyes misted with tears. She swiped at them.

"Destiny, I hardly think your true friends will think any such thing, but for now, I'd keep your gift a secret. It can be a little hard for people to embrace what we're able to do. Somehow they all seem to come around, though, especially when they lose someone and they want to find out what happened to them."

Destiny stared out across the yard. Butch nudged her hand with his cold nose, and Destiny's fingers slid into the soft fur. She rubbed his ears absently. "Grams?"

Rose looked at Destiny. "What is it, child?"

"Will Mom, Dad, and Elijah look like they did the night of the accident once they find their way back to us?"

Gently, Rose took Destiny's hand in her own. She held it firmly for a moment. "Maybe, sweetheart. I don't know for sure, but if they do make it back to visit, and I'm sure they'll try, we'll be prepared for whatever we have to face. If they managed to cross over, then that is a different story. They will appear in spirit form, and you will hear them, but all you'll see will be soft amber light. If they didn't cross over…then it could be ugly."

"What do you think happened? Do you think they crossed over?"

"I have faith that your mama knew what she needed to do. I only hope her love for you didn't cloud her judgment and keep her here. We'll just have to wait and see." Rose patted Destiny's knee and rose.

"At any rate, we need to fix some dinner. This old woman's hungry."

"I'll be in to help in a minute."

Destiny pondered her grandmother's words as she remained on the porch that warm afternoon. She shivered as she thought of what she'd seen in Amy's garage. That was horrible, but it wouldn't even compare to what she'd feel if she had to see her parents and her brother the way they looked when they died in the car crash. She prayed hard at that moment, harder than she'd ever prayed for anything. "Dear Lord," she whispered. "Please let them have crossed over."

CHAPTER ELEVEN

It was after dinner that night when Amy's father carried Sarah in from the car to her bedroom. Amy tucked in the soft powder blue covers around her mother.

"Stop it, Amy." Sarah pushed her hands away. "This is complete nonsense. I am perfectly fine and do not need to be treated as if I'm an invalid. The doctor said to rest. He didn't say I had to stay in bed."

Jeff looked at his wife and smiled indulgently. "Sarah, you know you need to stay in bed for at least a day or two. You took a pretty bad bump on the head, and it won't hurt you to give your body a chance to recover." He raised a hand when she started to protest again. "You've been working much too hard anyway. A few days in bed will do you good. Now, I'm going to go downstairs and fix you some tea. Would you like anything else?"

Sarah sighed, exasperated. "This is ridiculous. I've got to see to the store, and I've clients to shop for. I can't stay in bed like this, Jeff."

Jeff held up his hand again. "Not listening, Sarah. Do you want anything else from the kitchen?"

"Ugh. You drive me nuts." She slapped her hands on the quilted coverlet puffing it up on both sides, but she surrendered. "Bring me a sandwich, please. That hospital food was horrible."

Jeff smiled. "A sandwich and tea, coming right up. Amy, you stay with your mom and make sure she obeys orders."

Amy sat on the side of the bed. "I will, Dad."

The minute Jeff left the bedroom, Sarah leaned toward Amy

conspiratorially. "As soon as he goes back to work, you and I are going to get to work on that furniture again. I'll call a few clients, reschedule my buying trip for next week, and then we can get a good amount of work done before school starts. I want to finish it and have it in your room before then, and this…." she reached up and touched the bruise on the side of her face, "little accident has put me behind."

"Mom, you heard what Dad said, bed rest for two days. You have a concussion for crying out loud. Why can't you just rest for a while?"

"Because I'll go crazy lying here. I'm not the bed rest type. Besides, I'm excited to see how that furniture will turn out once it's finished."

Amy looked down at her bandaged hand. "Mom, how can you be so excited? That furniture nearly killed you."

"Amy, that is total nonsense, and you know it."

"Then how do you explain that mark on your face that looks exactly like the pattern on the drawer handle of that dresser? I bet if we went down there right now and held one of those drawers up to your face, it would be a perfect match. That's just spooky. You even said yourself that you could have sworn the drawer slid out and hit you. I didn't believe you at first, but now…." Amy looked down at her own bandaged hand.

"Oh my gosh, what happened to your hand?"

Amy began fussing with the pillows behind her mother's back, reluctant to get into the story of her injury.

"Amy, what's going on?"

"It's no big deal, Mom. I was trying to help you with the furniture, and I jammed a big splinter into my hand. Madame Rose helped me get it out. It's fine."

Sarah's eyes grew wide and misted with tears. "You were trying to work on the furniture?"

"Oh, Mom, get over it. It's not a big deal. I wanted to have the top sanded before you got home."

"I'm just surprised you took it upon yourself to work on it alone. You seemed so uninterested before. What brought this on?"

"I don't know. I felt guilty, I guess." She walked over to the chaise lounge by the window and curled up in it. She loved her parents' cozy room. She'd come there and read when her parents weren't home. The evidence of her mother's talent as a decorator filled the large space.

The large four-poster bed held the focal point of the room, surrounded by sky blue walls and handmade white silk drapes at the windows. The blonde hardwood contrasted nicely with the dark blue area rug with a white border. A flat-screen television mounted on the wall across from the bed showed CNN with muted volume. Amy's eyes moved from the TV to her mother's curious gaze.

"What?"

"Tell me how you hurt your hand."

"I told you already." Her mother glared at her. Amy glanced down at the bandage and then back at her mother. Sarah waited patiently. "Mom, it was so weird. When I came back to the dresser, there was this black sooty handprint right in the middle of the top where I knew I'd already sanded. It just came out of nowhere, burned into the wood, but ice-cold when I touched it. I tried to sand the handprint out, but it wouldn't go away. I kept trying, and I guess I pushed too hard. A big splinter jammed into my palm. I tried to get it out, but I couldn't. Dad was at the hospital with you, so I went down to Madame Rose's. She took it out for me."

Sarah's forehead creased with worry. "Are you all right? Come over here and let me see it. You may need to have your father look at it. I bet it's going to get infected. Did Rose get all of it out?"

"It's fine. I'll tell Dad about it later." Amy shifted positions on the chair, leaning forward with her elbows on her knees. "Mom?"

"What, honey?"

"You're going to think I'm crazy."

"What is it, Amy?" Sarah patted the coverlet summoning her daughter to the bed.

Amy joined her and leaned back against one of the extra pillows. "I think something is wrong with that furniture."

"Like what?"

"I don't know, like it's possessed or something."

Sarah snorted out a laugh. "Amy, that's absurd. Why would you say such a thing?"

Amy began to pick at the coverlet with her thumb and forefinger. "Well, don't you think everything that's been happening is weird? First you, then me...then Destiny...." She trailed off.

"Destiny? Rose's granddaughter?"

Amy nodded.

"What happened to her? Has the whole world gone crazy overnight?" Sarah said.

Amy shrugged. "Nothing happened to her, really. It's just…well… she walked me home after Madame Rose took the splinter out. I'm glad she did because we had to get some things straight about Jake. But anyway, she walked into the garage, took one look at that mirror on the dresser and freaked out."

"Amy, you know I'm not fond of slang. What do you mean?"

Amy looked at her mom and sighed. "I dared her to touch that handprint because she didn't believe me when I told her it was cold as ice. So she did, and all of a sudden, she went real stiff. She was staring into the mirror when her eyes got real wide, and she screamed. I couldn't see anything in that mirror. I thought she'd lost her marbles. I kept yelling at her, but it was like she couldn't hear me. She scared me so bad, Mom. Finally, I yanked her hand really hard, and she fell backwards onto the garage floor." Amy shifted on the bed.

"What happened then?"

Amy frowned. "She sat there for a minute and then looked up at me. I asked her what was wrong and what she'd seen in that mirror, but she wouldn't answer me. I asked her if she'd had a seizure or something. She said, 'yeah, that's it,' then got up and ran out." Amy glanced out the window, then back at her mother. "Mom, I know she saw something in that mirror."

Sarah sat in the bed, absorbing Amy's words. "I admit, that sounds very strange, but maybe you're right, and it was just a seizure of some kind. There are a lot of reasonable explanations for what happened, just like what happened to me. I simply leaned down too fast, got dizzy and fell into the dresser. The handprint was probably your own dirty hands, and soot is very hard to get off of wood, so that's probably why it wouldn't come off with the sander. The splinter was your own fault for not paying attention to what you were doing."

Doubt clouded Amy's expression. "Maybe."

"I'm sure that's all, Amy. The furniture is not possessed. That's just silly. Now go see about my sandwich. I'm starving."

Amy slipped off the bed to do as she was asked, upset that her mother didn't believe her. "I'm telling you, Mom, there is something weird about that furniture." She shut the bedroom door behind her.

Downstairs in the kitchen, her father was on the phone, and a half-finished sandwich lay on the kitchen counter. Amy sighed and completed the creation, adding the meat, cheese, mustard and lettuce to the bread.

Her father walked in just as she finished. "Oh, thank you, sweetheart. The hospital called about one of my patients, and I got distracted. Your mom is probably wondering where that is. I'll take it on up to her. You can bring the tea when the water starts boiling."

Amy rolled her eyes. "The water is boiling, Dad. Look." She pointed at the stove where a metal tea kettle whistled

"Well, so it is. Why don't you go ahead and make your mom a cup of tea then, and I'll take it up with the sandwich? She likes the way you make it better anyway."

"You're just saying that because you don't want to do it."

"I am not," her father said. "I just know she likes the way you put that cinnamon spice in it. I don't know how to do that."

"Like it's really hard, Dad. You shake the cinnamon and sugar into the tea and stir it."

Jeff laughed. "Yes, I suppose you're right. Hey, what happened to your hand?"

Amy rolled her eyes again. "It's no big deal. I was working on the furniture in the garage, and I got a splinter in it. It was pretty deep, so Madame Rose had to take it out for me. She did say you probably should look at it. You know, make sure it's not infected or anything."

"Well, let's have a look." He reached for her hand and began to unravel the bandage. He turned her hand over and studied Rose's handiwork. "Geese, Amy, how big was the splinter? It looks like she had to cut you open to get it out."

"I guess it was about the size of a toothpick. It really hurt until she mixed up some of this pasty stuff from some herbs in a pouch. Then I didn't feel anything at all. She spread that goo on my hand, and it numbed right up."

Now Amy's father rolled his eyes. "Oh boy, she went all natural on you, huh?"

"Well, sort of. She seemed to know what she was doing. Did you know that she used to be a nurse?"

"I'd heard something about that, yes. I think it was a long time ago, though. Although, it looks like she did a pretty decent job here. Looks like you could use a few stitches."

Just the thought of having more work done on her hand made Amy groan. "Do you have to? Won't those butterfly Band-Aid thingies hold it together? I really don't want to mess with it. It doesn't hurt now, but if you go and do all that, it will start to hurt again."

"Well, it doesn't look infected, but I want you to take an antibiotic just in case, and I'll keep an eye on it." He turned her hand to the left and then back to the right. "I guess we could wait a day or so and see how the butterfly bandages do." He reached into a kitchen cabinet, pulled out a roll of gauze and wrapped her hand again. "I'll check it again tonight and in the morning, but for now, it looks okay. Did you thank her?"

"Of course." Amy stirred the tea and put the cup and saucer on the tray. "Take this up to Mom. She told me she was starving. And whatever you do, don't give her a little bell to ring. She'll drive us both crazy with it."

Jeff laughed and picked up the tray. "You're right about that."

CHAPTER TWELVE

Rain spattered the darkened road and sizzled to steam on the burning car. Destiny faced the flaming coffin holding her baby brother, her feet rooted to the spot.

"Save him, Destiny," her mother's severed head pleaded from the center of the road. "Hurry...before he comes."

"Before who comes, Mama?" Destiny's head swiveled, examining the area. She saw nothing.

Her mother's head rotated away from Destiny, bone scraping against asphalt. "Oh God, there he is! Get Elijah, Destiny! Hurry!"

Destiny squinted into the darkness, and there he was. In the midst of the scrub palms and pines stood a tall cloaked figure. The laugh that emerged from beneath the black hood chilled her bones. Who was that? Death?

Her mother's head continued to scream. Destiny started toward the van. What should have been a full sprint felt more like a turtle crawl. Time slowed down for her, but not for the cloaked man. He reached the van before she did. Destiny screamed. "No! Don't take him!"

But she was too late. The cloaked figure reached a bony hand through the flames and pulled out a tiny body. But what emerged was not Elijah. It was....

Oh God, what was that?

His maniacal laugh echoed through the darkness as the cloaked man disappeared.

Destiny bolted up in bed, heart hammering. Taking deep, ragged breaths, she waited for the nightmare to fade. That laugh. She'd heard that before…at Amy's. Oh, God. That dream had been the worst ever. The cloaked figure was new. And what was that he'd pulled from the car? It certainly wasn't her baby brother.

Shivering, she ran a hand through her damp mop of hair and pushed back the covers. The small window unit could barely keep up with the heat and humidity in the small trailer. Sitting up on the side of the bed, she looked out the top of the window, letting the air from the window unit cool her sweaty skin.

She could have tried harder to save Elijah, and she knew it. Her mother was right. It was her fault her brother was dead. Tears slid down her cheeks as she remembered the last time she'd seen Elijah alive. He'd been singing, his bright little eyes shining with laughter. She fiercely wiped them away. "No, I'm not going to do this," she muttered aloud. "Grams is right. This was not my fault. That stupid cop pulled me out of the car before I could unbuckle the car seat. If he'd given me a few more seconds, I would have had it." She smacked her hand down on the top of the air conditioner. "Why didn't he just give me a few more seconds?"

She cried softly, her face in her hands, that overwhelming feeling of loss and loneliness spreading throughout her body. It hurt so bad that she just wished she could die. Why was she the only one still alive? It sucked.

Rose knocked softly. "Destiny, you okay? I thought I heard you moving around."

She wiped her eyes with the bottom of her nightshirt. "Yeah, I'm okay. I was just getting ready to take a shower. You still want me to go to the bookstore with you today, right?" She was glad her voice didn't sound as shaky as she felt.

"Yes. I need some help going through the inventory in the back room. I've had so many shipments come in lately that I haven't had time to check off all the orders to make sure everything is accounted for. I thought you could help with that first, and then I'll show you how to work the cash register. I only have one reading scheduled at eleven o'clock today, so we should be able to get a lot done."

"Okay, Grams. I'll be ready in about twenty minutes."

"You want some breakfast?"

"Not really. I'll just eat a bowl of cereal."

"Okay, honey. Take your time. We don't have to be there until nine."

Destiny was glad for the interruption. The nightmares had to stop. They were horrible, and the addition of Creepy Cloak Man didn't help one bit. She carried her basket of toiletries, a t-shirt and a pair of shorts down the short hall to the bathroom. Facing the mirror, the scene from Amy's garage replayed in her mind. Destiny closed her eyes and hugged her body. There was no telling what Amy would tell her parents or her friends about the way she'd reacted yesterday. She must've looked like a total idiot.

Destiny sighed and stepped under the warm spray. Making friends in this town wasn't going to be easy. First, she'd ticked off the most popular girl in school over her boyfriend and then acted like a complete and total retard at her house. What next?

Quickly, she finished her shower and turned off the water. Within ten minutes, she was dressed and walking into the kitchen. Rose was seated at the kitchen table, jotting down notes in a small spiral notebook.

"What're you doing, Grams?"

"Oh, I'm just making a list of all the things I want to get accomplished at the bookstore today."

Destiny leaned over her grandmother's shoulder to review the list. There were already ten items written down in Rose's neat looping script. "Wow, we have a lot to do, don't we?"

"Yep. Since I was out for the funeral, I let things pile up a bit. Just couldn't seem to find the motivation to get the work done. When Nila left to go to summer school in Gainesville, I lost one of the best workers I've ever had. I could give her the inventory order forms, and she would unpack, price and place everything in the store without me having to say a word. She was a blessing for sure. I haven't been able to keep up since." She dropped her pen on top of the table and faced her granddaughter. "Destiny, I'm really glad you agreed to work for me this summer. It's a relief to know I've got some help."

Destiny's lips curved. "I'm no Nila, but I'll do my best. I do have one question for you, though."

Rose smiled. "Only one?"

"Well, for now anyway. What attracts people to a store like yours?

Who would be interested in new-age magical stuff in a backwater town like this? You sure don't get a lot of tourist traffic. How do you keep the store in business?"

"Summertime will get busier than you think. Kids are out of school, and despite the fact that this is a small town, we do get some tourist traffic through here on their way to the east coast. Plus, we have three rodeos a year and the Watermelon Festival." She scribbled a few more notes on the pad. "The next rodeo is coming up in about a month. I've developed some regular customers from that rowdy bunch. I think the occult is always fascinating to people. Even if they are skeptical, they are curious. The fact that I do readings draws many people in. To some, the idea of contacting dead relatives is very exciting."

Destiny raised an eyebrow while pouring a bowl of cereal. "Really? Sounds creepy to me."

Rose nodded. "Back in England, during the Victorian times, they would conduct séances and treat them like we do playing board games. They thought it was great fun. Unfortunately, most of them had no clue what they were doing or how to tell a real medium from a fake one. Charlatans took advantage of a lot of people, giving us true mediums a really bad name."

"I guess so."

"Are you ready to go?"

Destiny poured her half-eaten bowl of cereal down the disposal and pulled her hair into a ponytail. To keep her bangs from falling in her eyes, she added a brightly colored yellow elastic band around her head. It matched the yellow of her tank top. She wiped her hands on her jeans. "Is this okay to wear?"

"You look fine to me. Let's get a move on then."

Rose pulled up in front of The Mystic Cat Book and Novelty shop just before nine o'clock. Easing into her normal parking space, she put the car in park and looked at Destiny. "Well, what do you think? It's not much, but it pays the bills."

Destiny stepped out of the car and went to one of the display windows. There was a storybook on a bookstand and a small black cauldron standing on a piece of black velvet, some small stones scattered at the base. The stones had strange markings on them.

"What are those?" she asked, pointing at the glass.

"Runes," Rose said, pulling out her keys. "They are used by some to tell the future."

"Really?" Destiny followed her grandmother into the shop.

She glanced around. Multiple bookshelves lined the walls, and a few stood in the middle of the floor. They were all clearly labeled with the name of the genre hand-painted on wooden cat-shaped signs. Destiny observed antique tables and display cases filled with items totally unfamiliar to her. A few things she recognized, like the pewter statues of dragons and wizards, decks of Tarot cards and candles of every color and scent. Other tables held weird items such as letter openers shaped like daggers and crystals of different sizes and colors.

"People really come in and buy all this?" Destiny asked, picking up a blue velvet pouch filled with some type of herb.

"They do. It is a unique shop for unique needs. Don't let it scare you, Destiny. People who use these items are just as sane as you and me. Many people think this stuff is used for devil worship, but that couldn't be farther from the truth." Grams picked up a few of the crystals and showed them to her granddaughter. She held them into a sunbeam streaming through the window. The blue and white pieces of glass shattered with light, dashing prisms of color all around the store. That was cool.

"As I told you before, I don't allow dark energy in my store. Those who practice the dark arts—and they do exist—are not allowed in here. Many of the items you see here are used for positive things like holistic healing. What I try to do here is support people's spiritual gifts, like yours and mine." Rose placed the crystals back on the table. Destiny blinked and met her grandmother's eyes.

"People are afraid of what is strange to them, and most treat the unknown with disdain rather than choose to become educated." She took an apron off a hook and handed it to Destiny, who slipped it over her head and tied it, grinning at the large Cheshire cat on the front.

"I encourage you to become educated. The more knowledge you have, the less scary things become."

Destiny wandered the store, still listening to her voice.

"I stay quite busy during tourist season. I told you about the rodeo in July, and I get a lot of regulars in here from the circuit. You being here will really help while I go upstairs to do my readings."

Rose headed toward the back of the store. Destiny had her doubts about how helpful she'd be. She didn't argue about remaining open-minded, having just found out she could talk to ghosts...who was she to judge anyone? Destiny pulled a book from one of the shelves to examine it when all of a sudden, something plopped on the shelf directly above her. She screeched, jumped back, and dropped the book, which landed with a loud *WHAP* on the floor. The creature atop the bookcase unleashed a vociferous meow.

She slapped a hand to her chest and took a deep breath to still her hammering heart. "Holy biscuits, you just scared the crap out of me," she said to the ebony cat staring at her with the greenest eyes she'd ever seen.

Rose came scuttling around the edge of the shelf. "Destiny, are you—oh, I see you've met Shamus."

Destiny huffed out a laugh. "Yeah. He just scared ten years off me." She glanced up at the cat again, swearing it grinned at her. "Hi, Shamus."

Rose smiled and snatched the cat from the shelf. "You bad kitty. This is Destiny. I told you about her. She's your family, and you've not made a very good first impression." She shoved the cat into Destiny's arms.

Shamus must have sensed Destiny was not much of a cat lover because he struggled to get down. She dropped him, and he landed on all four paws with a thud. He sat and peered up at Destiny with a dignified expression on his face. "Sorry," she said.

The cat sneezed, regarded the intruder with his disdainful emerald eyes, and stalked off, tail twitching.

"I don't think Shamus likes me," Destiny said.

Rose chuckled. "Shamus doesn't really like anyone. He's his own cat, but he is helpful at keeping mice away. He'll come around once he gets used to you. He's a great Shade alarm too." Rose headed toward the back of the store. Destiny scuttled to catch up to her.

"A Shade alarm? You mean he can sense them when they come around?"

"Yep," Rose said over her shoulder, pushing open a door that said

"Employees Only."

She swept her arms wide. "As you can see, I'm behind. I haven't had time to put out the inventory I ordered right before the accident. I'll show you where things go, but if there are any displays you want to change out, feel free to use your creativity. Nila was so good at that." Rose tapped the top of a box with a pen. "What I need for you to do first is unload the boxes. What you can't find room for, you can store back here. I'd start with the boxes of books because they will be the easiest to get out of the way." She handed Destiny a box cutter and a clipboard, who glanced at them with a dubious expression.

"The books I can handle, but I don't know about the displays. I don't know what items go with what. Maybe you should do that part."

"Oh, you'll get the hang of it quickly enough. I trust you. The bookshelves are labeled with the genre, so you should easily be able to tell where they go. Follow me, and I'll show you how to work the cash register and get you a pricing list. A smart girl like you should pick this up in no time." She slipped back through the swinging door.

Destiny learned quickly. She worked for two hours pricing and putting away books, all the while looking for titles about mediums and people with "gifts" similar to her own. She found a few to read later and placed them aside to ask her grandmother about them. Getting absorbed in the work, Destiny was already on the third box of books when the chime above the door jingled.

She leaned around the bookshelf, and her heart leapt. Jake sauntered toward the counter. Destiny ducked, unsure if she wanted to be seen.

"Hi, Madam Rose. What's up?"

"Hello, Jake. What can I do for you?"

"I'm looking for a birthday present for Andie. Do you have any suggestions?"

"Oh my, I'd forgotten your sister's birthday was so close. Is she coming home from college to celebrate?" Rose straightened a stack of papers and shoved them below the counter.

"She should be home later today. I think they were leaving earlier this morning to start back. Hey, Shamus," Jake said, reaching down to rub the black cat.

Oh…so the cat likes Jake. Destiny glared at the animal as it wove between Jake's jean-clad legs. She could've sworn it stuck its pink tongue out at her as it rounded his ankle. That cat was going down.

"Well, you be sure and tell her 'happy birthday' for me. Come over here. I think we've got some crystals she might appreciate. In fact, I just ordered some new ones. Let me see. Destiny!"

So much for the plan to remain anonymous. To make matters worse, when Destiny stepped out from behind the bookshelf, she tripped over the big box of books and sprawled onto the floor. Rose came hustling with Shamus on her heels. That cat had no intention of being left out of the festivities. He twitched his tail beneath Destiny's nose, causing her to sneeze.

"Shamus, shoo," Rose said, shoving the cat away with her foot. She reached down to help Destiny to her feet. "Oh my goodness, are you all right?"

Cheeks burning, Destiny replied, "Yeah, just clumsy."

"Hey, Destiny. That was some fall. You sure you're okay?" Jake said, holding onto Destiny's elbow while she brushed off her jeans. His blue eyes searched her face, further intensifying her embarrassment. She rolled her eyes. "I'm fine," she said, jerking her elbow out of his grasp. He grinned. Destiny sighed.

"You stay here while I go look for those crystals in the back. Don't want you falling over any more boxes." Rose chuckled as she toddled to the back of the store.

"God, I don't know what's more embarrassing, me falling, or her making jokes about it."

Jake smiled that killer smile Destiny loved. "Parents have the most unique way of humiliating us. Seriously, are you sure you're okay?"

"Yes, I only hurt my pride. So what are you doing in here?" They stepped around the cat on their way to the counter.

"I wanted to buy my sister a birthday present. She loves this store, so I thought I'd find something here she likes."

Destiny's jaw dropped. Jake's sister shopped here? She started to ask him a question when the chime above the door jingled again. A woman, who appeared to be about fifty years old, approached the counter. "Is Madame Rose here?" she asked.

"Yes, she just went to the back to get something. Can I help you?"

"Are you new here? I've never seen you before." The woman placed her purse on the counter and studied Destiny.

"Oh, there you are, Olivia," Rose said, coming out of the store room. "I'll be right with you. I see you've met my granddaughter. Destiny, this is Mrs. Kennedy."

"Why you're just pretty as a picture. I'm sure I'll see you a lot more this summer."

Destiny smiled and nodded.

"Destiny, I need to take Mrs. Kennedy upstairs for her reading. Here are the crystals I wanted to put out. Jake will want to look at them. Just mind the store until I come back down. We shouldn't be too busy today." Rose put her arm around Mrs. Kennedy and led her to a red door in the side wall. She opened it, and they disappeared up the stairs.

"She's right, you know," Jake said.

"Who's right?" Destiny asked, placing the box on the counter.

"You really are pretty," Jake said, grinning.

Oh my God, Jake's flirting with me.

She remembered Amy's warning. She would be so ticked off if she'd heard what Jake had just said.

Still thinking about how to respond, she jumped when Jake said, "Can I see the crystals?" He gestured at the box on the counter.

"Uh...sure." She handed him the box. He opened it and laid the crystals on the counter. She decided to ignore the flirt. No sense in asking for trouble. "You come in here a lot?"

"Yeah. My sister loves this store. She's studied alternative healing for the past year. She wants to go into medicine, but not the conventional kind if you know what I mean. She's into more holistic, spiritual, and herbal kinds of stuff. My parents don't quite understand it. It worries them," Jake said, holding the crystals up to the light. The colors danced on the wall. "Knowing Andie, it's probably just a phase. It doesn't bother me like it does some people, I guess."

Relief flooded through Destiny. Jake understood. He got it. Maybe someday, she'd share her secret with him.

"What does she use the crystals for?"

"I have no clue. For protection or something. What do you think of this one?" Jake held up a bluish-gray elongated crystal.

"It's pretty, but shouldn't you know what it does before you buy it?"

"Nah. Andie will like it anyway. I'll take it." Jake placed the crystal on the counter and reached for his wallet. "I also want to look for this book she said she wanted."

She opened her mouth to ask him the title when the door jangled again. In strode Amy and another girl, she'd not had the pleasure of meeting. "Uh oh," Destiny muttered.

"Jake, what are you doing here?" Amy asked, glaring at Destiny. Shamus hopped on the counter and hissed at the girls, causing them both to jump back.

Way to go, Shamus. Destiny grinned. *That cat may be worth something after all.*

"You should put that…thing…outside," Amy commented. Destiny shrugged and tried to hide her amusement. Amy turned to Jake, her eyes boring into him. He shifted uncomfortably.

"I came in to buy Andie a birthday present. What are you two up to?" He yanked some money from his wallet and returned her glare.

"We're doing a little shopping, and then we thought we'd ride into Sarasota and see a movie. You want to come with? That is if you can tear yourself away from this creepy bookstore. Honestly, Jake, I don't know why you have to come in here. The stuff here is just so weird."

Destiny watched the other girl roam around, picking up items and setting them down. She smirked and wiped her hand on her shirt.

Amy turned her gaze to Destiny. "So…what? Are you working here now?"

"Yep," Destiny said, determined not to allow Amy to rattle her. "I'm helping my grandmother over the summer."

She sneered and glanced around the store, disdain evident in her expression. Destiny hoped she wouldn't say anything about their last meeting, but she was quickly disappointed.

"Hey, I never got to find out why you freaked out in my garage the other day."

The other girl with Amy said, "You freaked out? What about?"

Jake introduced her, "Destiny, this is Jessica, Amy's best friend. She's also on the cheer squad."

"Hi," Destiny said, shifting from one foot to the other. She so wished they would leave.

"You should have seen her," Amy told Jessica. "One minute, she was staring into that ugly mirror and wouldn't respond to a thing I said. The next minute she's running home at lightning speed."

"Uh, I just wasn't feeling well," Destiny remarked, not knowing what other explanation she could have offered.

Jake must have sensed Destiny's embarrassment because he said, "Why don't you and Jessica go get a smoothie, and I'll meet you there. Then we'll head into Sarasota for that movie. I'll even drive." He put his arm around them both and steered them toward the door.

Amy glared back at Destiny and mouthed, "Stay away from my boyfriend."

Jake stopped at the front door. Amy said, "Ten minutes."

He returned, cheeks flushed with embarrassment. "I'm sorry, Destiny. I don't know what's wrong with her."

"Have you looked in a mirror lately?" Destiny asked. "You're freakin' gorgeous, you're sweet as sugar, and she's terrified of losing you." She clapped a hand over her mouth. Oops. She'd definitely not intended to say those words aloud.

Jake grinned. "You think I'm 'freakin'' gorgeous'?"

"Oh, shut up. What was the name of that book you wanted to buy your sister?" Heat burned Destiny's cheeks.

"I'll get it," he said. "I know right where it is."

Jake handed her the book. She stepped around the counter, checked the price list and rang up both the crystal and the book. "That's twenty dollars and twenty-seven cents with tax."

Jake slapped the money onto the counter, then inched his hand over Destiny's. She glanced up, captivated by his blue eyes. A soft sigh slipped from her lips.

"I'm really sorry about Amy."

"Don't be," Destiny said, lowering her gaze. She busied her hands straightening items on the counter. "She staked her claim the other night. I know what hands-off means."

"What are you talking about?" Jake asked, frowning.

"The other day, on the way to her house, Amy informed me that you belong to her, and I'm to have nothing to do with you. Apparently, I'm quite the slut, trying to steal her man."

"Oh jeez, Destiny...." He reached for her hand again and squeezed. Destiny expected Amy to walk back at any minute and see them. She removed her fingers from his grasp and rolled her eyes. "I'm sorry she treated you that way. Just ignore it, okay?"

"Yeah, whatever. It's not a big deal." She wrapped his purchase in tissue paper she found behind the counter and then placed it in a bag labeled "The Mystic Cat."

His lips curved. "So, are you going to work here all summer?"

"Yeah, I told Grams I'd try it for a while. To be honest, though, some of this stuff gives me the shivers."

"Really? I think it's cool," he flung his arms wide. "My dad throws a Halloween party in our barn every year, and we come in here and get all kinds of authentic stuff. Andie is friends with Nila, so when she's in town, she stops by to see her. I tag along with Andie, so I come in here a lot too."

"So what my grandmother does...it doesn't weird you out?"

"Nah, I think it's really neat. Madame Rose has been around for a really long time. People have gotten used to her talking with the dead. They come from all over to meet with her. During the rodeo, this place is always packed. You want to know what I think?"

Destiny nodded. She couldn't wait to hear this. The very balance of their very friendship hung on his next words.

"I like the idea of being able to talk to spirits," Jake said pensively.

"You do?" Destiny couldn't believe her ears. Inside she danced... an honest to God Snoopy dance. She loved that paw tapping, nose in the air jig Snoopy used to do when he was happy. Jake didn't think what she could do was freaky. He thought it was cool.

"Yeah. The thought that life goes on after death jazzes me. You know...that there is something more to live for, so to speak." He gave her one of his dazzling smiles.

Impulsively, Destiny reached out and hugged his neck. Jake hesitated for only a second, then squeezed.

"Now, who's flirting," he said.

Heat crept into Destiny's cheeks. It didn't, however, wipe the stupid grin from her mouth. Amy was going to kill her, but she didn't care. She was happy to know that Jake didn't think what she could do was weird.

Shamus, who'd been resting on the counter, suddenly leapt into the air, causing Destiny to jump. "God, I just started here, and already I hate that cat." The inky black puff ball rubbed his head against Jake's arm. "He seems to really like you, though."

Jake laughed. "Yeah, me and Shamus here, we have an understanding."

All of a sudden, the cat hissed, arching its back, looking toward the front of the shop. "What the…." Destiny said.

The door chime jingled, and she was sure it was Amy coming in to give her a good butt chewing. Jake rotated to see who'd come in the door.

"Didn't you just hear that door chime?" He asked, brows furrowed in confusion. "Huh, must have been the—"

Shamus yowled.

Destiny's breath caught in her throat, and it took all she had to stifle a scream. Standing at the door was a girl about eighteen or nineteen years old with bright pink hair. She wore tight black jeans and a pink t-shirt covered in blood. Her skin hung from her face like someone had pushed her into a shredder. A deep gash nearly severed her head from the rest of her body which explained all the blood. A squeak slipped from Destiny's lips, and Jake pivoted to face her.

"What's up with the ca—" he stopped.

Destiny slapped her hands over her eyes. She couldn't stand to look at the injured girl any longer. All that blood and the way her skin hung in strips…oh God.

Jake grabbed Destiny's arm. "What is it, Destiny? What's going on? First, Shamus wigs out, now you?"

She peeked through her fingers, lowering her hands as she saw the Shade had vanished. The cat settled down on the counter, emerald eyes narrowing. His gaze remained on the door.

"Um…nothing." Destiny staggered back against the counter. "I just had a sudden pain in my head." It was a lame lie, but she couldn't think of anything better.

"Oh, come on, something weird just happened. Are you going to tell me that you didn't hear those door chimes?"

She took a deep breath and cleared her throat, trying to get herself together. "Probably just the wind," she said, rubbing her temples.

Jake glanced at Shamus and then back to the door. "Maybe, but you have to admit that was strange. The cat reacts, the door chimes and then you all of a sudden get a headache?"

Even if he thought what her grandmother did was cool, Destiny wondered if he'd feel the same way about her. Her head throbbed. At least now, she wouldn't have to lie about the headache. She glanced at the door and saw Amy's face pressed against the glass.

"Hey, Amy's looking for you. You better go." She pointed to where Amy now stood with her hands on her hips.

"Are you sure you're okay? Want me to get Madame Rose?"

Destiny shook her head. "No, I'm fine. You'd better go."

"Okay, if you're sure...."

She nodded and motioned for him to leave.

Jake backed away. "Wow, that was so weird," he said, his glance roaming the store. "I'll see you later."

She waved and attempted a smile.

Jake reached the door, and just before he pulled it open, he stopped by a rack of hot pink book bags. "Maybe I should get one of these for Andie. It would match her hair." Laughing, he stepped outside.

Destiny sat down hard on the stool behind the counter. Her heart still hammered, and she drank in deep breaths of air. Only her nightmares scared her more than that girl just had. Rose had been spot on about Shamus being a Shade alarm. He'd seen her before Destiny had. Her face...holy biscuits! And her hair...oh God! She'd had pink hair. Didn't Jake just say his sister had pink hair? *Oh no...what if that was his sister and she's dead?* Destiny remembered the gash in her neck, and her hands flew to her throat. She hoped she was wrong.

Deliberately slowing her breathing, she tried to calm down. Lots of people had pink hair. It may not be his sister at all. That's what she wanted to believe anyway. She was pacing back and forth behind the counter, chewing on her thumbnail, when Rose and Mrs. Kennedy came down the stairs and stepped into the store.

Rose glanced over her shoulder at Destiny as she walked the

sobbing woman to the door. "It's okay, Olivia. We'll try again next week. Sometimes the spirits just aren't in a talkative mood. You know that."

Olivia Kennedy nodded and wiped her nose. "I know. I was just hoping to hear from him today, that's all."

"Well, we can try again next week if you want. Once spirits crossover, it's not so easy to summon them. They have to get in touch with me. If I hear from him, I'll call you immediately. Okay?"

Olivia nodded and pulled open the door. "Call me, okay? And put this visit on my account. I'll pay you when I come in next week."

"Don't worry about it. No charge for today. I don't feel right taking your money when the spirits are uncooperative." Rose smiled and held the door open for the woman as she went out. "Well, that was a frustrating session."

Destiny stopped pacing and looked up at Rose.

"What's gotten into you, child? You look like you've got the weight of the world on your shoulders. Want to tell me what's wrong?"

"I just saw another dead person, Grams. It was a girl, and she was all bloody, her face cut to ribbons, her head nearly chopped off. God, it was horrible. She popped up right when I was ringing up a book for Jake. I thought I was going to scream." She ran her hands through her hair. "He thought I'd lost my mind. He turned around, wondering what I was looking at." She looked pleadingly at her grandmother. "Do they always appear without warning like that? It's absolutely terrifying."

"They do tend to pop up, but once you get used to your gift, you will sense them in subtle ways before they appear. Sometimes it's a change in temperature, a rising of the hairs on the back of your neck, a smell—it could be anything. It's different for each medium. You just need to recognize yours." Rose walked behind the counter and put her arm around her granddaughter. She could feel the girl trembling.

"Can we work on that right away? This is going to give me a heart attack."

"Do you want to talk about it?"

"Well, I've told you what I saw, but what really troubles me is she had pink hair, and just as Jake was going out the door, he pointed to that pink canvas book bag and said he would come back and get it for his sister, Andie because it matched her hair."

Rose drew in a deep breath. "You think she might be Andie and that something terrible has happened to her?"

Tears stung Destiny's eyes, and she nodded. "I couldn't tell him what I saw. What if it is her? That poor family has lost their daughter, and they don't even know it yet."

"Well, we don't know for sure it was her. Can you describe her to me? She used to come into the store all the time to visit with Nila."

"She was my height, thin, and had short spiked pink hair. I couldn't see her eyes or the rest of her face because she was cut up so bad. Oh God, Grams, do you think someone attacked her?"

Rose's expression was grim. She was silent for a few moments.

"Grams?"

"I think that was Andie, Destiny." She sat down hard on the stool, the same way Destiny had. "Oh my. That poor family."

"What are we going to do?"

Rose's eyes brightened, and she popped up off the stool. She walked to the door and flipped the open sign to closed. Coming back around the counter, she grabbed Destiny's hand and pulled her to the red door that led to the upstairs room. "Come on. Let's try to contact her. Maybe she will be able to tell us what happened to her, and we can help the family."

CHAPTER THIRTEEN

Rose led Destiny to a comfortable sitting area with two overstuffed chairs and a low table between them. "Sit down, honey. Let's see if that girl will pay us a visit."

Destiny sat in one of the chairs and looked around the room. It was small, perhaps a storage room for a previous business, but it was clean. The lighting was soft and low, with several pillar candles glowing on wrought iron stands. A soothing, spicy scent wafted through the air. A thick rug covered the floor under the table. The entire setup was quite comfortable and cozy.

"This is nice, Grams. What do we do now?"

"All a medium needs to do is relax. The spirit world is all around us, and if there are spirits that want to talk, they will. Sometimes they appear, and sometimes they don't, but they're always here. Each of us has a spirit guide that watches over us while we are on our earthly journey. Many times I can send mine to find a spirit that I may be looking for. Let's see if it works."

Destiny watched as her grandmother closed her eyes and began to take slow deep breaths. Her shoulders relaxed, and she sank back into the softness of the chair. She was very quiet for several minutes, and Destiny thought she'd fallen asleep when suddenly she spoke.

"Madia, are you here?"

Destiny's eyes darted everywhere, looking for a figure. Both nervous and excited, she wasn't sure what to expect. Nothing happened. No figure in a flowing white robe appeared, no bright lights...nothing.

The room remained the same. Rose, however, kept talking.

"Thank you, Madia. Can you tell me if you've seen a young girl with bright pink hair? I think her name is Andie. We believe she died tragically, so she may be lost. Can you bring her to us?"

Destiny watched as Rose's eyes fluttered open.

"Madia is going to look for her," she spoke softly. "Since we don't know when she died, it might take a few minutes for Madia to locate her, and she may not be able to find her at all."

"This is so weird, Grams." Destiny's heart pounded, and she wiped her sweaty palms on her shorts. She really didn't want to contact this girl again. She didn't want contact with any dead person.

"Shades are beings just like us, Destiny. Many times they just want to deliver a message to a loved one they didn't get to see before they died. Sometimes they want to warn someone in danger. Rarely do they want to cause harm. That's a different type of entity altogether."

Destiny opened her mouth to comment when Shamus sprung to his feet, back arched. He hissed at the middle of the room.

"Shamus, stop," Rose said, tapping the cat with her foot. "You'll frighten her. Settle down."

The cat ceased his hissing, but his back remained bowed. The temperature dropped about ten degrees, and the hairs on the back of Destiny's neck stood on end. The air shimmered directly in front of her, and the form of the girl she'd seen downstairs appeared. Destiny gasped.

"Honey, you're really going to have to stop gasping every time a Shade appears. They will start to think you don't want them around."

Destiny raised one eyebrow. *Really?*

"Are you Andie Turner?" Rose asked the apparition.

The girl's head turned toward Destiny's grandmother and emitted a squishy sort of raspy sound. Her face was a mess, flutters of skin flapped loosely around her jaw, and Destiny thought for a minute that her head might even fall off. Her heart leaped to her throat. If that left her body, Destiny was so going to be so out of there.

Rose saw the difficulty the Shade had responding to her, so she said, "Just raise one finger for yes and two for no. Do you understand?"

One finger popped up.

"Are you Andie Turner?" One finger rose.

"Do you know that you're dead?" A tear slid down the torn-up face, and she kept one finger in the air.

"I'm so sorry, Andie. Was it a car accident?"

Andie raised one finger. Another tear fell.

"We're going to try to help you. Because you're unable to speak, I want you to think of your answers." Rose pointed at Destiny. "This is my granddaughter, Destiny. She knows your brother, Jake. Between the two of us, we should understand your thoughts. Think really hard now. What happened to you?"

Destiny closed her eyes and tried to concentrate. She had no clue how to make it work, so she listened intently, trying to hear any sound at all. After a few minutes, she heard a whisper, soft as a breath, then after more intense focus, she heard three words.

Car, roommate, drunk

Destiny opened her eyes and glanced at her grandmother. Rose nodded. "I heard her, Destiny. Go ahead, Andie. We're listening."

The bloody ghost closed her eyes in concentration.

Head went through windshield. Couldn't breathe. All I remember.

Rose smiled. "That's very good, Andie. I'm sure the cops will be contacting your family soon. Let me ask you a question. Did you see a bright white light?"

Andie held up one finger…yes.

"Why didn't you go into it?" Rose's eyes narrowed, and the tone of her voice relayed concern.

I'm not sure. Felt pulled to stay. Work to do here.

Destiny gazed at Rose, then back at Andie. "What does she mean?"

Destiny, I'm here. You can ask me.

Destiny's breath caught. Andie had actually spoken directly to her instead of her grandmother. Embarrassed, Destiny said, "I'm sorry, Andie. This is all new to me. What did you mean by work to be done?"

Not sure. Very strong feeling.

Shades could be very cryptic and mysterious.

"So you had a very strong feeling you were needed here, and that's why you didn't cross over?"

One finger went up.

"I know you and Jake are…*were* close. Is it because of him?"

Andie sighed, a wet bubbly gurgle. Destiny swallowed. Yuck.

Rose leaned forward in her chair, a matronly expression on her face. It was a sweet look, and at that moment, Destiny admired her grandmother. In her pale blue eyes, she saw a glimpse of how much the work Rose did meant to her. The ability of her new gift struck home with magnitude.

"Andie," Rose said. "I want you to know that you can come to me or Destiny any time you need us. We'll help you through this. It's important that you go to the light if you see it again. Everyone here'll be fine. They'll miss you and mourn for you, but they'll be okay. I hope you can finish what you need to do before you see the light again. Let us know how we can help you."

I will. Andie shimmered and faded away.

Rose relaxed in her chair, turning sad eyes on Destiny. "That poor family. This is going to devastate them. She was such a bright and warm ray of sunshine. She came in here a lot because she knew Nila and was trying her hand at alternative healing."

"I know. Jake told me. He said it was freaking her parents out."

The corners of Rose's mouth twitched. "I imagine it would if you don't know anything about it. But as I've said before, once you take the time to learn, these alternative methods aren't so mysterious."

"Well, what do we do now?" She wanted to know. "Do we go to Jake's house and tell his family?"

"No. We'll let things play out the way they should. Many people aren't very receptive to mediums. I prefer to wait until people come to me. Knowing Jake's folks the way I do, I'm not sure they'd be very receptive to a reading. I don't think they believe in what we can do."

"Jake does. Should I tell him I saw Andie?"

"Not yet. Let's wait and see how things go. Just be there for him as a friend. He's going to need you and his other friends to help him through this."

Destiny nodded. "I will. He's a really nice guy. I'm not sure Amy deserves him."

"I know. That girl has her hooks in him pretty tight. She should be careful. Some boys don't respond to being smothered."

Destiny sighed. "She definitely doesn't want me hanging around him. I haven't even given her any reason to be jealous." Rose raised an eyebrow. Guilt tugged at Destiny. "Okay, so I hugged him once, but that was because he said he thinks what you do is cool. Maybe I'll have at least one friend who doesn't think I'm a freak."

"I'm sure you'll have more than that. Sometimes things have a way of working out the way you least expect." Rose stood and clapped her hands together. Destiny blinked at the unexpected gesture.

"Let's go get some lunch. I'm hungry. There's a great pizza parlor down the street that has the best pepperoni around."

The two left the cozy room and went back downstairs. Rose opened the door and then relocked the shop.

"I hope Jake is going to be okay."

"Me too, honey."

Later that night, Rose drove home past Jake's house. Destiny noticed two police cruisers in the driveway and other cars lining the street. Her eyes burned, chest tightening. Her own grief still all too fresh, she knew that utter sense of loss. In her mind, Destiny said to Andie, *Don't worry, Andie. I'll watch out for him.*

I know you will.

Destiny jerked, not expecting an answer. Whoa, that was wild.

I'm counting on you, Destiny.

CHAPTER FOURTEEN

Arcadia is one of those towns where a sense of community holds the place together, so the news of Andie's death hit with hurricane force. Matthew and Ellen Turner owned the oldest hardware store in two counties and had managed to keep it prospering in spite of all the Home Depot and Lowe's stores sprouting up around them. People in Arcadia supported their own, and they really stepped it up for the Turners.

On the day of Andie's funeral, the town council asked all the business owners to close their offices and shops, and all the local government offices were closed. The local Church of Christ was filled to the brim with people there to support the family. The minister delivered a moving service covering all of Andie's accomplishments. While she wasn't the most popular girl in town and had a few strange habits that a lot of people were wary of, they still were there to support the family and remember her.

Destiny sat with her grandmother toward the back of the church. She could just see Jake as he sat with his head bowed on the front row. She knew his pain and could physically see the grief in the slump of his shoulders and his sagging body. Tears leaked down her cheeks, memories of her own family's funeral all too fresh in her mind. She was thankful for him that he didn't have to deal with the guilt she'd struggled with over not being able to save Elijah.

Gazing over the sanctuary, her eyes stopped when she saw a girl with bright pink hair seated in one of the chairs on the pulpit. Her body was still the same bloody mess that it had been the day Destiny saw her in the book store, but it didn't seem quite as shocking this time. Maybe she was getting used to seeing some of these horrific sights. Destiny leaned over to her grandmother.

"Andie's here," she whispered. "Can you see her?"

Rose nodded. "She's sitting in the preacher's chair on the pulpit. Doesn't look much better, does she?"

Destiny shook her head. "Do you think she knows we're here?"

"Probably. The dead often attends their own funeral. Sometimes they cross over soon afterward. I don't think Andie will, though. I have a feeling she's sticking around for something. I just don't know what."

Destiny nodded. She continued to watch as Andie rose from the chair, walked through the preacher and down the stairs to her closed casket. Her high school senior picture was mounted on a small stand atop the casket because her body had been too horribly mutilated for viewing. She trailed her hand along the smooth wood.

Destiny watched as she approached each member of her family. She placed a hand on top of each one's head in a gesture of love and sorrow. When Andie reached Jake, Destiny gasped when he raised his head at the exact moment her hand touched his face. Did he feel her? Could he see her? She could tell something had passed between them, but she didn't know what.

The minister continued his eulogy as Andie walked down the aisle. She seemed overcome with emotion at the attendance. Destiny was surprised to see the look Andie gave Amy and her parents. She must not have thought much of Jake's girlfriend.

Andie's head still flopped around on its loose tissue as she glanced from side to side while gliding down the aisle. Destiny shuddered, wishing the body would return to its recognizable state at some point. Even though she was growing somewhat accustomed to the sight of Andie's mangled body, it was still gross. So far, that was the worst part of the Shade Sight.

Finally, Andie reached Destiny's row. She stopped and stared at Destiny and Rose. Destiny closed her eyes and concentrated. Andie's thoughts came through loud and clear.

Wow, I never knew so many people cared about me.

Destiny nodded and smiled, brushing a tear away from her face.

She aimed her thoughts at Andie. *You were obviously well thought of. So is your family.*

Yeah, Andie replied back. *They're wonderful people. I'm going to miss them so much. Especially Jake. He and I were buddies.*

Destiny nodded once. *I know. He was just telling me about you the day you died. He was buying you a book for your birthday.*

Andie's head rolled on its loose tendons as she focused on Destiny more intently. The folds of cut skin swung on her face like fringe on a shawl. Destiny swallowed down the bile rising in her throat.

Was he really?

Yes, Destiny thought. *He wanted you to have a pink book bag that was in our shop that matched your hair.*

Andie laughed, which came out in a wet gurgle, but then her expression grew serious. Her head swiveled, faced the back of Amy's head for a moment, then swung back toward Destiny. *Destiny, there is something weird going on with Amy. Please watch over Jake and make sure he doesn't get hurt.*

Destiny drew her brows together. *What do you mean?*

I'm not sure what it is, but I get this really bad feeling every time I'm around that girl. It's kind of spooky, really. I know I don't know you very well, but you and your grandmother are the only ones who can see and hear me, so I've got to trust you. Something evil is happening in this town. I can't explain how I know that. I just do, and somehow Amy's involved. I just don't want Jake getting hurt, okay?

Chills ran down Destiny's spine, and she physically shivered. Rose looked at her and then saw Andie standing at the end of the row. "What is it, Destiny?" she whispered.

"Nothing," Destiny whispered back. "I'll tell you later."

When Destiny turned back to Andie, she was gone. What a strange thing for her to say. Did she know about what Destiny had seen in the mirror the other day at Amy's house? It seemed impossible, but maybe not. She had felt the same way as Andie, though. The dark and ominous shadow that loomed over that burned girl had scared Destiny senseless. Perhaps it was evil. All Destiny knew was she didn't want to be anywhere near that furniture ever again.

People in the church rose as the minister said a final prayer, and the pallbearers rolled the casket down the aisle. The men were followed by Jake and his parents. Destiny's heart broke when she saw the raw grief on Jake's face. His skin was pale and tear-stained, his eyes red and puffy from crying. He looked nothing like the strong athletic guy she knew him to be.

Jake saw Destiny and shot her a weak smile. Destiny's lips curved, and she held up a fist as a sign of strength. Jake returned the gesture and exited the church. Destiny wiped more tears from her face with the wad of tissues she held in her hand.

The other attendees filed out row by row and went to their cars. There was to be a graveside service in the cemetery on the outskirts of town, but it was reserved for immediate family only. Destiny and her grandmother got into their car. Destiny rolled her window down to let out some of the insufferable Florida summer heat.

"Whoo. It's hotter than a furnace in here." Rose copied Destiny and rolled her window down as well. "Let's get some air started." She started the car, and hot air blasted them from the vents. "When it's this hot, it takes a while for that air conditioner to cool things down. We'll probably be home before it even begins to work."

"I know. It's awful. Did you see Jake, Grams? He looked so torn up. I felt so sorry for him. I know exactly how he feels. It's just terrible to lose someone you love."

Rose looked at Destiny and placed a hand on the side of her face. Destiny leaned into it. "I know, baby. It is terrible. Maybe in time, as the worst of the grief fades, you can tell him about Andie. That will probably give him some comfort. But it will have to be when he's ready. Not before."

"I know, Grams. I won't say anything. I'm not really so sure I want him to know what I'm capable of doing. It's still really weird, and people don't get it."

"I know they don't. I saw Andie standing at the end of the aisle. What did she want?"

"You couldn't hear her?"

"No, I didn't tune in this time. It looked like she wanted a private talk with you, so I didn't want to butt in."

"She asked me to watch out for Jake." Destiny turned and looked out the window. Her grandmother waited for the hearse and all the other cars to pull out before she followed.

"Did she say anything else?"

"Not really." Destiny sighed. "I don't think Andie likes Amy very much."

"Why do you say that?"

"I saw her scowl at her when she passed her row."

Rose smiled. "You did, huh?"

"Yeah…Grams?"

"Hmm?" Rose pulled into the parade of cars filing out of the church parking lot. Instead of turning left to follow the procession, she turned right and headed home.

"Will Andie ever look normal to me again? Looking at her the way she died is really giving me the creeps."

"If they stay on Earth long enough, they begin to transform. My spirit guide, Madia, told me that if a spirit doesn't cross over right away and lingers earthbound, the energy begins to regenerate after a time, and they learn to project their appearance as they had once been in life. They learn quickly that if they manifest the way they looked when they died, it scares the people they want to see. It's a trick they have to learn."

"You make it sound like learning to roller skate or something."

"Well, I guess it's like that in a way. They have to learn how to manipulate their energy so they can get their message across."

"What about once they cross over?" Destiny asked. "Don't they have to learn to do it then too?"

"No, once a spirit crosses over to the Great Beyond, they are able to communicate with their thoughts. If they appear physically at all to someone, it is more as a memory or a dream than an apparition."

"Hmmm. That's interesting."

"Did Andie say anything else?" Rose could tell by Destiny's expression that she was troubled.

"Just that I needed to watch out for Jake because something evil was going on with Amy. She said she couldn't tell what it was, but she seemed worried."

Rose didn't respond right away. She focused on the road. "You think she's referring to what you saw in that mirror?"

"I don't know how she would know about that, but maybe. It's the only thing going on with Amy that I know of."

"We'll keep a sharp eye out without doing too much interfering. If things get worse, or if we are asked, then we might step in. You be careful, though, Destiny. You're new to your gift and not quite sure how to control it yet. You may open a doorway to something you're not ready to handle. For the time being, if you are going to try to channel any spirits, let me know, and I'll be with you, okay?"

Destiny looked at her grandmother. "That's fine by me."

CHAPTER FIFTEEN

Amy dropped the sander and sat down with a huff in a folding chair. Sarah Morgan glanced at her tired, sweaty daughter. "Had enough, Amy?"

Amy responded with a scowl. She lifted the bottled water next to the chair and took a long swallow. "I've worked up a sweat sanding this old furniture, Mom. It seems like I have to keep doing the same area over and over. That old smoky soot just doesn't want to come off. I'm gonna have the arms of a UFC fighter if this keeps up."

Sarah laughed. "Re-finishing furniture is hard work, that's for sure. What's that buzzing noise?"

With sudden renewed energy, Amy jumped up from her chair and hustled to the workbench. She grabbed her cell phone and flipped open the top. Her thumbs flew over the keys.

"My goodness. You've only had that thing a short time, and you can send messages on it that fast already?"

"It's Jake. I don't want him to feel neglected. He's really sad right now."

"I'm sure he is. I'm so sorry about what happened to Andrea. She was such a nice girl and so young to die so tragically. Jake's parents are devastated. I can't imagine what it would be like to lose a child. It would be the most horrible thing on Earth."

Amy was only half listening as her thumbs flew across the cell phone keypad. "He wants to come by later. That's okay, isn't it, Mom?"

"Well, we need to get this dresser fully sanded so we can start staining it tomorrow, so I'd make it a little bit later. Now put that phone down and come over here and help me. I'll start on this right side while you finish the front."

"Aw, Mom, I'm really tired. Can't we quit for the day?"

Amy received her mother's best "Don't Push Me" look.

"Okay, okay." Amy put down the phone and retrieved her sander. "You know it still hurts my hand to do this."

Sarah rolled her eyes. "I know. Don't push so hard on the sander, or you'll get another splinter."

"I'm telling you, Mom, this crap just will not come off." To prove her point, Amy swiped the sander across the handprint on the top of the dresser. "See?"

Sarah stepped over and examined the top of the dresser. She took the sander from Amy and rubbed it across the sooty handprint. Amy crossed her arms against her chest. "I told you."

Sarah rubbed harder. Still nothing. After a few more swipes, she stood with her hands on her hips. "Well, you know it does give the dresser character. You could tell your friends that it's from the original owner who died in a fire."

Suddenly, a blast of frigid air struck both women. They stared at each other as their hair settled back into place.

"What the heck was that?" Amy asked.

"I don't know. Where would it have come from?" Sarah began to look around the garage and could find no source for the forceful wind. The temperature in the room had dropped by at least twenty degrees, crystallizing their breath into frosty puffs.

Amy shivered. "I'm really cold. I told you that air conditioner was broken. It shouldn't be that cold in here."

"You're right. It shouldn't, but I never heard the air conditioner turn on, did you?"

Amy thought a minute. "No, I didn't." Her eyes grew wide. "Where did that come from, Mom?"

Sarah strolled around the garage. Her brows drew together. "Well, maybe I'll have to call Climatek to come and check it. There must be a hole in one of the ducts or something. That's all I can figure out." Sarah shook her head, baffled. "That was weird."

"I'm telling you, Mom, there has been a lot of weird stuff happening since you brought this furniture in here. I've said it before, and I'll say it again, this stuff is possessed."

"Oh, don't be ridiculous, Amy. Furniture cannot be possessed. You act like it's alive or something. I'm sure there's a reasonable explanation for that blast of cold air. We just don't know what it is yet. You will feel terribly foolish when you find out it's just what I think it is, the air conditioner."

"I'm just saying…." Amy trailed off and picked up the sander. Instead of worrying about the handprint, she worked around it. Within the hour, she and her mother had finished sanding the entire dresser.

"There," Sarah said, satisfied. "We're done with this piece. Once we put the stain on it, I bet you won't even be able to see that silly handprint. Go ahead and text Jake and tell him he can come over."

Amy didn't waste any time. She dropped the sander on the workbench and snatched up her phone. Instead of texting, she punched in his number and waited for him to pick up.

He answered on the first ring. "Amy?"

"Hi, Jake. Mom says we're done. You want to come on over?"

"Yeah. I'll head out now and be there in a few."

"Okay. See you soon, drive safe."

She punched the end button and slipped her phone into her shorts pocket. "When do you want to torture me some more with this stuff? You know sanding those creepy little cherubs is going to be a pain in the butt."

"I know. I thought I'd leave those for you." Sarah smiled.

"Gee, thanks. I can hardly wait. I'm going to run up and get a quick shower before Jake gets here. Tell him I'll be down in a few minutes."

Jake pulled into the driveway ten minutes later. Sarah put her broom and dustpan aside and enfolded Jake in her arms. "How you doing, Champ?"

"I'm hanging in there, Mrs. Morgan. It's so hard. All those people at the house, and my mother is just a mess. She can hardly finish a sentence without crying. I just had to get out for a while."

"I know it's hard, Jake. I can't imagine what you and your parents must be going through. Is there any more information on what caused the accident?"

"Not that I've heard. They think the girl was speeding and overcorrected. That caused the car to flip over. Andrea was thrown halfway out the window, and the car apparently landed on her."

Sarah's raised her hands to cover her mouth. "Oh my God, who told you all that? That's information you didn't need to know."

Jake shrugged. "Word gets around. I'd rather know she didn't lie there suffering, waiting on someone to come and rescue her. Somehow it's easier knowing she died instantly."

Sarah looked doubtful. "I guess. Seems to me someone is sharing information better kept to themselves. I plan to go over and visit with your mom tomorrow. I didn't want to descend on her right away. You need family around at a time like this."

"I'm sure she'd love to see you anytime. I just hope she can eventually cope. She seems so out of it since it happened."

"She'll be okay, Jake. Just give her some time. She'll need you more than ever, so you make sure you're there for her. I'll try to keep in touch after everyone is gone. That seems to be when things get rough. Oh, here's Amy."

Both Sarah and Jake turned to face the door to the garage as Amy stepped out wearing a beige sundress. Her long blonde hair, still wet from the shower, hung down her back in a tight French braid. She hugged Jake and kissed him on the lips.

"What do you two plan to do this evening?"

Jake put his arm around Amy. "I don't know. Do you want to go into town and get some dinner? Maybe we'll head into Lakewood Ranch and catch a movie. What do you think?"

"That's fine by me. Let me get my purse and my cell phone. I left them in the kitchen."

While Amy backtracked into the house, Jake strolled over to the dresser. "This is going to look good when you're done. I think Amy will be happy with it when she sees it finished."

"I hope so, Jake. She certainly doesn't like it now." Sarah placed the sanding tools back on their hooks above the workbench.

"What's with the handprint?"

Sarah laughed. "That's becoming the signature of the entire piece.

Amy said it just showed up the day she hurt her hand, and we can't get it to come off. Both of us have tried very hard. I think I'm just going to stain over it. That should blend it in enough."

Jake laid his fingers lightly over the print. The coldness of it startled him. He jerked his hand back and glanced at Sarah. She faced the workbench putting away her supplies. Tentatively he touched the edge of the print again. Something caught his eye in the mirror. Glancing up, he saw his reflection, but he wasn't alone. A black shadow swept across the front of the glass. Jake blinked and spun around, convinced something had passed behind him in the garage. Nothing. He peered at the mirror, wondering if he would see the shadow again, but he didn't.

Amy came up behind him and wrapped her arms around his waist. "Ready." She stopped, puzzled by the expression on his face. "What? What's wrong?"

"Nothing," Jake said slowly. "I just thought I saw something in the mirror."

"What is it with that mirror?" Amy said impatiently. "Everyone who looks in it sees weird stuff. First, there was Destiny, now you. Mom, I'm telling you, there is something really creepy about this furniture."

Sarah returned to glance in the mirror with the two teens. "Jake, will you tell Amy that she is being totally ridiculous about this bedroom suite? I've never heard such nonsense. There is nothing in that mirror. It is just plain glass." To prove her point, she took her finger and tapped on the glass.

Half expecting it to shatter, Amy jumped back. "Don't do that, Mom. The thing might smash into a million pieces, and then we'd have thirteen years of bad luck or something."

Sarah laughed. "When did you become so superstitious? You two go on now and have fun. Have her back by midnight, Jake."

He reluctantly turned from the mirror to face Amy and her mother, his expression still puzzled. "Yes, ma'am. I'll have her back right after the movie is over. You ready, Amy?"

"Yep. Bye, Mom."

"Bye. Have fun." Sarah opened the door and stepped into the house

CHAPTER SIXTEEN

Amy and Jake climbed into his Jeep, and he backed out of the driveway. Passing Destiny's house, he leaned forward and peered out the windshield. He'd hoped to catch sight of Destiny on his way out. He couldn't help wondering what she had planned for tonight. He'd not seen her with any other girls in town, and Amy certainly hadn't been very helpful in the friend department. Jake worried about her. Now that he'd lost Andie, he knew about true loneliness. He couldn't imagine losing his entire family.

"What are you doing, Jake?"

Jake looked at Amy, confused. "What do you mean? I'm driving."

"You were looking for Destiny, weren't you?"

"So what? Is that a crime all of a sudden?"

Amy's eyes narrowed. Jake had seen that look before. He steeled himself for impending argument.

"It's not a crime, Jake. It's just that you've been very interested in her lately. I find out you've been by her house the other night. I caught you in the bookstore with her. And now, when you're on a date with me, you're looking for her as we drive by. What is it with you and Destiny? Is there something you need to tell me?"

Jake kept his eyes on the road, and his expression warned Amy that he struggled to keep his temper under control. "Amy, I just want to go out and have a nice time. I don't want to fight about Destiny or anything else. I just lost my sister, and I'd like to have an evening where I can escape reality for a little while and spend some time with my girlfriend.

If you're going to be a pain in the butt, tell me now, and I'll just take you home."

She folded her arms and sat back against the seat. "I'm not being a pain in the butt," she sulked, but she didn't bring up the subject again.

Jake drove in silence the rest of the way to town. He took Amy for a burger at the local Applebee's. Following dinner, they ran into Steve and Jessica, and the entire group decided to go bowling at the Super Bowl, a sports bar bowling alley combination.

***

As they bowled, Jake appreciated the fact that his friends seemed to know what he needed. They did their best to help cheer him up. The jeering at the gutter balls, the half-hearted insults flung at each other, and high fives for strikes improved his mood tremendously. By the end of the game, he could say he was actually happy for the first time in days. Immediately, the guilt assaulted him. Here he was having fun when he should be home with his family, but he just couldn't take all the sadness and tears. He knew Andie better than anyone, and she wouldn't want any of them sad. Celebrating life was what she did best, and Jake bet she'd give them all hell if she could. He sure wished she could.

Amy rolled another gutter ball and suffered the heckling of Steve and Jessica. She plopped on Jake's lap and smacked his lips with a strawberry-flavored kiss. He granted her a smile and a tight hug. Good times.

The foursome wrapped up their evening at the local ice cream shop. Jake and Amy shared a banana split, and Steve handed Jessica the second of two chocolate cones as he straddled the wrought iron chair.

"Hey, Jake, you gonna ride in the rodeo this year?" Steve asked, catching a drip of ice cream falling from his cone.

"I guess. I had planned to. Shasta is ready for the barrel race, and I might enter the bronco event. My parents might be a little more cautious now, so I don't know."

"Yeah, I know what you mean. I bet they'll let you ride, though. They know how good you are. You practically won last year, even with all those circuit cowboys competing against you. I've never seen anybody work a horse like you. You are like that horse whisperer guy in the movies."

Jake laughed. "Hardly," he said. "I just love to ride. It helps to think like a horse, too."

Steve whinnied, and they all cackled.

Amy laid her hand on Jake's arm. "I wish you wouldn't ride in the bronco contest. It scares me. Those horses are so mean."

Jake put his arm around Amy. "They aren't mean, babe. Just misunderstood. As long as you talk to them first, they won't hurt you. Doesn't mean they don't want you off their back, though."

Steve laughed. "You talk to them, do you?" He took his fingers and waggled them in front of Jake's face. "Wooooo."

"Very funny, Steve. I don't know how it works. I just know it does."

"Jake and I will be riding Samson and Goliath in the horse show that same weekend," Amy said. "We're working hard at training them. I hope they win."

"They're coming along great. They need some more practice, though. Goliath still shies away from that third jump, and I have to force him over it. We should work them this week. I don't want him to throw you the day of the show. That would be embarrassing."

"Duh. He won't throw me. He likes me."

Jake rolled his eyes. "Well, just the same, he needs practice." Jake glanced at his watch. "I guess we better go. I promised your mom I'd have you home early, and I need to get home myself. Don't want my parents to worry. They have enough on them right now."

Amy gathered her purse and stood. She hugged her best friend Jessica and then gave Steve a kiss on the cheek. She waved to a few other friends that had stopped by for ice cream and walked with Jake out to the Jeep. As they passed Destiny's house, Jake sensed Amy staring at him again. He deliberately glanced out the window to see what she'd say.

"Jake, I swear, why do you always look at *her* house? I'm beginning to think you like her more than me."

Jake, not surprised by her reaction, responded, "Amy, don't be stupid. I don't like Destiny more than you. I feel bad for her, that's all. I wondered what she was doing in that little trailer all alone. We really should start asking her to go a few places with us. You know…introduce her around some."

Amy growled in frustration. "Why do you care so much about whether she has friends or not? You know what? I'm beginning to think Jessica is right, and you have a crush on Destiny." Amy glared at Jake. "I bet she's put a spell on you."

Jake's mouth dropped open. "What?"

"Oh, come on, Jake. Everyone in town knows Madame Rose is a witch. It stands to reason that Destiny is one too. Don't be so naive."

Jake snorted. "Oh, for God's sake, Amy. You're an idiot."

She stared at him, her eyes filling with tears. He immediately regretted the harshness of his words, but at times she infuriated him. He parked the Jeep in the driveway, unbuckled and swiveled in his seat. "Look, I'm sorry, but you've got to know how ridiculous that sounded."

"I want you to stay away from her, Jake. She's trouble. Everyone in town knows it."

He sighed and gripped the steering wheel. "Amy, don't tell me who my friends should be. I am your boyfriend, but that doesn't mean you own me. Jessica is my friend too. You don't seem to be jealous of her."

"Jessica is my best friend. She wouldn't dare move in on you. Destiny, on the other hand, has her sights set on you, and she's ready to aim."

He rolled his eyes. What Amy didn't know, and he wasn't going to tell her, was Jessica had tried to make a move on him at Amy's birthday party last year. "Destiny does not have her sights set on me. She is a nice girl in need of a few friends. Why can't you just be friends with her too?"

"Jake, honestly, I don't know why you're so blinded by her. She's weird. Who in their right mind would work in that creepy bookstore? That stuff is way beyond bizarre. If you ask me, I think her grandmother is half crazy."

"Amy, stop it. If it weren't for Madame Rose, you'd have been in serious trouble when you injured your hand. Just because the stuff she sells in her bookstore is different does not make her a witch. I know what everyone in town says, but they're wrong. Andie loved going in there, and I still do. Their stuff is really cool. Are you saying Andie and I are witches too?"

"Of course not. Don't be stupid." She huffed and crossed her arms.

"Then listen to yourself. You know Destiny isn't a witch any more than I am. You act like doing something different is a crime. As long as people cause no harm to anyone else, I don't see what business it is of anyone's what they do. I think you are a snob, Amy Morgan. That's what I think." Jake leaned close to her, pointing a finger. "I'll tell you this. If you go spreading rumors about Destiny all around town and make it difficult for her to make friends, you and I won't have a future together. I don't want a girlfriend who would act that way."

Jake got out and opened the door for Amy. She stepped out of the Jeep and put her arms around Jake's neck. "I'm sorry, Jake. I know I can be jealous. You are just the most perfect boyfriend, and I don't want anyone else to steal you away from me."

He reached up and removed Amy's arms. "If you trusted me and weren't so insecure, you'd see that you have nothing to worry about. I've got to get home. I don't want my parents to worry."

He walked her to the front door. She took out her key and waited for him to kiss her goodnight. When he reached around her and opened the door, her eyes widened. "Aren't you going to kiss me, Jake?"

"Goodnight, Amy."

Jake went back to the Jeep, turning the engine to life. He'd shocked Amy by not kissing her, but she'd ticked him off. As he drove by Destiny's house, he looked for a light. Seeing none, he continued home.

CHAPTER SEVENTEEN

It was Sunday, the store was closed, and the sun blazed through the morning clouds. After a lazy breakfast with her grandmother, Destiny left her reading the paper and wandered onto the porch. She grabbed an apple from the basket by the door and bounded down the steps. "I'm going to go visit the horses," she called over her shoulder.

Samson and Goliath grazed at the center of the paddock. Destiny clucked to them and held the apple out over the railing. Goliath snorted, stamped a foot and turned his head away. Samson, however, pricked his ears forward and approached, blowing air through his nostrils.

"I think you're Samson, and between you and your brother, I think he's got the brawn, but you've got the brains, don't you boy?" she said and held out the apple in the palm of her hand. Samson took it from her politely. He stood crunching while she rubbed the white blaze on his otherwise black face.

"You gonna spoil that beast."

Destiny jumped. She'd not heard nor seen anyone approach, yet there the old farmer stood, right foot on the bottom rail of the fence, elbows resting on the top rail.

She faced the Shade. "You're Patch, right?"

"Yep, that'd be me," he answered.

"You sure know how to sneak up on people. Next time, clear your throat or something. Jeeze."

"Didn't mean to scare you, young'n. Thought you'd be used to us by now."

She glanced at Patch, still marveling at how real he seemed. She didn't reach out to touch him, though she wanted to. "I'm not sure who you mean by 'us,' but the last time we met, you could have warned me that you were dead. I fainted in my grandmother's kitchen when I found out I'd been talking to a ghost. I could have been seriously injured."

Patch laughed a deep, hearty laugh. Destiny found herself liking him even if he was a Shade.

"I reckon you would have fainted a lot sooner had I told you the truth, and I couldn't even catch you. I figured it'd be better coming from your grandmother."

Destiny nodded. "You might have a point. What are you doing down here?"

Patch surveyed the field. "I was about to ask you the same question."

She scratched the horse's neck. "I came down to visit with the horses. They're so majestic. Especially these two. Even though Goliath, at least I think that's Goliath, won't have anything to do with me. He must not be the smartest horse in the barn."

"Don't let him fool you. He's just making you work for his affection. Last time I saw you, the look on your face wasn't too happy. How you doing now?"

Destiny sighed and didn't answer him right away. She rubbed Samson's soft velvet nose. Patch waited for her to respond. "Things could be better, I guess."

"What ails you, girl?"

She mocked his stance by putting her elbows on the top rail and her foot on the bottom. "Thanks to Miss Snootfull up there, I'm going to be the laughing stock of the entire town. She thinks I'm after her boyfriend, so she's trashing my name with all her friends. And if word gets out about this new little 'gift' of mine…well, you know…."

"Well, are you?" Patch asked.

"Am I what?"

"After her boyfriend?" He threw her a grin, causing her to wince. For a Shade, he was pretty sharp.

The corners of her mouth turned up slightly. "No," she said without much conviction. Patch raised a ghostly eyebrow. "Well, okay then. If the opportunity presented itself and they broke up, I might turn on the charm, but I'm not a boyfriend stealer." Destiny was surprised at how Patch could get her to talk about things she'd had no intention of telling anyone. "Jake has been the only one nice to me since I moved in. And now, after what happened in Amy's garage the other day and the fact that she saw me working in Grams' bookstore, she's gonna tell the whole town I'm a witch."

Patch put his hand on his chin, rubbing it slowly. "I see your predicament, but I don't think being related to your grandmother is a problem. She's very well respected in this town. Has been for a long time." He shifted position. "Oh sure, there're people who don't understand her gift and are afraid of it. Those people…you just have to ignore their ignorance. What you and your granny can do is special." Using his tongue, Patch flipped the piece of straw from one side of his mouth to the other. "Not many people are blessed with being able to talk to the dead. We need help over on this side sometimes more than the living. People get lost over here in my world and often need someone to show them where the road signs are. That's what your granny does. The extended benefit is she gives the living peace of mind about their dead."

She thought about what he said. It was the same thing her grandmother had told her, but for some reason, she understood it better coming from Patch. "It's so scary, though, Patch. Take what happened at Amy's. I still am not sure what I saw, but it scared the crap out of me."

"You've mentioned that twice. What happened up there, child?"

She told him, explaining about the handprint and everything she'd seen in that mirror. When she finished, he seemed worried.

"I've sensed a disturbance around here lately. Something evil this way comes. Gives me the shivers."

Destiny widened her eyes. "Gives *you* the shivers? It can't hurt you. You're already dead. By the way, why do you still hang around here? Weren't you supposed to cross over into some light or something?" Destiny had the urge to poke him in the chest but resisted. She was certain her finger would pass right through him, and she wasn't sure she could handle that.

Patch chuckled. "Well, missy, that's complicated and my own business. Now, after so many years, I'm not even sure I remember why I didn't go into that light. But lately, I get the feeling I'm needed for something, and that evil I've been sensing at the Morgans might have something to do with it." He stroked the horse, and Samson shook his head, stamped a hoof on the ground, and rolled his eyes to see the source of the touch. Destiny wondered if horses could see spirits. It certainly seemed they could feel one's touch. "Or maybe I just enjoy watching over my horses."

"Are you lonely? Wasn't there someone up there waiting for you?" Destiny didn't want the old Shade to be lonely. He seemed so nice. She scratched Samson's ears, and the animal settled down.

"Naw. I never jumped the broom. Never had any kids. Nobody but me and these smelly old horses." He sighed, his eyes filled with sadness. "See, I had me a drinking problem back in the day. It cost me quite more than I care to admit. I had me a woman I was quite fond of, and we planned to get married. Then I got drunk one night and got into a bar fight. Didn't know my own strength, and I killed a man. Because it was self-defense, I never went to jail, but the idea that I could kill a man must have scared Elsie 'cause she left me. Left town with her mama and daddy, and I never saw her again." Patch stared off across the paddock, chewed his straw, and then swiveled his head toward Destiny.

"Old man Morgan, he gave me a chance when no one else would. He brought me on to work with his horses. Seems I got a way with the beasts. I tried to stay away from the booze after that. I love these animals, and I didn't want to do anything to endanger them. Then one day, I just up and died, right there in that very barn. Guess you could say I died doing what I loved most."

Tears welled in Destiny's eyes. "That's quite a story. Did you ever try to look up your girlfriend?"

"Nope. After about a year, I learned she'd married somebody up in the next county. Didn't think much about it after that."

"That's so sad," Destiny said, rubbing Samson's nose again. Suddenly, the horse tossed his head and snorted.

"What's a sad story, Destiny?" Jake suddenly appeared behind her. She jumped for the second time that morning. She'd been so involved in her conversation with Patch that she didn't see or hear Jake's approach. She casually swiveled her head to the left, and of course, Patch was gone. Now she looked like an idiot.

"Oh, I was just talking to the horse here," she lied. "Thinking about him and his brother over there and what a sad story it is that they aren't with their mom and dad anymore."

Jake smiled. "Horses don't think about their relatives the same way we do. Samson here would just as soon bite Goliath as look at him. He's not a brother as much as he is another male rival to challenge for the fillies. As long as we keep them away from the ladies, they get along amiable enough. Actually, the stallion and mare that gave birth to them are still on the farm, so you don't really have to worry about them being separated from their parents."

Destiny's lips curved. "I know you think I'm silly." *Better than crazy,* she supposed.

"No, I don't. I think you're sweet. Samson here sure seems to think so too." Jake looked down and spotted the piece of apple core on the ground. "Did you give that to him?"

Destiny blushed and offered a sheepish grin. "Yes. Am I spoiling him for you?"

"Naw. Horses love apples, and Samson here is a real sucker for them. He'll be your friend for life now." Jake reached out and scratched the horse's ears. Goliath trotted over to receive his share of the attention.

"Oh sure, now you come over here," she said. "Must be a male bonding thing."

Jake laughed. "Goliath, here, is a little shy. Especially around a beautiful girl. Samson's the flirt, and he's greedy. He can smell apples from a mile away."

Destiny blushed. Jake thought her pretty...boy, wouldn't that tick off Amy. "What's going to happen when your girlfriend spots you down here talking to me?"

"Well, since she's at church, she won't see me, but even if she did, I've already told her she can't pick my friends for me."

Destiny scuffed one shoe in the dirt. "Look, Jake, I don't need any trouble. It's going to be hard enough to fit in around here because of who my grandmother is. I don't need to make the most popular girl in town mad at me. Maybe we shouldn't be seen together. She might come home any minute." Destiny spun to head toward her house. Jake placed a hand on her arm, halting her progress.

"Please don't go, Destiny. I really enjoy talking to you and think of you as a really good friend. I hope you think the same about me."

She faced him. "I do, Jake, but I can't have Amy turning all the other kids in town against me because she thinks I'm trying to put voodoo on her boyfriend. I have to go to school in this God-forsaken town for two more years before I can graduate and get out of here. Life's hard enough for me. I don't need more trouble."

"I'm your friend, Destiny. There won't be any trouble. I've already told Amy to back off, and if she kept up the gossip, I was going to break up with her."

Destiny rolled her eyes and sighed. "Oh, great. That helps. Thanks a lot, Jake."

Jake leaned against the fence with his hand on the post. Samson nudged his hand for a rub, and Jake obliged. "Look, Destiny," he said. "It's not right for Amy to be so jealous and make snap judgments about you. She doesn't even know you. I'd say the same thing about anyone she was acting jealous over. It just so happens that I really do enjoy your friendship."

Destiny walked along the fence line, and Jake followed. She needed to keep moving, or she might throw her arms around him right then and there. "Thanks, Jake. I enjoy having you for a friend too. I just don't need any drama. It's weird enough starting a new school. I don't need to add to my stress by ticking Amy off."

"You haven't done anything to tick Amy off. She's always been the jealous type. It's just who she is. I don't know why I put up with her. I guess it's because she was the only interesting girl around here until you came."

"Jake, she's your girlfriend. You should be with her on a beautiful Sunday morning, not down here with me." Destiny glanced back at him. His face was drawn tight with concern. Samson followed both of them along the fence, probably hoping for another apple. Goliath watched with disinterest. She thought it funny how two horses could have totally different personalities and come from the same parents. Much like people, she guessed.

She sighed as she dragged her shoe through the sand. She couldn't let herself care for Jake. No matter how handsome or how sweet he was to her, she had to let it go. That wasn't easy with the way he just kept showing up. If Amy got home and found her with him, it would cause more drama than an MTV reality show.

"I told you she went to church. I came down to exercise the horses. We are going to train them some this afternoon. Hey," Jake stopped. "Do you want me to teach you how to ride?"

Destiny's eyes widened, and her heart raced with excitement. She'd never really been on a horse, and she peered at Samson and Goliath. She swallowed...they were so huge. Jake caught her expression and started laughing. Destiny's cheeks flamed.

"I didn't mean these guys," he said quickly.

"No, that's okay. I'd rather stay on terra firma and watch." She didn't want to run the risk of being seen riding with him, just in case Amy came home. That just begged for trouble.

"Dr. Morgan has a shy little filly up in the barn that I think would be perfect for you. Her name is Ginger." Jake grabbed her hand and dragged her toward the barn.

"Jake—wait!" Destiny protested.

"Oh, come on. It'll be fun. I love teaching, and I can tell by the look in your eyes you want to learn. We won't do much, just ride around the ring. It'll be fine, you'll see."

Together they went into the barn, Destiny still loudly objecting. "Jake, no...I don't think this is a good idea...." And then she spotted the little horse. Ginger peeked out of her stall with expectant soulful brown eyes, her ears pointed forward. Her brown face with its white star warmed Destiny's heart. She grinned at Jake. "She's beautiful."

Jake laughed out loud. "I knew you'd like her. Listen, if you really don't want to do this, I won't push you, but I think it will be fun."

It was a sunny Sunday, and Destiny had nothing better to do. She knew she was playing with fire by spending this time with Jake, but she was only human. "Okay, let's do it," she said.

Jake laughed. He led Ginger to the mounting block and put on a blanket and saddle. He showed Destiny how to put her foot in one stirrup and swing her leg over the back of the horse. Once she was in the saddle, he took the reins.

"Here, let me lead her around for a bit so you can get used to what it feels like sitting in that saddle. Practice putting weight on the balls of your feet in the stirrups. Just get used to the feel of her beneath you."

Destiny did as instructed and found that riding really wasn't that bad. She held on to the pommel of the saddle as Jake led Ginger around the paddock. After two trips around, he handed her the reins. Instructing her on the different commands she needed to use, he walked beside Destiny as she guided the horse. It was more fun than Destiny had imagined. In fact, she got so into it that she was surprised to look up and see Jake standing against the fence on the opposite side of the paddock.

"Ride her toward me," he shouted.

"Okay, here I come," Destiny gently nudged Ginger's sides, and the horse clopped over to where Jake was standing. "I did it!" she declared.

Jake reached up and helped her down. "You sure did. Now come with me to the other field while I give Goliath a workout. Then I have to ride Samson. We'll tie Miss Ginger near the feedbag and bucket of water. She'll be perfectly content for a little while."

Most of that morning, Destiny watched as Jake put Samson and Goliath through their paces. For such large horses, they were extremely nimble and graceful as they soared over the pre-set jumps. She was quite impressed that Jake didn't end up on his butt with the height of some of those jumps. She found herself sucking in her breath more than a few times. When he'd finished with both horses, he unsaddled them and turned them loose in the pasture. He put the saddles away, and then she followed him back to the barn, where they retrieved Ginger and put her comfortably in her stall.

Jake took the brush and showed Destiny how to groom Ginger. He checked her feet for pebbles and cleaned out around her shoes. He turned to Destiny when he'd completed the task. "Next time, we'll go out to the fields," he promised.

Destiny found herself excited that there would be a next time and then remembered her promise to Amy.

"Jake, there won't be a next time. This was really fun, but it's not right. Amy will get mad."

"Oh, stop. I'm just teaching you to ride. No big deal."

"I don't know, maybe. Hey, are you thirsty?"

"Very," Jake said.

"Come on up to my house, and I'll grab some drinks out of the fridge."

"I'm right behind you."

Jake and Destiny strolled to her house. She noticed Grams's car wasn't in the driveway. She must've gone to the bookstore.

"I'm sure this is not what you're used to," Destiny said, opening the door and letting him into her tiny home. To his credit, Jake didn't miss a beat.

"This is great. Efficient," he said.

Destiny huffed out a laugh. "Efficient, huh? Well, that's an interesting word to describe this...." She waved her arms around. Destiny went to the fridge and took out two cold sodas. She gestured to a seat at the kitchen table. "Let's sit here. You can feel the air conditioner better."

"Okay." Jake grinned and sat next to her. He looked around the trailer. "This is nice. It's bigger than it looks from outside."

She blushed, embarrassed. "Yeah, it's a real palace." Jake laughed, and Destiny joined him, then grew serious. "I miss my house in Naples. There I had room for friends to come hang out, it had a pool, and my bedroom was bigger than this entire trailer."

"Yeah, I'm really sorry about your family, Destiny. I know now how much you must miss them."

She put her hand on Jake's arm. The pain swimming in his eyes tore at her heart. "I know, you know. I'm so sorry about Andie. If you ever want to talk, I'm here. Just find a way to do it without Amy knowing."

Jake frowned.

"I'm sorry. I shouldn't have added that part. Listen, I know the pain of losing someone you love, and it sucks. So just call me when you feel like you're losing it, and I'll talk you through."

Jake's eyes welled up with tears. Destiny raised an eyebrow. She hadn't expected that from the macho football star. "I miss her so much, Destiny. She and I were really close, you know? Sure we had our fights like most brothers and sisters, but she was so cool to hang out with. It was tough enough when she went to college, but now that it's permanent...." Jake grabbed a napkin and angrily swiped at his eyes. "It's all so stupid. It shouldn't have happened."

"I know, Jake. I'm sure she wouldn't want you so torn up about it, though. She'd want you to remember her the way she was when she was with you."

Jake held her gaze. Destiny stared deep into his blue eyes and fell in love. She knew she shouldn't, but the heavy emotion took her by surprise. She blinked, and Jake glanced away. With her heart lodged in her throat, Destiny remained quiet. Jake shifted his eyes back to hers, and for just a second, she thought he was about to kiss her. He didn't, and the moment passed.

"I must look like a real girl," he said, swiping at his eyes again.

Hoping her voice wouldn't betray her emotions, Destiny said, "Nope. More like a real man."

Jake smiled. "Do you think about your family a lot?"

"Every day," she replied. "At least for you, Andie died at the hand of someone else. My brother didn't live because I couldn't get him out of the car seat before the car exploded into flames. I've been having nightmares about it since the accident. No one knows about this but my grandmother. They scare the crap out of me."

"Tell me about them," Jake said, taking a long sip of soda.

"Oh, trust me…you don't want to hear about them. They're pretty gruesome. I started having them the day after the funeral. In my dream, my mother is furious with me because I didn't get Elijah out in time. Both my parents were killed instantly when they were thrown from the car, but Elijah and I survived the initial wreck." Destiny paused to take a deep, steadying breath. "I tried to get him out, but the buckle on his car seat was jammed. A cop jerked me out of the van before I could save Elijah. The cop went back to get him, and the car blew up. We were both thrown several feet from the blast."

Jake stared, wide-eyed. "God, Destiny. That's horrible. I can't imagine going through something like that. You gotta know, though, it's not your fault. That stupid cop yanked you out too soon. You can't blame yourself for that."

Now Destiny's eyes filled with tears. This wonderful guy was trying to make her feel better when he suffered so much grief himself. Still, his words didn't absolve her guilt. "I should have gotten him out, Jake."

Jake slid his chair over and wrapped his arm around her shoulders. Destiny leaned her head on his shoulder and let the tears come. A drop plopped on her head, and she realized he cried too. At that moment, the two teens connected in a way no two people can unless they've shared the loss of someone they loved.

Destiny didn't know how long they cried, but once she got control of herself, she lifted her head. "Feel better?" Jake asked.

She nodded. "You?"

He said, "Yeah, honestly, I do. In fact, this is the best I've felt since Andie died. Why don't you tell me about your dreams?"

Destiny hadn't planned to tell anyone other than her grandmother about her dreams, but in the safety of that moment, the words started flowing before she could stop them. She told Jake about the crash scene and how she tried to get to Elijah. She knew the next part sounded crazy, but she told Jake anyway. She described seeing her mother's decapitated head rolling in the street, turning and accusing her of not saving her brother. Jake's eyes went wide, his eyebrows rose, and his mouth dropped open as he listened to her recount the nightmare.

"She blames me, Jake. I know she does. She's somewhere, wandering around, blaming me for not saving Elijah."

"Destiny, that's just nuts. No mother would blame her child for what happened in that crash unless she's just cruel. Your mother wasn't cruel, was she?"

"No, she wasn't, but these dreams just feel so real."

"Of course they do. I think you feel so guilty that you're projecting a lot of this onto yourself. Your mom loved you. She doesn't blame you for your brother's death. There is no way you could control that situation."

He's right, Destiny. You don't need to worry about it.

Destiny's head whipped around so fast that she nearly hit Jake in the nose. Standing in her kitchen was Andie. She looked a little better than she had at the funeral, but she hadn't quite mastered that mind over matter thing yet. Her clothes were still bloody, the wound in her neck gaped open, and her head still listed to one side.

Well...maybe it wasn't that much better, but at least Destiny didn't gasp this time.

Maybe she'd get used to this gift after all.

"What is it, Destiny? You jumped like you've seen a ghost or something."

It's okay to tell him, Destiny. Jake will get it.

She shook her head. *He'll think I'm a freak.*

"What are you shaking your head for? Destiny, what's going on?"

Tell him.

Destiny glanced at Jake. He watched her with curious eyes. "You promise not to think I'm crazy?"

"Yes."

She sighed, knowing she was going to regret this and looked at Andie, who nodded encouragingly.

"I am not as different from my grandmother as you might think."

Jake drew his brows together. "What do you mean?"

"I can see, hear, and talk to spirits. There is one in the room with us right now." Destiny waited for him to jump up and run out of her home, never to return, but to her surprise, he didn't. In fact, he looked intrigued.

"Really?"

"Really. Listen, I know this sounds completely strange, and you're probably all freaked out, but it's true."

"I'm not freaked out, Destiny. This is cool! I told you before in the bookstore that I believe in these things. I believe your grandmother can do all the things she claims. In fact, I was thinking about going to her about Andie. I want to make sure she's okay."

"Well, you don't have to go to my grandmother. Jake, Andie's here."

Now that shocked him. His mouth fell open, and his eyes popped wide. "Andie? She's here? Oh my God, is she okay? Andie! Andie!"

Tell him to stop shouting, Destiny. I'm not deaf.

Destiny smiled. "Andie said to stop shouting. She's not deaf."

Again, Jake's jaw dropped. He stared at her. "She really is here, isn't she?"

"Yes, she's standing by the sink."

Jake whipped around and faced the kitchen sink. "Why can't I see her?"

"I don't know. It's just one of those things, I guess. Maybe I'm just more in tune to it than you are. But trust me, you wouldn't want to see her like this."

Thanks, Destiny.

My pleasure.

"Is she okay? I mean, she's not scared or anything?"

Tell him I'm okay. I'm not scared or cold or sad.

Destiny told him the words Andie sent to her mind.

"That's good, Andie. I'm glad you're okay."

Destiny stared at Jake. He grinned at the kitchen sink like a loon. "You really are okay with this, aren't you? You're acting like she's right in the room with us."

"Well, you said she was."

"I know, but this doesn't freak you out at all?"

I told you he was okay with it. You should have trusted me.

"I know, I know," Destiny said.

"You know what?"

"I was talking to Andie."

"Tell her I love her and miss her very much."

"You just did, Jake. She can hear you; she just can't speak. I hear her through my mind. It's a little unsettling when you don't know it's coming."

"I bet. Hey, Andie, what's it like where you are?"

Tell him it's nice. I don't want him to know I haven't moved on yet. It will make him worry.

Destiny looked doubtful. "She says it's nice."

"Good," Jake replied. "I'm really glad. Mom and Dad are going to be glad you're okay."

Tell him it's not a good idea to tell Mom and Dad he's spoken to me. They wouldn't get it.

"Uh, Jake?"

"Yeah?"

"Andie thinks it wouldn't be a good idea to tell your parents about this. I happen to agree with her. This really needs to be our little secret. I can't have it getting out around town that I can do this. People already think I'm freaky enough just because of who my grandmother is. If they find out that I can see ghosts and spirits, they will treat me like I have some kind of plague. Please don't tell anyone."

"Destiny, what you have is a gift. It's not something to be afraid of or hide."

"Yeah, well, if it'd happened to you, you would feel differently, I promise."

"I guess, but I worry that Mom and Dad are so sad. This might make them feel better."

Tell him I'll find a way to let them know that they will understand and be able to cope with.

"Andie said she'll find a way to help them cope. Jake, please don't tell anyone about this. I really trust you as my friend." She took his hand in hers. "Please?"

Jake apparently grasped the urgency in her tone because he said, "Okay. I won't say anything, I promise. Will you still talk to Andie for me?"

"When I can. Maybe if you come to the bookstore some, we can use my grandmother's reading room. Just please don't let this get out. You also can't tell Amy when you meet with me. She'll freak out. She hates me, Jake."

Jake sighed. "I've already told you not to worry about Amy. She doesn't control who my friends are."

"And I've told you that she could ruin things for me here in Arcadia. Jake, if you want to stay my friend, you will respect this, okay?"

He nodded. "Okay, Destiny. I'll keep all this to myself. I know how much it means to you to fit in with the other kids here. I still think you're cool to be so different, but if you don't want it spread around, I won't say anything."

If he says he won't say anything, he won't. Destiny, you can believe him.

"Spoken like a true big sister."

"What did she say?" He continued to stare hard at the kitchen sink. Destiny could see that he so desperately wanted to see his sister again.

"She was reassuring me that you keep your word."

He reached for Destiny's hand. "I do."

"I'll have to trust you. If you let me down, I'll sick one of these spirits on you."

You won't have to. I'll haunt him for you.

Destiny laughed. "I like your sister, Jake. She's a real pal."

Jake frowned. "Yeah, I just wish I could talk to her like you do. I really miss her."

Destiny watched as Andie crossed the room and ran her hand over Jake's head. She saw a few hairs stir. Did he feel it?

Jake jumped. "Was that her? I think I felt something. I felt the same thing at the funeral. It was like a puff of air right on the top of my head."

"Yes, she just laid her hand on your head. She did the same thing the day of the funeral. I saw her."

Jake laid his hand on top of his head. "Wow, that is so cool. I love you, Andie."

I love you too, Jakey.

"She says she loves you too."

"Wow," Jake said again and sat back in the chair. "Is she gone?"

Destiny nodded. "She comes and goes. I think it has something to do with the energy they can expend to appear. My grandmother says it takes a lot for them to be able to control it."

"That is just so cool. Thank you, Destiny. Thank you so much for talking to her for me."

"You're welcome, Jake. Please keep this our secret, okay?"

"Wild horses couldn't drag it out of me. Speaking of horses, I better get up to Amy's house. She will be home by now and ready to ride."

"Okay. Why don't you go out the back and around to the stables? That way, it will look like you were coming from the barn. I don't want her to know you were in my house."

"Okay, I get it." Jake got up and walked to the back door. He stopped, turned and pulled Destiny into his arms, hugging her tight. "Thanks again."

She grinned, her heart soaring.

CHAPTER EIGHTEEN

"Amy, this looks so nice. I can't believe how well this furniture turned out. It looks even better than the way I pictured it." Sarah wandered through the bedroom, lightly touching each piece with the reverence she'd hold for a museum artifact. Amy wished she shared her enthusiasm, but her skin crawled, and the hair stood up on her arms whenever she entered the room. She had to admit the furniture did look better, but those angels on the mirror still creeped her out, and the stain didn't cover the handprint as Sarah assured her it would. Something just didn't feel right about any of it, but her mother wouldn't listen. Sarah stood staring, anticipating Amy's response.

"Okay, it does look better than it did when you bought it," Amy said. She couldn't think of anything else to say, wanting to love it as much as her mother did, but she didn't.

Amy and her mother had picked out a white comforter set that really stood out against the richness of the dark wood. They'd chosen red pillows and a throw of buttercup yellow to accent the bed, adding a colorful classy touch.

"Well, you must admit it does look better than Winnie the Pooh."

Amy laughed. "I was just thinking that."

"You two did a fabulous job," Amy's father said, standing in the doorway. "I must say when I first saw that bedroom suite in the garage, I thought your mother had lost her mind, but she knew what she was doing. Very elegant and grown-up."

"Oh ye of little faith," Sarah said, smiling. "In spite of all our little mishaps, we got it done and in Amy's room without any major disasters."

"Thanks, Dad," Amy said. "It'll do. It was a lot of hard work, though. If Jake hadn't helped finish the headboard, it would still be sitting in the garage."

Jeff nodded. "Jake's a good guy, Amy. Is he going to ride in the rodeo this year?"

Amy sat down on the bed and motioned for her father to come into the room. He sat in a small armchair on the other side of the nightstand. "Yes, he's riding the broncos again and doing the barrel racing. I wish he wouldn't do the Bronco event, though. I'm really afraid he'll get hurt. He wants to win that prize money to help with college." She picked at the fringe on the yellow throw, her eyes darting from one corner of the room to another. She wished she could relax. Amy glanced at Sarah, who still roamed around admiring their handy work. She shook her head and faced her father. "I think he has a good chance of winning, though."

"He certainly does. He has a way with horses, and his grandfather did too. William Turner's the reason we have such good horses on this farm. He was quite the horse trader. Jake has the same ability to recognize good horse flesh when he sees it." Jeff crossed his legs and relaxed in the chair. He picked up a copy of Wuthering Heights, flipped it open, turned a few pages, then placed it back on the nightstand. "He's also quite the horse charmer. I'm sure he'll be fine. I'm a little surprised at his parents, though. After what they went through with Andie, it's a wonder they let him ride."

"Yeah, Jake said that he had to do some convincing. Are you coming to the horse show on Saturday?" Leaning forward, Amy searched her father's face. Jeff glanced away and shifted in the chair. Uh-oh, here came the lie. Attempting to head him off, she said, "I want you to see me put Samson through his paces and ride him in the steeplechase. People think he's too big for that, but he's actually very nimble on his feet for such a big horse. I can't wait to win and prove to everyone how wrong they are about the Morgans."

Jeff smiled. "I'm sure you will, honey. I'll be there unless I'm called to the hospital for an emergency. You know how my life goes. I can never make any promises."

Amy rolled her eyes and mumbled, "Don't I know it."

"Amy," Dad chastised. "You know if there's an emergency, I have to be there. You may have everything you've ever wanted, but that comes with a price. Being head of the trauma center means I go when I'm needed. I want nothing more than to see you ride in that show, and hopefully, all the fools out there will cooperate and not get into trouble on Saturday."

"I know what you do is important," Amy whined. "But can't you get someone to cover for you? I mean, there are a few things more important than that hospital."

His expression grew dire. She'd crossed a line, and she knew it. His brows drew together, and he frowned. According to her father, nothing was more important than saving lives, but Amy disagreed. Growing up, no matter what she got involved in, he'd missed it. She knew he'd regret it someday, but she couldn't push. "Okay, whatever."

"Amy, don't give your father a hard time. You'll have plenty of friends there to cheer you on, and I'll be there." Sarah fluffed the curtains at the window.

"I know that Mom, but I want Dad to see me ride. I've worked so hard with Samson. Jake has taught me so much. I really want to win the steeple chase this year."

"Hello," Jeff said, waving his arms. "I'm still in the room. Listen, Amy, I promise I'll do everything I can to be there and watch, okay?"

Amy met his gaze and then nodded. Hope was something she'd learned to doubt.

"Good. Now we'll leave you to enjoy your new furniture," Jeff said.

"I really enjoyed doing this project with you, Amy. It was so much fun. I'll find something else for us to work on. You know, a nice antique table would look good under that window," Sarah said, still talking as Jeff dragged her out of the room.

Amy rolled her eyes behind Sarah's head and patted her on the shoulder. "Yeah, sure, Mom. Whatever you want." She closed the door after them.

Amy turned and glanced around her room. The atmosphere grew heavy and pressed against her chest. Something was watching. Not the angels...as Destiny had pointed out. The faces were directed at the mirror. Amy couldn't say why the angels bothered her, but she half-expected their heads to turn and show mouths full of sharp little teeth. She shivered.

The fact the handprint wouldn't come off that dresser unsettled Amy. She wondered what Destiny had seen in the mirror that day in the garage. Something had scared the crap out of her, and Amy needed to know what it was.

All of a sudden, the mirror darkened. Amy's eyes widened as she watched the glass turn smoky black and smelled burning wood. Flames appeared at the corner of the mirror frame, and Amy bolted to the bathroom, filled a plastic cup with water and dashed back into the room. She heaved the water on the frame. Nothing happened. Then she realized the flames were *behind* the glass. She leaned forward, studying this bizarre event.

The pressure built in her chest as the air in the room thickened. The orange flames flickered against the black background of the mirror. BANG! Amy yelped and jumped at the loud noise emanating from the mirror. The black smoke previously contained in the mirror shot out across the room. It hovered in a cloud above the closed door for a few seconds and then zipped right through solid wood into the hallway.

Amy dashed to her door, flung it open and poked her head into the hallway. She swiveled her head from right to left, but nothing was there. What the hell—

Her cell rang, and she jumped inches off the floor, a scream escaping her lips. Amy's hand covered her pounding heart. She pulled the phone out of her pocket.

"Hi, Jake," Amy said, voice shaky.

"Hi, Ames. What were you doing?"

"Um…nothing." She sucked in a breath of air and walked back into the bedroom. The mirror glass showed only her terrified reflection.

"Are you okay? You sound a little weird." Jake's voice sounded concerned. Was she okay? What had she just witnessed? She knew no one would believe her…she'd didn't even believe it herself. Deciding to keep it to herself, for now, she cleared her throat and said, "I'm fine."

"You sure?"

Amy plopped on the bed, her heart still racing. "I said I was fine, didn't I?"

"Okay. Okay. Why are you so testy today? I mean, you've got that beautiful furniture in your room. Life should be glamorous."

"Shut up, Jake," Amy said, growing exasperated. That last comment wasn't funny. She changed the subject. "I was talking to Dad, and he wanted to know if you were riding in the bronco event this year. I told him you were, but I'm hoping you've changed your mind."

"Why? You know I can win it." She detected offense in his tone.

"I know, but I don't want you to get hurt."

"I went down to the arena and checked out the stallions they are using this year. They've got some wild-eyed horses down there, but I don't think there's one I can't handle. I really want to win this, Amy. I need that money for college. My parents have some money left from Andie's fund, but that won't be enough for all four years. In this economy, Dad's store hasn't done that well, and things are a little tight for my parents right now. I've got two more years to save, and then it's here."

"Why can't you just go to college with me? We could stay together. It would be fun."

"Amy, you know I can't afford to go out of state. I have to stay in Florida, where it's cheap. You know your dad will want you to go to some Ivy League school that I can't afford. I'm really hoping to get a football scholarship. That'll help a lot, but if I don't, then I have to pay for at least two years on my own."

"Well, maybe I'll just go to college where you go, and I won't do what my dad wants me to do." She kept her gaze glued to the mirror, but nothing more happened.

"Yeah, right," he scoffed. "Like your dad is going to let you go to a state school. He went to Harvard, for crying out loud."

Amy blew out a breath. "Jake, you and I both know I'm never going to get into freakin' Harvard. My grades aren't good enough."

"You've got money, Amy, and money talks. I'm sure your dad will get you in regardless of what your GPA is."

"Well then, maybe Daddy will pull some strings for you too," she said, warming to the idea. "I just want to be with you, Jake."

"Amy, we don't even know if we'll still be dating our senior year. Don't you think all of this is a little premature?"

Amy sat up, stunned. What had he just said? Her mind took off in all different directions. This sudden doubt had to do with Destiny Dove. She just knew it. Her temper flared. "What do you mean we might not be dating senior year? Why wouldn't we be?"

He didn't answer right away, flaring her temper further. Finally, he said, "Amy, that's two years away. Let's not worry about it right now."

"I'm sorry, Jake, but I *am* worried about it. Are you saying that you plan to break up with me? This has to do with Destiny, doesn't it?" She hated herself for bringing up that skank's name, but she couldn't help it. Enough was enough.

Jake sighed. "Amy, I'm not planning on breaking up with you, and it has nothing to do with Destiny. You really need to stop being so paranoid and jealous."

"I don't know, Jake," she pressed. "You two have been pretty chummy lately. I've seen you in that creepy bookstore talking to her. What is it that you two have so much in common? You don't read, so I know you're not in there looking for books, and your sister is gone, so you're not buying presents. What is it, Jake?"

He cleared his throat. She knew he only made that sound when he fought to control his temper. Maybe she regretted saying so much...sort of. She spoke the truth. He had been spending a lot of time in the Mystic Cat with Destiny. He thought she hadn't seen him, but she had.

"Amy," Jake finally said. "I really don't want to fight. Destiny and I are just friends. You really don't need to be jealous of her."

Heat flooded her face, anger growing from a source deeper than the current argument. Rationally, she knew this wasn't a big deal, yet she couldn't stop the fury. Glancing in the mirror, she sucked in a breath. The same smoky mist that had just flown into her room was back, reflected in the glass. It hovered in the corner. Rather than turn and face it directly, she stood up and stepped closer to the dresser. As she watched, the mist darkened to ruby. A stabbing pain struck her chest, and her temper blew.

"I'll be jealous of who I want," Amy raged. "You should be more considerate of how I feel and not hang around with someone you know I don't approve of." She watched her eyes grow dark in the mirror. Something controlled her brain. She wanted to stop the ranting, but she couldn't. The words continued to flow, laced with anger. "She's a witch, and you know it. She's not a good influence on you, keeping you interested in all that freaky stuff she's involved in with her grandmother. I forbid you to see her anymore." Amy shouted now. The sharpness of her words surprised her.

The red mist evaporated from the corner of the room, and immediately her anger faded. She blinked, struggling to remember what she'd just said. Jake was so silent on the other end that she feared he'd hung up. "Jake, are you still there?" she asked, fear gripping her gut. Why couldn't she remember? She knew they'd been discussing Destiny. Oh, God. She'd done something stupid.

"I'm here," he said in a frosty tone. "You and I have already had this discussion once, and I told you then, you don't tell me who my friends will be. Neither Destiny nor her grandmother is a witch, and you're way out of line for saying it. They help people. They've even helped me with Andie's death, something you've never seemed interested in doing."

"What?" Amy paced the room. She may have been out of line with the witch comment, but what was this crap about her not being there for him? "What do you mean? I was there for you every step of the way. I sat behind you at the funeral. I went to the graveside service with you, and I helped organize the reception at your house. How could you even say that I wasn't there for you?"

"You were there, Amy, but you weren't there for *ME*. You did all that stuff to help, that's true, but every time I needed to talk about Andie, you didn't want to listen. You'd brush me off and change the subject."

The red mist swirled and re-appeared, covering a larger portion of the glass in the mirror. It brightened in intensity. Amy stared at the swirling mass, feeling her emotions change. The brighter it grew, the angrier she became. Soon the mist filled the entire room. Amy watched it, mesmerized, her heart pounding, her fists clenched. She squeezed the phone so hard she heard the plastic crack. When she spoke, her voice sounded deeper. "Oh, so that's what Destiny does for you? She listens to you go on and on about your dead sister? What else does she do for you, Jake? Does she kiss you and make it all better?"

"WTH, Amy. Are you drunk or something? I'm not going to talk about this anymore. I'm going to bed." Jake hung up.

She sat on the bed, fuming. What did he see in that little tramp?

She was a nobody. Destiny could never offer Jake the things her family could offer him. Amy knew she was the best girlfriend he could ask for. She grabbed the pillows on the bed and hurled them across the room, murderous thoughts filling her head. She needed some air.

She opened the door and stepped out into the hall. Immediately, the anger dissipated. The expulsion of it left her weak, and she slumped against the wall. She studied the floor, then the cell phone in her hand, and struggled to orient herself. How'd she get out here? What the heck had just happened? She checked the last call on her phone...Jake. Memory poured in. Oh God, she'd acted like some super stupid jealous idiot. Something possessed her to say those things. She'd never have done that in her right mind.

Chills wiggled their way down Amy's spine. Her body trembled so hard she had to hug her knees to stop the quaking. Amy sat for several minutes. Confusion swirled through her brain. None of it made any sense. She crawled into her room, climbed into bed and cried herself to sleep.

CHAPTER NINETEEN

Amy woke several hours later to the sound of someone crying. Deep darkness enshrouded the room, preventing her from seeing the source of the noise. The sound of soft weeping followed by a moan from someone in terrible pain came from inside the room. Her heart pounded, her breath quickening as she strained to listen. The sound repeated, closer this time. She reached for the comforter to cover herself against the chill. Her dad really needed to see about that air conditioner.

Something moaned right next to Amy's ear, and she scrambled upright, scooting against the headboard, grabbing her pillow and hugging it tightly to her chest. She tried to convince herself it was a dream. Pinching her arm, she mumbled, "Wake up. Wake up. Wake up." But she was awake. Whoever belonged to that moan stood right by her bed.

She strained to see, her eyes adjusting to the deep gloom. A watery beam of moonlight streamed in through the window, the result of a wandering cloud. She saw movement. The very air in front of her shimmered and slowly, a shadowy shape formed in the frosty air. Amy's eyes widened from both fear and the perverse desire to observe the transformation occurring right before her. Pale moonlight bathed the shape of a girl, her face and hands badly burned. Skin peeled away from her chin and jaw, and Amy actually saw a strip fall to the floor. But the worst part was her eyes…oh God! Nothing but empty sockets stared at her, the girl's cinder charred hands reaching out to her. Bony fingers clutched at the comforter, and she saw the covers move, inching the blanket down from the top of the bed by about three inches.

Amy screamed, loud and long. The door to her room flung open, and her father flipped on the light switch, flooding the room with bright yellow light. He grabbed her by the shoulders and shook her, trying to end her terrified screaming, but Amy couldn't stop. Her entire body quaked as he rocked her. Her mother rushed through the door seconds later. She scrambled onto the bed and wrapped her arms around her terrified daughter. In an attempt to arrest her attention, Jeff grabbed Amy's chin between his thumb and forefinger and forced her to meet his gaze. "Shut up," he commanded harshly. Amy focused on his sharp features, ceased her screaming and drew in air in giant gulps.

"Jeff, maybe you should go look around the house. I have no idea what scared her, but something could be inside," Sarah said.

Jeff nodded and left the room, his robe flying out behind him. "I'll be right back, baby," he called over his shoulder.

Amy heard him moving through the house, opening and closing windows and doors, but all she cared about was the safety of her mother's arms as Sarah held her, rocking, while they waited for her dad to return. Amy buried her face in her pillow and wondered how she'd ever explain to her parents what she'd seen.

"What happened, Amy?" her mother asked, smoothing the hair from her face.

Amy couldn't speak. Her throat was raw and sore from screaming.

"Amy...talk to me. Was it a nightmare?"

Jeff came back into the room and sat at the foot of the bed. "What's wrong with her?" he asked. "I didn't find anything out of order. All the doors and windows were locked."

"I can't get her to talk to me," Sarah told him. "Whatever or whoever it was terrified her. I think she may have had a horrible nightmare."

Amy shook her head. "No," she croaked, her voice muffled by the pillow over her face.

"What, honey?" her mother asked.

Amy raised her head and faced her parents' worried expressions. "It wasn't a nightmare," she squeaked.

Her father grabbed her hand. His grasp was warm and comforting. "What was it, Amy?"

"She was right there," Amy said, pulling her hand away and pointing to the other side of the bed.

"Who?" Sarah asked.

"I don't know who she was…a young girl. Her face and hands were burned and her eyes…." Amy re-covered her face.

"What about her eyes, Amy?" her father asked.

Amy rocked her head from side to side, burying her face deeper in the pillow. Both parents waited patiently for an answer. Eventually, Sarah gently removed the makeshift shield and lifted Amy's chin. Finding courage in her mother's gaze, Amy said, "Her eyes were gone."

Had Amy not been so petrified, the shock on both her parents' faces would have amused her.

Jeff said, "Amy, I've been through the whole house. There's no one here. It was just a very realistic nightmare. I've had those before, and they can be terrifying."

"It was not a dream, Dad. Her crying was what woke me up. Then I heard this moaning right beside my ear. I sat up and moved to the other side of the bed. When the moon came out, that's when I saw her. She just appeared out of thin air. Then she started reaching for me." Amy's glance dropped to the wrinkled comforter. She pointed. "She actually pulled at the bed covers. Look, you can see where her hand was…oh God." She grabbed the pillow from Sarah and hid her face again.

"Amy," her father said, his hand smoothing the comforter. "You know there is no such thing as ghosts. It was just a bad dream."

Amy glanced up at him, temper rising. "I've been trying to tell Mom that something is wrong with this furniture, and she won't listen. It caused both of us to get hurt, Destiny saw something in that mirror, and I just bet it was that gruesome looking girl. You can just feel the difference in the air when you come into my room. I'm telling you, something is wrong."

"Amy," Sarah said, her tone ringing with disbelief. "I know it seems real to you because the dream is still so fresh in your mind, but that's all it was. Just a dream."

"I'm going to go get you a sedative so you can go back to sleep," Jeff said.

"That's a good idea, honey," Sarah said to her husband as she tucked

Amy back under the covers.

Amy knew she'd never go back to sleep. What if Gruesome Girl came back?

"I did not dream this, Mom. I will never forget her face. How awful to have been burned like that. I know that's what happened to her."

"Amy, settle down. Your dad will be back with that sedative, and you'll be able to go back to sleep. When morning comes, you'll be able to laugh about this."

Shock bolted through Amy's system. Laugh? She would never laugh about what she'd just seen. Never. A terrorizing thought occurred to Amy. If that thing can touch and move the bed covers, could it touch her? Her pulse raced. What if it wanted to hurt her? Thoughts of the red mist popped into Amy's mind. She hadn't even told her parents about that yet. Glancing at her mother's expression, Amy decided now was not the time to bring it up.

It really hurt that her own parents didn't believe her. Why would she lie about seeing a ghost? She wasn't crazy. There were just too many weird things going on to not have something in common, and in Amy's mind, that was the furniture.

Returning to the room, Amy's father offered her a little blue pill and a glass of water. "Here, honey, take this."

Amy swallowed the offering, then scooted down in the bed and yanked the comforter up to her chin. As soon as her parents went back to bed, she planned to sleep downstairs.

Sarah sighed. "Do you want me to stay with you till you fall asleep?"

Amy nodded, figuring that if the thing came back, then her mother would see it too and know she wasn't crazy.

Jeff said, "That's probably a good idea. I'd feel better if you were with her until we get to the bottom of what's causing these dreams."

"It wasn't a dream," Amy said through clenched teeth.

"Okay, Jeff. I'll stay with her."

He started out the door and reached to turn out the light.

"NO!" Amy screamed, causing her mother to jump. "Please leave the light on. Okay?"

"Okay, baby." Her father smiled. "I love you both."

"Love you, Dad," Amy said, cuddling next to her mom.

"We haven't done this in a long time. You were probably four or five years old the last time we slept in the same bed. It's nice."

"I'm telling the truth, Mom. I think it was a ghost."

She rubbed her hand up and down Amy's arm. "Okay, Amy. Just try to get some sleep. Things will seem much brighter in the morning."

Amy closed her eyes and pretended to sleep but inside the anger stirred. She couldn't believe that her parents didn't think she was telling the truth. Something very wrong had just happened in her room, and it scared the crap out of her.

CHAPTER TWENTY

The Monday before the big 4th of July rodeo event dawned hot and sunny. Amy stretched in her new bed and sat up. Her mother was already up and out of her room, and Amy could hear her parents talking in the kitchen, their voices abnormally loud. Amy really didn't pay all that much attention to it. Her parents had argued before. That was nothing new.

If Amy had to guess the reason for the discord, she imagined it had something to do with her father's job and him missing the horse show on Saturday. His frequent absences were a source of strain on her parents' marriage, with her father always off tending to some patient or urgent business at the trauma center. Amy vowed never to marry a doctor.

She looked around her room, remembering the terrifying night before. Her mother was right; in the bright sunshine, the room didn't look nearly as frightening as it had last night. She could almost convince herself it was a dream…almost. Amy knew what she'd seen, though, and that girl was a ghost. No doubt about it. It was not a dream or her imagination. It had really happened, and she had no explanation for it. It still made her angry that her parents didn't believe her. Sure, she'd lied about things in the past, but she was definitely not lying about what she saw last night. It still scared her senseless just to think about it.

Throwing back her comforter, Amy approached the dresser and leaned close to the mirror. She would need serious makeup today to cover those dark circles. She picked up her hairbrush and went to work on her hair. She thought about giving it more blonde highlights for the summer while brushing the night's snarls away. Flipping her hair forward, she brushed the tangles from the base of her neck over her head. Running her fingers through the smooth strands, she tossed her hair back out of her face. Amy checked the mirror and yelped, dropping her hairbrush where it landed with a soft thud on the carpet. Her heart banged against her rib cage, and she stumbled away from the dresser. Directly behind her, a dark shadow figure hovered in the air. It had no face, but clearly, a pair of arms flowed from the dark mass.

The shadow struck, wrapping long, black hands around Amy's neck, closing off her airway. She tried to scream, but the invisible hand squeezed tighter. Amy clawed at her neck, trying to pull the hands away, but only succeeded in digging deep scratches into her skin. Spots developed before her eyes, and she sank to her knees. The sound of her father's voice drifted in from the hallway, and immediately the grip on her throat disappeared. She sucked in great gulps of air as her father found her seconds later.

"Amy, what the hell are you doing on your hands and knees like a dog?" he asked.

Amy couldn't respond, her neck on fire where she'd scratched herself, and her knees wouldn't support her.

"Amy, I said, get up off the floor." Jeff reached down and jerked Amy to her feet by her elbow, and she stumbled into him.

"Dad," she gasped as he shoved her away. "Something was choking me. I couldn't breathe. There was this shadow in my mirror, and it wrapped its hands around my neck. Couldn't you see I was choking?"

"All I saw was you acting like a fool. I've had about enough of this play for attention. It's clear to me you've scratched your own neck. Now get dressed and come downstairs for breakfast. Your mother has cooked enough food to feed an army. I don't know what goes through her head." He stomped off toward his bedroom.

The air reeked of vodka in his wake. When had her father started drinking in the morning? Amy twisted to look at her neck in the mirror. Deep scratches oozed red. Entering the bathroom, she grabbed a cloth, wet it, and dabbed at the wounds. Her mind reeled at what her father had just said to her. Amy couldn't believe he thought her being attacked by some evil entity was a play for attention. Just because no one could see this thing but her, didn't mean it wasn't there. Those were real hands on her neck. What the heck was in that room? This presence differed from the horrifying ghost girl Amy had seen last night. It was darker, more evil. It wanted to harm.

Amy slipped on a pair of jeans and a t-shirt. On her way to the kitchen, she heard her parents arguing again. She snuck down the stairs, hoping her dad would leave for the hospital without seeing her again. No such luck. He marched into the foyer just as Amy hit the bottom step.

"Amy, I don't want any more talk of spirits, ghosts or any such nonsense. Do you understand?" He glowered at her.

Amy's jaw dropped. "Dad, what is wrong with you? You've been in a bad mood all morning."

"Having your mother sleep in your room last night was ridiculous. You're far too old for that kind of behavior." His bloodshot eyes glared.

"Dad, it was your idea."

He raised his hand to hit her, and Amy flinched.

"JEFF!" Sarah stepped into the foyer just in time to see him.

He glared at her too. "Sarah, if this behavior of hers continues, I'm calling Dr. Beaumont. It's obvious she wants to hurt herself. This is not normal for a teenage girl. You better talk to her." He stalked out, slamming the door behind him.

Sarah rushed back to the kitchen. Taking a moment to recover, Amy shook her head. Something wasn't right. She'd never seen her father act that way, and he never drank in the morning. She'd seen him have a glass of wine with dinner or a cocktail with her mom when he got home from the hospital late at night, but she'd never known him to drink in the morning.

Amy followed her mother to the kitchen and saw her standing over the kitchen sink, her shoulders shaking. Hearing her come in, Sarah grabbed a paper towel from the rack and swiped at her eyes. She cleared her throat and said, "Do you want some breakfast? I cooked plenty."

Amy sat down at the table. "I'll take some eggs with bacon and toast if you have it." She paused. "Mom?"

Sarah scuttled around the kitchen, putting together the plate of food. She kept her back turned until she placed the plate on the table. Her eyes were red and puffy, tears staining her cheeks. "Here you go, Amy." The plate clattered on the table. "Those scratches look deep. Did you put some antibiotic ointment on them?"

"Mom, I don't care what Dad said to you. I didn't do this to myself…I mean, I did, but not on purpose. Mom, there was a shadow figure in my room. I saw its reflection in the mirror. It had me by the neck. I didn't know ghosts could harm people, but this thing can. Suddenly it wrapped its hands around my neck, choking me."

"Amy, stop. Don't say any more. Don't you realize how crazy this sounds? Your father is ready to drag you to the hospital to see Dr. Beaumont."

"Why would he want me to see a shrink, Mom? I'm telling you both the truth. You just won't listen to me."

Tears sliding down her face, Sarah pleaded, "Amy, please, just stop this, okay?"

Amy stared. She'd never seen her mother so upset. "Mom, let me ask you something. I've never ever tried to hurt myself, have I?"

Sarah shook her head.

"Okay, so when was the last time Dad started drinking before nine o'clock in the morning? Could it be that he was just a little drunk? And why would you let him say those things about me?"

"Just because your father has one Bloody Mary before he goes to work, Amy, does not mean he's drunk. I wouldn't let him go out of the house if I thought for one minute he'd had too much to drink." She sat down hard in the chair next to Amy and then covered her face with her hands as she started to cry again.

Amy squeezed her mother's shoulder. "Mom, I'm not making this up, but I'll stop talking about it while Dad's around if it will make you feel better. I just want you to know that I'm not lying. There is something in my room, and it has to do with that furniture. I am not trying to harm myself. I promise."

Sarah's sigh expressed her relief. Hurt, Amy turned to look out the kitchen window. She didn't ever want to go back into her bedroom again, and all Amy's mother cared about ensuring her daughter wasn't crazy. Amy sighed and finished breakfast. She couldn't win this battle with her parents and had no clue what she was going to do, but she had to find a solution. Whatever that thing was, it wanted to hurt her and possibly everyone in her family.

She rose and placed her plate in the sink. "Thanks for breakfast, Mom."

Sarah's lips curved. "What are you going to do today?"

"Jake and I are going to work the horses some, and then I guess we'll go to the pool at the country club. It's supposed to be really hot today."

"Why don't you invite Destiny to go with you?"

Amy swung around and faced her mother. Where had that come from? Her mother hadn't mentioned Destiny in weeks. Amy put both hands on her hips and said, "You've got to be kidding."

"What?"

"I can't believe you just asked me that," she said, planting herself in front of her mother. "You want me to invite the one girl that Jake has been spending way too much time with to the pool...with Jake...and me."

"Don't you think you're being way too silly about that? She knows Jake is your boyfriend. I feel really sorry for her. She has no friends, and school will be starting soon."

Raising her eyebrows, Amy said, "You don't know her, Mom. I'm not so sure that she didn't curse that furniture in my room that day in the garage. She's a witch just like her grandmother."

"Amy!"

Sarah's eyes widened, and her face actually turned red, reminding Amy of a cartoon character from Nickelodeon, which almost made her laugh. She didn't regret anything she'd said. In fact, now that she'd said it out loud, she was convinced it was true. Destiny was to blame for everything that was wrong in this house.

"I raised you better than that, Amy. If I hear you've gone around spreading such a nasty rumor, I'll ground you for the entire summer. And there you go with that furniture again. Destiny had nothing to do with it, and you know it. Madame Rose is one of the nicest women I've met in this town, and you'd do well to treat her with respect."

"You believe whatever you want, Mom, but I know what I know."

"Honestly, Amy," Sarah said, throwing her napkin on the table and scraping her chair backward. "You infuriate me. I'm going to call

Destiny and invite her to go to the rodeo with us. I'm sure no one else will ask her. Once you get to know her, I'm sure you'll feel differently."

Oh crap. That was so not going to happen. "Mom, don't do that. I'm sure she will find someone to go with. I'm sure she hates rodeos."

"Have you asked her?" Sarah faced Amy with her hands on her hips.

"No, but she doesn't seem the type that would. Besides, Mom, she's trying her best to steal my boyfriend. Why do you want to put her right in his path? Don't you care about me at all?" Fury flushed Amy's cheeks.

"Enough, Amy. You *will* be friends with Destiny, and you *will* treat her better than you have been, or I'll see to it you have a miserable summer. Do you understand me?"

Amy understood, all right. She knew at that moment her mother was crazy, but when she got that hard look in her eye and her lips became one thin line, she knew not to push her luck. "Yes, ma'am."

Sarah dropped her head in a quick nod and then glanced at the clock on the wall. "You better get ready if Jake is coming over soon." She started to load the dishwasher.

Amy dashed for the stairs. A miserable night had led to a miserable day. She wanted to break something. Reaching her room, she hunted for the hairbrush, knowing she'd left it on the floor after the attack, but she couldn't locate it now. She searched the bathroom; perhaps she'd moved it without thinking. The light in the bathroom popped on just as her iPod sang out from its docking station, both seemingly on their own. Amy gasped, jumping back from the counter. Then she heard the giggle.

CHAPTER TWENTY-ONE

Destiny nearly jumped out of her skin when the phone rang. That didn't happen very often, and it reminded her to ask her grandmother for a cell phone. If she had one, she could at least text some of her old friends. Scuttling across the couch, she answered on the second ring.

"Hello?"

"Destiny?"

"Yes?"

"This is Sarah Morgan, Amy's mom. I'm calling to invite you to go to the rodeo with us this Saturday. It's a big day. They close off downtown and fill the streets with vendors where you can get everything from Krispy Kreme Doughnut Burgers to funnel cake. As you probably already know, Jake will be riding in some of the events, and Amy will be in the horse show with him. We'd love it if you would spend the day with us."

Stunned into silence, Destiny stared at the phone. No Shade or spirit from the Great Beyond could have surprised her more. A vision of Amy's face, red with fury, popped into her mind.

"Destiny?" Sarah Morgan's voice inquired.

"Um…I'm here. I'm sorry, I just wasn't expecting this. I really do appreciate the invitation, but I'll probably have to work at the bookstore helping my grandmother. But thank you anyway." She never thought she'd be grateful for The Mystic Cat, but working there during the rodeo seemed far more appealing than spending the day with Amy and her family.

"Oh, well, I'm sure if I talk to Rose, she'll let you have the day off. She usually closes half the day anyway. Is she there? I'll ask her now."

Her eyebrows rose at Sarah's persistence. "No, Mrs. Morgan, Grams isn't here. She went to the store," she said as she shifted from one foot to the other, trying to decide if she should tell Amy's mom the truth.

"You can have her call me when she gets home." She sounded so authoritative.

"Um...." Better now than later, Destiny thought as she pressed on. "Mrs. Morgan, are you sure Amy would like to do this? I mean, no offense, but she and I aren't really on the best of terms. I'm sure she'd rather I not come to the rodeo with you. If Grams closes the store early, then I can come with her. I really do appreciate the offer, but—"

Sarah interrupted, "Nonsense. Amy is thrilled about it. I'll not take no for an answer. If your grandmother has a concern, have her call me about it. Otherwise, you just march your little self right up here at eight o'clock on Saturday. Wear some really comfy clothes and shoes. It'll be fun. I may need some company if Jeff gets called to the hospital while Amy is riding in the horse show. Call me if your grandmother needs to talk. Bye, Destiny." She hung up.

Holy crap. She stood there staring at the phone. Mrs. Morgan was a steamroller. Mrs. Morgan had to be lying. Amy had to know. But...she did want to go and see Jake ride. Oh boy, did she want to see Jake ride.

She shook her head. This had to be the most insane thing she'd ever contemplated. No, she decided. She wouldn't go. She'd just call Mrs. Morgan back and tell her she was sick or something. Rose opened the door and stumbled her way through with two bags of groceries just as Destiny picked up the phone with the intent of improvising some excuse. The excuse could wait, she decided, as she hung up the phone to help relieve her grandmother of her burden.

"Is that it?" she asked.

"No, there are two more out in the car," Rose said, puffing as she put her purse on the counter.

"I'll get them," Destiny said, bouncing out the door and down the steps.

"Who was on the phone?" Rose asked when she came back in.

Destiny unloaded the soup and placed it in the cabinet. "Mrs.

Morgan. She invited me to spend Saturday at the rodeo with them, but I told her I had to work."

Rose put down the bag of flour and stared. "I'm not making you work on Saturday for that very reason. Why did you lie to her?"

Destiny sighed, heat creeping into her cheeks. "Because, Grams, you have no clue what a really bad idea that is. Amy hates my guts. She's convinced I'm trying to steal Jake away from her, and she'll be ticked if I'm stuck with her all day. Not a very comfortable spot for me."

Rose turned, pausing a moment before she spoke again. "I'm sure Sarah wouldn't have asked if they didn't want you to join them. I think it's a good idea. Go with them for the morning, and then once I close the store, I'll come find you. Then if things aren't going well, I can rescue you."

Destiny shook her head. "Nah, it's so not a good idea. I'm going to call her Friday night and tell her I'm sick."

Rose smacked her hand down on the counter. "You're not going to lie, Destiny. It's a nice offer, and you'll accept. You've got to face this thing with Amy sooner or later. You can't hide from her. It's best to clear the air now before school starts. It would give you a good chance to meet people in town and maybe make a few more friends. Does Sarah need me to call her?"

She started to protest but stopped. "Only if you have a concern," she mumbled.

"Well, it's settled then."

"I just hope you have insurance." Destiny leaned against the counter, her arms crossed. Her grandmother was just as stubborn as Mrs. Morgan.

"Why?"

"'Cause Amy's going to pulverize me if I so much as peep at Jake. Now that Jake wants to talk about Andie, he's been coming around more often, and Amy will have a fit if she catches him."

Rose dropped the can opener from where she opened the coffee can. "Whoa, wait a minute. Did you just say that you've been having conversations with Jake about Andie? Does that mean you told Jake what you can do?"

Destiny sat down at the kitchen table, picked up the blue recyclable grocery bags and folded them. "Yes, I told him." She enlightened Rose about the day Jake came in for a drink, and Andie showed up. "Andie was actually the one who encouraged me to tell Jake. She said I could trust him."

Rose stopped putting coffee in the canister and sat down at the table. "And how did that work out for you?"

"It was actually scary. I thought he'd think I was a freak, but he didn't. And you know, Grams, it turned out pretty cool." Propping her chin on her hands, Destiny continued, "Jake was so excited that he could communicate with her. Andie even came up to him and put her hand on his head." Her voice rose in pitch. "I think he even felt it. It really made me feel good to know I'd helped him."

Rose's lips curved. "Now maybe you can understand why I do what I do, what our gift allows us to accomplish for others. It's sort of a healing power, really."

"I think I understand what you mean now," Destiny said, leaning forward. "I've been happy to help Jake. He comes to me a lot, and sometimes Andie is there, and sometimes I have to call her."

Rose sat up straighter at the table, her eyes filled with concern. "Destiny, I don't want you channeling when I'm not with you. I haven't taught you how to shield yourself from the Great Beyond yet. It can be very dangerous when you have no protection. Promise me you won't try to contact Andie again unless I'm with you."

Destiny's eyebrows shot up at her grandmother's firm tone. "I'm sorry, I didn't know I was doing anything wrong."

Rose reached out and took her hand and squeezed it. "You're just following your instinct, but you need some training first. I need to show you a few techniques that will help you protect yourself. Not everything in the Great Beyond is good, Destiny. I need to teach you to build a shield to block out the more negative energies you may summon when you're channeling."

"Ugh, sounds creepy."

"Not if you know what you're doing and build the strength of your protection. Maybe we can practice after dinner. Right now, I'm hungry." She patted Destiny's hand and stood.

"Hey, Grams,"

"Hmm?"

"When we practice tonight, do you think we could try to contact Mom, Dad and Elijah?" She swallowed hard. She'd wanted to ask about them but didn't really know how. Her heart pounded every time she thought about it for fear her nightmares would be true. Fear that her mother would hate her for not saving the baby.

Rose's eyes softened. "We can try, but I don't want you to get your hopes up. Many times when people die suddenly, they go straight into the light. Madea tells me that it's so beautiful there that most forget about who they left behind for quite some time." Rose swiped at the tear leaking from Destiny's eye. "That doesn't mean they don't find their way back. It just takes time, that's all."

She didn't want to ask, but Destiny squared her shoulders and said, "What if they didn't go into the light?"

"Then we will find them and help them," Rose said with resolve. That settled Destiny.

"Okay. I don't want them to be lost."

"I know, honey. I know."

The two ate spaghetti noodles with sauce from a jar and a salad. It wasn't great, but satisfying. They talked about the rodeo, and Rose explained what a boost it was for the town every year. She said some of her best clients traveled to her every single year when the rodeo came to town. As they ate, they talked about some changes to make to the bookstore, and Destiny even contributed a few suggestions that Rose admired. Destiny reveled in the praise her grandmother gave her. Maybe she could fit in after all.

Destiny finished the dishes and joined Rose in the living room, where she'd positioned candles and crystals all around the big square coffee table. She'd turned off the lamps, and the room glowed while shadows danced from the flicker of the candle flames. Destiny raised an eyebrow.

"Just a little something I picked up from one of my books in the shop," Grams said. "Your true protection needs to come from within, but it doesn't hurt to cast a circle now and again."

She motioned for Destiny to step up to the coffee table and then mumbled some chant. When finished, Rose gestured at the chair. "You have been blessed—" Destiny rolled her eyes, and Rose sighed. "Yes, Destiny, blessed...blessed with the ability to channel more psychic energy than the average person. Your brain works differently because of the Shade Sight." She reached for the girl's hand.

"What I will try to teach you tonight is how to use that energy to surround yourself with a white light of protection. This will shield you from anything negative that you happen to encounter. You may be lucky and never run into anything like that, but I doubt it. Evil will find us. They are drawn to our power."

Little tingles started at the base of Destiny's neck and worked their way down her spine. Having a gift was all well and good, but being an evil magnet was not part of the plan. "Grams, I'm not so sure about this."

"Don't worry," Rose said, keeping eye contact and grasping her other hand. "I'm with you, and although I've never shared this with you, I'm actually quite a powerful medium. I control a great deal of energy and have had years of practice on how to use it. My shield is nearly impenetrable, and I can protect us, but it is very important that you learn to protect yourself. Are you ready?"

Destiny wanted to find her parents, but all this woo-woo talk set her teeth on edge. She took a deep breath, met Rose's pale blue eyes, squeezed her hands and said, "Okay, let's do this."

Rose nodded. "Relax and close your eyes." Destiny heard her take a deep breath and followed suit. She closed her eyes, forced her facial muscles to relax and kept breathing until her body loosened.

"Good," Rose said. "Now, focus on the white space right in front of your eyes. Imagine you're staring at a whiteboard like they have at school, but the white is all you can see. Tune out all the other things around you. Can you see it?"

"Yes," Destiny said softly. It wasn't very bright, but a white glow illuminated her inner vision.

"Okay, now picture that warmth blanketing you. Wrap yourself in it, Destiny. Keep concentrating...imagine yourself bathing in it... there... that's good."

She had no clue how her grandmother could see what she saw, but warmth began to spread over her body, and the light grew brighter behind her eyelids.

"I can see your shield forming," Rose said. "Keep concentrating. What do you feel?"

Destiny swallowed. "A little light-headed, and I'm starting to get a headache. I'm warm all over, like when I lay out in the sun."

"Good, you've got the beginning of a good shield. Now I'm going to join mine with yours so we can take a peek and see what we can see in the Great Beyond. Can you see a difference?"

"Wow, the light just got a lot brighter, and now it's slightly orange."

"Good," Rose said. "Now, I'm going to open a doorway. Open your mind and think about your parents and Elijah. Think of a happy memory and reach out with your mind. Similar to what you do with Andie, but maintain that focus on the white light. Don't drop your shield."

That was easier said than done, and Destiny had no clue if she'd done it right or not. In her mind, she called out to her parents and told them to come forward so she could see them.

"That's good, Destiny. Keep calling for them."

The white light shimmered. Gray shadows entered in and then floated out again, but her parents never materialized. She called to them again. "Teresa, Frank and Elijah Dove, please come forward so I can see you and know that you're alright."

More shimmering, then nothing. Destiny sighed.

"Don't get discouraged, honey," Rose said. "This takes a lot of practice, and your spiritual voice will grow stronger with time. Let me try…Teresa, Frank, Elijah, this is Grams. If you can hear me calling for you, come forward. Let us see you."

The light shifted again, and a darker shadow loomed just on the edge of Destiny's field of vision. The pounding of her headache grew worse. Something pushed against the shield, a pressure resembling a strong wind against a closed door.

"Um…Grams?"

"I see it, Destiny. Crank up the power to your shield. Imagine it covering you."

Not sure how to do that, she imagined pushing back against the door. Without warning, the head of the black shadow burst through the white light. The eyes were yellow with black slits for pupils running vertically in the iris. Heavy horns protruded from a red scaly face with sharp, wicked teeth. Destiny screamed, scooting back away from the table. Rose reached out and grabbed her arm hard. Destiny winced. Her grandmother had quite a grip.

"Hold your shield, Destiny. Push against it. Now!"

Terrified, she tried to do what her grandmother suggested. She squeezed her already closed eyelids more tightly shut and thought hard about the white light. Her heart pounded, and she breathed in short quick pants. "It's a blanket. It's a blanket. It's a blanket," she muttered.

The light blazed, and Rose shouted, "I don't know who you are, but you're not welcome here. We have no quarrel with you and have caused you no harm. Leave this place and return from where you came."

A blast of energy hit the monster in the face, and he roared. Destiny slapped her hands over her ears, uncertain if the sound had only been in her head or in the room.

"Hold your shield, Destiny," Rose commanded.

Destiny dropped her hands to the table and concentrated. The pressure and the pain in her head eased. The light of the shield stayed white but softened to a glow.

"Is he gone?" she queried.

"I think so. Let me say the closing ritual prayer before you let down your guard."

Rose muttered some more words in a language Destiny didn't understand. The light faded and winked out. "You can open your eyes now, Destiny."

Destiny fell backward on the floor, too exhausted to move. At that moment, she didn't care if she never talked to another Shade again. "Holy biscuits, what was that?"

"That was the very reason I don't want you channeling alone."

"Well, you've convinced me." Destiny held a hand to her chest, where her heart still battered her rib cage. "That was scarier than Mom's head in the dream."

"It was very evil, I agree. Not sure what he's after here. Our energy must have attracted his attention."

A thought sent chills straight down Destiny's spine. "What if he comes back when I'm asleep or something?"

"I'll teach you a protection prayer and a ritual that you'll say every night before you go to sleep. It'll keep you safe." Rose got slowly to her knees and blew out the candles.

"You know, it seemed familiar," Destiny said, helping her gather the crystals.

"What do you mean?"

"Like I've felt this presence before. But that's not possible, is it?" she asked. Then a sudden thought pierced her foggy brain. "Amy's! That was the shadow I saw in Amy's mirror."

Rose's brows furrowed. "Are you sure?"

She nodded. "I could feel him pushing against my head. You know how a door bows in from a strong wind? That's how it felt, and it hurt too."

Rose got to her feet and took Destiny's hand, drawing her body up into a hug. "You need to practice your shield as often as you can, honey. Whoever that entity was, he wanted possession of you." Destiny opened her mouth, but Rose held up her hand. "I'm not sure why, but you must promise me no more channeling alone. If Jake wants to talk to Andie, you let her come to you. Don't try to summon her. Do I have your promise on that?"

Destiny hugged her grandmother tight. "I promise."

"I'm worried for Amy. If you saw it at her house, then the Morgans are vulnerable."

"Is there anything you can do?" Destiny sure didn't want that thing coming back again.

"I'm not sure. I'll work on it. Stay away from up there in the meantime, though. He now knows what you're capable of, and if he gets the chance, he'll target you again."

Destiny saw a potential escape. "I guess I shouldn't go to the rodeo with them then," she said, hopeful.

"No, that will be fine. In fact, it might be good for you to observe them away from the house. Let me know if you see anything strange."

Crap. "Are you sure?" She tried one more time.

Rose gave her granddaughter an agitated glance. "You're going to that rodeo on Saturday."

Destiny sighed. "Okay. Okay."

Rose reached for her hand. "I'm sorry we couldn't contact your parents."

"That's okay. This was enough drama for one session. I think I'm going to bed."

Rose taught Destiny the prayers she'd need to say and made her promise she'd say them faithfully. Destiny promised. She sure didn't want a return visit from that…that demon.

CHAPTER TWENTY-TWO

Destiny parked her butt on the edge of the bed, too wired to go to sleep. Seeing that demon, or whatever it was, had shaken her to the core. She shivered, thinking of the face that poked its way through the white curtain of her shield. The eyes held hatred and menace, and they'd glared straight at her. There was a message there. She'd seen the entity, for lack of a better word, twice now, once in Amy's mirror and next through her own shield. He wanted something. Destiny wondered what this thing was doing at Amy's house. Had she and her parents experienced the threat? Was the demon going after them too?

Hi, Destiny. What's going on?

A yelp escaped her throat. Pulse racing, she turned and saw Andie standing just inside the closed bedroom door.

"I wish you'd give a girl some warning before popping in," she said, her hand pressed against her chest. At least this time, Andie appeared a little better. She must have mastered the image projection thing because her head managed to stay anchored to her neck, and her face appeared more normal. She still couldn't talk, so Andie spoke to Destiny's mind.

What's wrong with you? You don't look so hot.

"I don't feel so hot either. Grams and I were channeling in the living room, trying to find my parents, and we had an unexpected visitor."

Tall shadow guy with a really ugly goat-looking head?

"Yes! Have you seen him?"

That's why I'm here. This guy is bad news to the max. Andie drifted over to the bed and sat down. Destiny observed a slight indent in the covers.

"Who is he? This is the second time I think I've seen him. Once at Amy's and the other time here."

I don't know who he is, but he is not from the Great Beyond, and his intentions are far from good. He is very strong. I know I've not had time to build any energetic strength over here yet, but in his presence, you think he's going to suck out your soul. The pressure is unbearable. I've started hiding when I sense him coming. Andie's ghostly eyes held terror and concern. *I want you to tell Jake something for me.*

"What?"

There are some really bad things happening at Amy's house. They have to do with this...this...aw crap, I don't even know what to call it. It's not a spirit or Shade. I've learned to recognize those right away. There can be some Shades with mean intent, but this thing is worse than all of that. I just know it.

"I think it's a demon," Destiny said, running a hand through her hair. The thick black tresses weighed heavily on her already throbbing head.

I need you to tell Jake to stay away from there. I'm afraid whatever that thing is will hurt him. It doesn't care who it possesses as long as it gets its way.

Destiny gawked at Andie's ghostly form. Did she have any idea what she asked? "Andie, I can't do that. Amy already thinks I'm trying to steal Jake away from her. There's no way I'm going to tell him to stay away from her house."

Destiny, I have no way of telling him myself. You're my only link. If you don't tell him, no one will, and I think he's really in danger. She touched Destiny's arm, and goose pimples covered her flesh up to her shoulder.

"Well, if he's in danger, isn't Amy in danger too?"

Yes, but I can't do anything about that. They invited this thing into their home. I can't control that, but I can control Jake if you will tell him that message for me. Her ghostly eyes resembled Jake's. The beseeching glance worked on Destiny's conscience. Then she pulled out the big guns.

Personally, I don't like the fact that he's seeing Amy at all. I think she's a selfish, spoiled brat. I'd rather he see someone with your personality.

Oh boy. Destiny shifted on the bed and squirmed under her gaze. She didn't like Amy either and would've jumped at the chance to have Jake as a boyfriend, but she had too much honor.

You like him, don't you? Andie's gaze held Destiny's. A grin broke out across her still-tattered face. Destiny hoped she wouldn't do that often.

Relieved that Andie couldn't communicate with Jake, Destiny knew her secret was safe. "Listen, Andie, I want to help you, really I do. But it's just not my place to come between Jake and Amy."

Don't be such a wimp. You're a lot closer to his type than Amy. I've seen his face when he's with you. It wouldn't take much for him to fall for you. Just a little nudge.

Destiny's heart skipped a beat. She so wished that was true, but she didn't need the hassle at school. Besides, she didn't want to be anybody's sloppy seconds, and Destiny knew she couldn't hold a candle to Amy in either beauty or background. Amy may not be the ideal match for Jake, but she could offer him a lot more than Destiny could.

That's bull crap, and you know it. Andie fisted her hands and smacked them to her hips.

"Shut up, Andie. And get out of my head." Destiny stood up and stepped to the window, letting the air conditioner blow on her hot, sweaty body.

Not until you promise to tell Jake to stay away from Amy. Seriously, Destiny, if you care for him at all, you'll do this. If it weren't important, I wouldn't ask. I know you don't know me well, but I'm not the type to beg for anything. Please say you'll talk to him. I'll haunt you relentlessly until you do.

Positive Andie was true to her word. Destiny agreed, but not before she set conditions of her own. "Okay, Andie. I'll do it, but you have to do something for me in return." She turned from the window and faced the Shade.

This doesn't sound good. Andie had moved to stand right behind Destiny, and she almost walked right through her. Weird.

"I want you to try and find my parents," Destiny said. "You have access to the Great Beyond and people who come in and out. You can also travel among the Shades and see who's crossed over and who hasn't. I need to know that my parents and my baby brother are safe. If they aren't, then I want you to lead them to me and Grams. We can help them cross over. If you do that for me, I'll talk to Jake."

Andie remained silent for a moment. Destiny tapped her palm against the side of her head. "I didn't hear you."

Okay, I'll try. You know I'm new to this spirit world stuff. I'm not sure how to even begin looking, but I'll figure something out. What are their names?

Destiny told her and the hair on her arms raised. Excitement flooded her heart. She might actually get to see her parents again and tell them how sorry she was about not saving Elijah.

Listen, I've gotta go. This apparition stuff is a lot harder than it looks. I'll keep an eye out for your family, but you call me as soon as you talk to Jake.

"Uh…I can't do that anymore without Grams. Not until my shield gets strong enough. I don't want that demon to get a shot at my mind. You come to me when you can."

You're probably right about that. I'll be in touch. Oh wait, by the way, do you know a Shade named Patch?

"Yeah, I've talked to him. Why?"

He's cool, Destiny. You can trust him. Andie stood and went back to her place by the door.

"Good to know." Her lips curved.

He's watching over things at the farm. If he visits you, listen to him. Okay?

Destiny nodded as Andie faded away. She twisted back to the window and jerked the curtain aside. She stared at Amy's house, goose bumps forming on her arms.

CHAPTER TWENTY-THREE

"Where is that stupid iPod?" Amy rummaged through her closet, tossing clothes over her shoulder.

Jessica, Amy's best friend, sat on the bed, leafing through the latest Glamour magazine. Her voice muffled by the closet walls, Amy heard her say, "Maybe you left it in the pool bag or your purse. You had it yesterday when we were at the pool."

"I know," Amy shouted. "I had it on my nightstand last night too, and it's not there now." She stomped out of the closet, kicking clothes out of her way.

"Is it under the bed? You could have knocked it off the nightstand during the night and then kicked it when you got up this morning." Obviously not concerned, Jessica continued to leaf through the magazine.

"No, I already checked there." Amy faced her friend, smacking her hands on the top of her thighs. "Would it kill you to put that mag down and help me look for it?"

Jessica glanced up, eyebrows raised. "My, my, aren't we cranky."

"Shut up," Amy said. "I'm so tired of stuff disappearing from my room."

"What are you talking about? Maybe you have gremlins." She laughed.

Amy knew then that she couldn't tell her all the weird things that were going on. Jessica would think she'd lost her mind, and she wouldn't be alone. Amy had her own doubts. "Very funny. I'm really getting steamed."

Jessica got up and started picking up the clothes and checking the pockets. "Okay, calm down. I'm helping. Why are you so wound up all the time lately?"

Amy didn't respond right away but continued opening and closing dresser drawers with a slam. She stomped into the bathroom, poked her head in, returned, and searched under the bed one more time—still no iPod. "I know I had it this morning."

Jessica moved a t-shirt off a chair. "There it is," she said.

Amy spun around. "Where?"

"Right here on the chair." She handed Amy the device. "I knew we'd find it."

Amy glared at her. "Thanks," she said, snatching it from her hand.

Shrugging, Jessica sat back down on the bed. "Are you and Jake going to the dance after the rodeo on Saturday?"

"Of course. Who are you going with?" Amy put the iPod in her pocket and joined her best friend on the bed. She apprised the mess of clothes on the floor and decided it could wait until tomorrow.

"I've been asked by two guys, but I'm not sure which one I want to go with."

"Well, don't keep me in suspense. Tell me." Amy clapped her hands on Jessica's shoulders and shook her.

"One is Steve. And the other was...."

Amy waited, and Jessica remained silent, smirking. "Jessica, for God's sake. Who?"

She lowered her head and peered at Amy through her lashes. "Andrew."

Slapping the bed with both hands, Amy squealed, "What? When were you going to tell me? That's big news! You've wanted to go out with him all year."

Jessica's grin widened. "I know, right? I've been hoping and praying he'd ask me out, and I thought he didn't even know I existed. My mom and I were in Best Buy the other day, and I saw him." Jessica shivered and leaned toward Amy. "He came right up to me. We talked about music for a minute, and then he just came right out and asked if I was going to the dance with anyone."

"Oh my God," Amy breathed. "He just came right out and asked?

What did you say?"

Jessica cocked her head to one side, a familiar gesture to express exasperation, and put one hand on her hip. "Duh…what do you think I said, you dope?" She hit Amy on the arm. "I said yes."

Amy squealed again, hugged her friend, and eased back, searching her eyes. "What about Steve? What are you going to tell him?"

"I don't know. What do you think I should tell him?"

"Tell him Andrew asked you first." Amy dragged the magazine over and turned a page.

"That might be a problem. See…Steve asked me first, and I told him I wasn't going with anyone. I didn't really say yes to him, but I didn't say no either. Now what?" Jessica jerked the magazine away from Amy and closed it. "I don't want to hurt Steve's feelings."

Sighing, Amy said, "Just do what I do. Tell him you forgot or you didn't think he was serious. Boys get along better when you let them think you're stupid. Then you get what you want."

Jessica gaped at Amy, and then her lips twitched. "You know, that just might work. Steve's polite enough that he wouldn't say anything anyway. It's not like we're going out. You're a genius, Amy." She lay back against the headboard. "You're so lucky that you have Jake and don't have to worry about all this stuff."

Amy wasn't so sure her friend was right about that and didn't respond right away.

Jessica, drawing her brows together, jumped on her hesitation like a dog on a squirrel. "What's wrong, Ames? Are you and Jake fighting again?"

"No," she said, moving to lean against the headboard with Jessica. "We aren't fighting. It's just that he spends a lot of time at the Mystic Cat with Destiny. I've asked him not to, but he gets mad and says I can't pick his friends." Amy sighed. "I've tried to explain to him how weird everyone thinks she is, but he's not listening."

"Wow. Really?"

"I know, right? Ever since Andie died, he just seems so distracted. He almost got kicked by Goliath today because he wasn't paying attention." She put her hand on Jessica's leg. Her gut clenched. "I'm afraid he likes her."

Jessica made a rude noise. "Amy, that's ridiculous. Why would he go for a weirdo like her when he's got you? You're just creating problems where there aren't any."

The tension around Amy's heart eased a little. "That's what Jake says. He gets really mad, though, if I say anything bad about Destiny. He's always so quick to defend her."

"You're jealousy's just running away with you. You need to watch that. The more trapped he feels, the more likely you are to lose him. Just ease up a bit. It'll be fine."

Amy knew she was whining but didn't care. "He's mine, Jess. I can't let her think for one minute that she can have him. Jake's the best thing that's ever happened to me."

Jess hugged her friend. "I know, Amy, but just don't push too hard, okay?"

Amy opened her mouth to say something else when the door flew open and banged against the wall. Her father rushed in, red-faced and furious.

"Amy! I thought I told you to get down into the kitchen and help your mother."

Amy gaped at him, shocked. Her father had never been so angry, and never had he barged into her room when she had company. How rude. "Um…Dad, I was going to help Mom when Jessica left." She indicated her presence with a wave of a hand.

"Hi, Dr. Morgan," Jessica said, tension creeping into her voice.

"Tell your friend to go home. She's been here all day, according to your mother. Get downstairs." He left the room, slamming the door behind him.

"Well, hello to you too," Jessica said to the closed door. "What is up with him? He's never treated me like that."

Mortified, Amy grabbed Jessica's hand. "I'm so sorry. He's been acting really weird lately. He went off on me the other day for no reason. I'm not sure what's going on."

"I guess I better go," Jessica said, sliding off the bed and placing her feet into flip-flops.

"Yeah, I guess. I'm really sorry." Amy followed Jessica out of the room and down the stairs.

"No biggie. I'll text you later."

"Okay," Amy said and closed the door behind her. Her father was coming down the stairs, and Amy turned to face him. "How could you be so rude to Jessica, Dad? You've never talked to her that way before."

Amy sucked in a breath. Her dad's eyes were so dark she could see her reflection. How weird. He frowned, drew his eyebrows down and glared at her. In spite of the heat of his gaze, Amy shivered.

"You spend entirely too much time with that tramp. She's not a good influence on you."

Amy's jaw dropped. For a moment, she was struck dumb. In the few seconds it took for her to recover, Jeff had reached the bottom of the stairs. "What?" Not an earth-shattering argument, but all she could manage due to the shock radiating through her brain.

"You heard me," he brushed past her, bumping her shoulder none too lightly. "I don't want you spending any more time with that girl."

"But Dad, she's my best friend. You never had a problem with her before. What is wrong with you? You're acting uber strange."

Jeff whirled on his heel and stomped back to his daughter. He shook his finger in her face. "You watch your mouth, young lady. You've had it entirely too easy around here. I think it's high time you started pulling your own weight. If you want to ride in that horse show on Saturday, you'll need to earn the privilege." He grabbed Amy's arm and steered her toward the kitchen. "After you help your mother, head down to the stable and see what Thomas needs help with. Mucking a few stalls would be good for you to learn some responsibility. No more riding and just hopping off the horse, either. You put your animal away and groom it properly."

Amy's blood boiled. Never in her life had she been so humiliated. First in front of her friend, and now her father assumed she never did anything to help around the house or with the horses. There were plenty of times she'd groomed her own horse. Well...sort of. "Then what will you pay the groomsmen for if I do all their work?" she snapped.

Jeff reared back his arm and slapped Amy across the mouth. She staggered back several steps and caught herself against the door jamb before landing on her butt. Her father had never struck her before. Stunned, she gaped at him, unable to move a muscle.

"Amy, go to your room," Sarah said, entering from the dining room.

Amy unfroze, pivoted and dashed up the stairs. She slammed her door but then decided she wanted to hear what her parents said, so she eased the door open a crack.

"Jeff, what the hell is the matter with you?" Sarah demanded.

Amy couldn't see them, but her mother's sudden scream froze her blood.

"Jeff! Stop!"

Amy heard the shuffling of feet in the foyer, and all was silent for a few seconds. Having no clue what had just occurred, Amy crept out of her room and knelt at the top of the stairs. She still couldn't see them, so she scooted two steps down. Her mother faced her father with both hands on her hips. She glared at him, her face beet-red. Amy's dad just stood there blinking, like he'd just woken up from a deep sleep. Amy rubbed her sore cheek. Not a hard slap, it stung her pride more than her skin.

"Why are you yelling at me, Sarah?" Jeff asked, his eyes rapidly blinking again.

"Oh, you're not going there," she said, an expression of disbelief on her face.

"What are you talking about?"

"You just slapped your daughter in the face, and you don't know what I'm talking about?" Sarah poked him in the chest with each word.

Jeff's brows drew down, and he frowned. "I would never slap Amy. You know that."

Amy saw the anger drain from her mother's face. Her shoulders sagged, and she cocked her head. "You don't remember, do you?"

"I guess not. I've got a terrible headache."

"Jeff, tell me what you do remember about the last few days. What's the last thing you remember doing?"

He sat on the bottom step, and her mother sat down beside him, putting her arm around his slumped shoulders. Amy relaxed. She had no clue what happened when her mom screamed, but maybe the worst was over. The sound must have jarred her dad out of some kind of trance.

"I remember leaving here to go to the hospital the day of the surgeon's meeting. After that, it gets really blurry."

Sarah gasped. "Jeff, that meeting was three days ago. You've blacked out for three days?"

"What day is this?" he asked, alarmed.

"Thursday. The rodeo is Saturday." Sarah rubbed his back. Amy couldn't believe her father had lost three days, but thinking back, she had to admit he'd been acting really strange since the day he left for that meeting. What was up with that? Amy leaned forward to hear what her mom was saying.

"I came into the foyer a few minutes ago, and you had just smacked Amy in the mouth. You two were arguing about something, and I came in just in time. I've never seen you so angry over nothing at all. You just haven't been yourself the last few days, and now you tell me you don't even remember. Jeff, what's going on?" Amy saw her mother rest her head on her dad's shoulder.

"I don't know. I'm just shocked. I can't believe I would actually hit Amy." Jeff propped his head on top of Sarah's. It seemed so sweet, but Amy didn't totally buy his *I don't remember* gag. He seemed pretty lucid when his hand had connected with her cheek.

"You've been under so much stress at the hospital. Maybe you should have a checkup. It's been a while," Sarah said.

"I think I will. This is just so weird. What else have I done that I don't remember?" Jeff shivered. "The prospect is terrifying. I better go say something to Amy." He hugged his wife and turned to mount the stairs.

Amy scrambled up and scuttled back into her room. She'd just closed the door and leapt on the bed when her dad knocked.

"Go away," she said.

"Amy, honey, can I come in? I want to talk to you."

He sounded sincere, but Amy didn't totally trust him. "It's open."

He pushed the door open and stepped in. "Hey, kiddo. I'm really sorry about what happened. I don't know what came over me." He approached the bed and sat.

Sitting with her back against the headboard, knees up against her chest, she shot him a doubtful gaze.

He reached out with both arms. Amy hesitated. "Amy, really, I'm sorry. Forgive me?" His eyes were sad, and his mouth drew down at the corners.

"Why did you hit me? What is going on with you lately?"

Jeff dropped his arms and sighed. "I was just telling your mother, I've lost a few days, and I don't remember what happened. I have no memory of smacking you, and I couldn't tell you why I did it."

"Gee, that's a little scary, don't you think?" She only half believed him, suspecting he just wanted to make up to get out of hot water with her mother.

He dropped his head to stare at the floor, his hands limp in his lap. He drew in a deep breath and sighed. "I know you have no reason to believe that, and truthfully, I don't blame you. All I can say is I'm sorry. I shouldn't have slapped you."

She glanced at the mirror, mulling over his words. Her reflection shocked her…cherry-red scratches on her neck, puffy eyes and lips, and a pink tint to her cheek, where her dad had smacked her. As she stared at her face in the mirror, a light grey mist swirled in the top corner of the mirror. She squinted, unsure of what she saw. "Um…Dad. What is that?"

He raised his head. "What is what?"

She pointed. "That."

His gaze followed Amy's finger, and he eyed the mirror. He rose and stepped to it. "I don't know." He reached out a hand.

"Don't touch it!"

Jeff jerked his hand away. Then his reflection frowned at Amy in the mirror. He leaned closer to peer at the mist, but it disappeared. Poof. One minute it was there, the next clear glass.

"Well?" Amy demanded.

He rubbed a hand on his chin. "I don't know what that was. Is it smoke? I was afraid something might be burning from the wall socket." He moved the dresser away from the wall and leaned behind the mirror. His muffled voice said, "I don't see anything."

"I've been telling you and Mom that weird things are going on around here, and you don't believe me. I think it has something to do with the way you've been acting lately and the fact that you don't remember anything for the last few days."

Jeff moved the dresser back to the wall and faced Amy. His

expression showed exasperation for a few seconds, and then he just appeared confused. He sat on the bed again. "Amy, I don't know what caused my lapse of memory, but I intend to find out. And I'm sure there is no supernatural reason for it. I'm very sorry I hurt you. Are you all right?"

Amy let him lift her chin with his hand and study her face. "I'm fine."

"Okay. I don't think it will bruise, and those scratches appear to be healing fine." Jeff opened his arms and raised one eyebrow. His lips twitched at the corners. "Forgive me?"

Amy never could stay mad at her father for very long. She crawled into his arms and hugged him. "I love you, Dad."

"I love you too, Amy."

A blast of cold air rushed through the room, rattling the blinds at the window. Amy and her father sprung apart, and he gaped at her. "What was that? Is your window open?"

She just raised her eyebrows. "I'm just sayin'…."

CHAPTER TWENTY-FOUR

After dinner, Amy and her parents watched a movie on TV. The day had been chock-full of emotion, and once the movie ended, they all headed up to bed. Amy told her parents good night and entered her room. Once she heard their door shut, she stepped back out into the hall and turned on the light. No total darkness for her. No way. No how.

She grabbed the remote, and the TV winked on. She started her nighttime ritual by listening to MTV. Exiting the bathroom and not wanting to deal with that mirror, she dragged her comforter off the bed and tossed it over the dresser. Finally feeling somewhat secure, she crawled into the bed and tugged the sheets up to her neck. She channel surfed for about an hour, finally settling on old reruns of *The Fresh Prince of Bel-Air.*

Amy dozed. A noise jarred her awake, and she glanced at the clock. The digits read 3A.M. Heart hammering, she lay perfectly still, hands clutching the sheets. What had she heard? The TV screen scratched out sound from the digitally snow-covered screen.

"Aimeeeee."

Amy flinched, heart leaping into her throat. Had a voice coming from the television just said her name?

"Amy, help me. He's coming." The voice of a young girl filled the room, growing louder with each spoken word.

She froze, grasping the covers so tight her hands hurt, and her knuckles turned white. Thank God she'd covered the mirror.

The voice came again, louder this time, "Hurry, please, Amy. Please save me."

She swallowed and closed her eyes. Whoever or whatever it was, she didn't want to see it. The temperature dropped in the room by ten degrees. Amy shivered. As lightning flashed from a brewing storm outside her window, the hall light winked out. The room became shrouded in inky blackness. Thunder boomed, and at the same time, a blood-curdling scream filled the air. Amy drew up in a ball and clapped both hands over her ears to block the sheer agony of the voice.

Before the scream completely faded into the night, Jeff burst into the room. "Amy! Are you all right?" He rushed to the side of the bed. She lifted her head to peer at him from behind her knees. "You were screaming. What's wrong?"

Sarah dashed through the door. "What is it? What's wrong?" She landed on the other side of the bed.

Under her parents' intense gaze, Amy tried to speak, but her voice wouldn't work. Her heart pounded, and her entire body trembled.

"Why were you screaming?" her mother demanded.

"It wasn't me," she managed in a whisper.

"What do you mean it wasn't you? Who the hell else could it have been?" Jeff placed his hands on his hips, frowning.

Okay, this was ridiculous. Amy'd had the living bejeezus scared out of her, and her father was angry with *her*? Clearly, they didn't believe she hadn't screamed, and if she had to be honest with herself, she wasn't sure she believed it either. The truth was just too terrifying.

"Would you care to explain what you mean?" Her father sat on the edge of the bed, his expression still hard.

"I didn't scream. Someone did, that's obvious, but it wasn't me."

"Amy," Sarah said, putting her hand on her daughter's arm. "Did you have another nightmare? Maybe you woke yourself up screaming. I swear, your dad and I thought someone was killing you."

Amy shook her head. The stupidity of her parents amazed her. "Have you forgotten what's happened to you, Dad? How you lost the past few days? I'm telling you, it really wasn't me. There was someone in this room. Why don't you believe me? Someone or something called my name and asked for my help. She said, 'He's coming,' then she screamed like the hounds of Hades were after her." She shivered, wrapped her arms around her legs and tucked her knees up under her chin.

Jeff and Sarah exchanged glances. Then the blanket over the mirror caught Amy's mother's attention. Worry filled her gaze.

"I'm sure you just had a nightmare, and the storm woke you. There is nothing wrong with your room, and," he waved his arms wide, "as you can see, there is no one else here but us."

"Why don't you two ever listen to me?" Amy shouted. "This house is haunted. This furniture that you ordered came with something that doesn't belong to this world." She straightened her legs and smacked both hands on the bed. "And before you can think it, no, I'm not crazy." Anger boiled beneath the surface, but Amy struggled for control

"That's enough nonsense for one night. Go to sleep, and we'll talk about this in the light of morning. I do think we should make that appointment with Dr. Beaumont," Jeff said to Sarah. She winced and avoided facing Amy's gaze.

Anger surged through Amy. "Dad, how do you explain what happened to you today? Do you think that was just random? Something is going on in this house, and you're both stupid if you don't believe it."

Her father's expression grew dark. Had she gone too far with the stupid comment? Probably, but she really didn't care. They'd ticked her off.

"Just because I can't explain it doesn't mean there isn't an explanation," Jeff said through clenched teeth. "You screamed in your sleep. That…I can explain. I've got an early shift at the hospital. If we're done with all this foolishness, I'm going to bed." He stalked out of the room.

Sarah glanced over at Amy. "You going to be okay?" Her face crinkled with concern.

"Mom, I really am telling the truth. You believe me don't you?"

She sighed. "I don't know what to believe." She ran her hand through Amy's hair. "Do you want me to stay with you tonight?"

"No, I'll just watch TV or something. I don't want to get Dad's panties all in a wad."

"Are you sure?"

She scooted down under the covers, not really wanting to be alone, but she didn't want her parents around either.

"Okay," Sarah said, scooting off the bed. She stopped at the door and glanced back, offering a weak smile. "Goodnight." She clicked off the light.

Amy grunted, keeping her eyes on the television that now had a picture. She scanned the room, her first instinct to flee downstairs and sleep on the living room sofa. But she figured the thing would only follow her, so she stayed put. Saying a quick prayer, Amy snuggled into her sheets. Exhausted from all the events of the last few days and wrung out emotionally, she welcomed the oblivion of sleep.

But…sleep wouldn't come. Lying in bed, she observed the dancing shadows the light from the TV made on the ceiling and waited for what would happen next. She didn't have to wait long. A soft rustle reached her ears from the direction of the dresser. Amy's heart leapt to a thundering pulse. The air in the room changed, the oppressive weight of it pressing on Amy's chest and pushing into her ears. This was not the ghost of the young girl. This was bigger and meaner. She could feel the evil all around her.

Another rustle. Was it crawling across the carpet, and any minute she'd see some ghoulish head pop up at the foot of the bed? Another rustle, heavier than the first. Amy glanced at the dresser just in time to see one corner of the comforter lift up into the air. She gasped and scooted up against the headboard.

How could that happen? Something had to be holding it. Her jaw dropped, and she watched the comforter slip from the dresser and land on the floor with a soft whoosh. Her eyes were inescapably drawn to the mirror. Amy wanted to look away, but some unseen force compelled her to keep looking. The face that materialized in that glass nearly stopped her heart. Red eyes appeared first, and then the head of a horned goat with jagged teeth formed around those evil eyes. She tried to scream, but her vocal cords were robbed of air. Gaping like a fish, she was too terrified to move a muscle. A bony hand appeared beside the horrific head and pointed at her.

In the voice of the devil, it said, "You are mine."

Black mist built behind the figure, and all of a sudden, head and hand merged with the mist, roiled and shot out of the mirror straight at

Amy. The impact of the mist slamming into her chest stole her breath. Pain shot through every nerve ending, yet she couldn't scream. It only lasted a moment before she started growing warm. Heat radiated from the inside outward to her frozen limbs, and she relaxed. Strange, dark thoughts swirled through her mind. Thoughts about harming her friends and parents, magnifying past feelings that Amy knew were wrong. Only this time, those feelings didn't seem so wrong. Justice…that was it. She'd get justice. Her lips stretched into a grin.

No longer afraid, Amy slept.

CHAPTER TWENTY-FIVE

Amy found Jake in the barn rubbing down Goliath. He glanced up from behind the horse's rump when she stepped across the threshold. Plagued with a bad mood she couldn't explain, Amy leaned against the doorframe, unable to appreciate the beautiful day.

"Hey. I thought you weren't going to ride today." He stepped around to Goliath's neck, rubbing him with the brush. "I already ran Goliath through the course and was getting ready to ride Samson. You want me to saddle him up for you instead?"

Amy entered the barn and approached the stall. Goliath's head snapped up from munching grain and nearly caught Jake on the jaw. He jumped back just in time. The horse faced Amy and whinnied, yellow teeth and tongue exposed. Goliath rapped one hoof on the barn floor and lowered his head, his entire body quivering.

"That's weird," said Jake. He rubbed the horse's neck and whispered in his ear. "Easy boy. What's got you fired up all of a sudden?"

Amy took a step closer, and Goliath's head shot up again, and he backed up. Jake grabbed the reins and held him. She glared at the horse. "What's wrong with him?"

"Whoa, Goliath. Whoa." Jake tightened his grip and led the animal to a nearby stall. "I don't know what's spooked him, but I'm going to put him up until I figure it out." He shut the stall door. Goliath kicked the wall, causing both teens to jump. Jake rubbed the horse's nose and whispered soothing words. Once the stallion settled down, Jake glanced over at Amy. "So, you going to ride?"

Irritation prickled. "No, I'm just standing here dressed in my riding gear for looks. I knew how hot you think I look in these jeans." Amy stomped to the tack room door and wrenched it open. Boys could be so stupid.

Jake approached Amy, turning her body to face him. With two fingers, he lifted her chin and gazed into her eyes. "Wow, you look tired. Come here." He enfolded her into his arms, but she stiffened. Never had she felt so out of control. She wanted the hug, but some unseen force from within her shoved Jake roughly away.

"Let's get this over with. That stupid horse isn't going to get any younger." Amy grabbed the leather equipment from the pegs. "You get the saddle."

"Yes, ma'am," Jake said, his tone cold. "I'll get right on that." He reached for the saddle and carried it over to Samson. "Who peed in your Cheerios this morning?"

Amy glared at him. "Just saddle the horse." She knew her words were harsh, but she couldn't control them. Her brow furrowed. What was wrong with her? It was like being at war with her own mind. "I'm sorry, Jake," she said. "I guess I'm just really tired."

"What's going on? Why aren't you sleeping?"

She sighed. "You wouldn't believe me if I told you. Just hold me a minute, okay?"

He nodded, placed the saddle on the barn floor and snuggled her close. Amy raised her face, expecting a kiss. Jake moved in, meeting her lips with his own. All of a sudden, a rake flew from the loft and landed within inches of their feet. She jumped back, a stream of curse words flowing from her mouth. Jake stared at her in surprise.

Amy's hand covered her mouth. "I'm sorry," she muttered, but that dark mood slithered over her again. She stared at the loft, squinting. The air shimmered just at the edge of the hay. Her heart skipped a beat as the weirdest feeling overcame her. Whatever was up there wanted her out of that barn.

"That was weird," Jake said, stepping over to the ladder to the loft.

"Don't go up there," Amy said, a harsh tone grabbing her voice. "It doesn't like me," she said.

Jake had climbed halfway up the ladder. He twisted and said, "What did you just say?"

"You heard me."

Jake shook his head and proceeded to the loft, mumbling, "Crazy."

Amy's temper flared, though her rational mind told her she had no reason to feel this angry. Clamping down on the emotion, she stepped to the foot of the ladder, gazing up at Jake. Jake examined the wall that held several tools, from rakes to pitchforks. "I see what happened," he called down to her.

"What?"

"The nail slipped out of the wall."

Amy studied where Jake stood, about four feet from the edge of the loft, and then glanced down at the rake. There was no way that rake just slipped off a nail. Something threw it at her.

Agitated, she paced the barn floor, running her hands through her hair. She must be losing her mind. She was hearing voices and screams, and now objects were being hurled without any source of propulsion. Her head filled with ominous thoughts that she'd never before experienced. She swore her brain belonged to someone else. Maybe her dad was right, and she needed to see Dr. Beaumont.

Jake climbed back down the ladder. "I'll tell Charlie to replace those nails and make sure the other tools are secure." He placed an arm around Amy. "You okay?"

No, she was not okay. She was terrified and tired of being haunted. Amy desperately wanted to tell someone what was going on, but who in their right mind would believe her? Amy led Jake to the front of the barn and plopped on a bench.

"What's going on, Amy?"

She sighed, fighting the war going on inside her. Part of her struggled to keep this a secret, while the other half really needed to tell someone. She didn't understand the mix of emotions fighting for attention in her body. Since that horrific experience in her room…Amy jerked, her muscles seizing. Jake's brows shot up.

"What's wrong?" he asked, concern filling his eyes.

She didn't answer. A diabolical laugh filled her mind. She clapped her hands to her ears, but the sound remained. Terror crawled down her spine, and her face paled. That's it. Something must have happened to her after she saw that really creepy face in the mirror. She trembled and opened her mouth to speak but coughed instead.

Jake patted her back. "You look like death. Are you sick? You've been acting really weird."

Her coughing fit ended. Swallowing hard, she forced the words out. "You're going to think I'm crazy."

Jake's blue eyes softened. "Try me."

"I think we're being haunted," she blurted and quickly glanced away, waiting for Jake to laugh. Surprisingly, he didn't.

"What makes you think that?"

Something lodged in her throat, and she coughed again. Managing to get the words out through clenched teeth, Amy said, "Ever since my mom bought that stupid furniture, some really strange things have been happening at our house." She shifted on the bench, leaning away from Jake. He waited for her to continue. "You remember when Mom got hurt, then I got the splinter in my hand, and we had all those cold blasts of air in the garage?"

Jake nodded but didn't say anything.

"Well…." A voice in Amy's head interrupted her thoughts.

I wouldn't tell him. He's going to think you're off your rocker. It's best to save all this for the surprise.

She jumped. Had something actually spoken? Her eyes widened, and she twisted on the bench to see if someone stood behind her. No one. Had she actually heard a voice? She rubbed her temples with her fingers. Oh God, now she was hearing voices in her head.

"What?" Jake grabbed her hand and followed her gaze, concern now evident on his face.

"I've seen a ghost," she blurted out, wincing as the pain in her head worsened.

The voice returned. *He thinks you're a loon. Look at his eyes. He's going to tell your parents that you're crazy, and they're going to lock you up. I warned you about telling him. I tried to stop you.*

She ignored the voice and glanced at Jake. She got a reaction, but nowhere near what she'd expected.

Jake jumped up off the bench and spun around. "No way! Really?"

Amy frowned in confusion and nodded.

"I've always wanted to see a ghost or talk to one. I know Des—"
He stopped. He sat back down. "Wow, that is so cool."

Amy's eyes narrowed. He'd been about to say something about
Destiny…again. A topic she meant to discuss, but right now, she needed
to tell him everything about what had happened to her. Before she could
speak, the voice in her head returned.

*He's in love with Destiny. You know he is. You can see it in his eyes.
He's going to dump you for her.* Fury burned in her soul. This time she
agreed with the voice but needed time to think about what to do.

I'll help you. He'll pay for what he's done to you. I promise.

A slow smile stretched across Amy's face. "Never mind," she said.
"Let's go ride." She jumped off the bench and strode back to the barn.

Jake sat back and blinked at her abrupt change of subject. "Wait,"
he said, following Amy into the barn. "I want to hear more about the
ghost. I think I know a way I can help."

She ignored him. He was stupid if he thought he could help with
her problem. It was bigger than all of them—her parents, Jake, Jessica.

Soon, the voice in Amy's head said. *They'll understand soon.*

"I don't want to talk about it anymore."

Jake leaned in. "What did your parents say when you told them?"

Her head whipped around, and her mouth opened, poised to tell him
to leave her alone.

Let's not be so hasty, the voice cautioned before Amy could snap
out words she'd regret.

*Use this to your advantage. Let him see your vulnerable side. Draw
him in. We can use him later.*

The voice was right. Maybe she could use this to her advantage.
Amy softened her expression, batted her eyes, and said, forcing out a
single tear, "They don't believe me. They want me to see a shrink."

"A shrink? Really?" Jake reached for her hand. "Listen, Amy, this
stuff really does happen, and I do think you do need to talk to somebody,
but not a shrink."

"And my dad has been acting really weird too," she continued,
not really listening to Jake's response. She knew just how to draw Jake
in. "The other night, he started acting really mean for no reason." She
stopped and pushed her hair behind her ears for effect.

"Yeah? And?"

"We were arguing about how I never do any work with the horses. You know…how I never groom them and put away my stuff. Things like that. I told him that's what the grooms are for, and…he hit me."

"He what?" Jake's eyes widened, and he scooted back on the bench.

Amy fought the curve of her lips. He'd bought it. She swiped at a leaking tear. "I know. He's never done that before. He practically threw Jessica out of the house the other day."

Jake shook his head. "Man, this doesn't sound like your dad at all. What do you think is going on with him? Does this have anything to do with the ghost?"

"I don't know."

Good, the voice said. *Keep reeling him in.*

"He'll be really mean and then have these periods where he can't remember anything that happened. He can't remember what he did or said. It's really weird."

Now ask for his secrecy. You need his promise not to tell anyone.

Amy questioned the stupid voice in her head. *Why? What if—*

Don't question me! A pain rocketed through her skull. *I will lead you to great heights, Amy, and Jake will be yours forever, but you must listen to me. Do exactly as I say.*

That got her attention. Jake, hers forever?

"Listen, Jake," Amy said, following directions. "Don't tell anybody about this, okay? I don't want people thinking I'm a nut case." She grabbed his face in her hands, forcing him to maintain eye contact.

"You need to talk to someone, Amy. Maybe keeping it a secret is the worst thing you can do."

Panic rose in her throat, her heart racing. "Jake, you've got to promise. You can't tell anyone."

He stood and paced in front of the bench, then he stopped and snapped his fingers. "What about Madame Rose?"

NO! The voice shouted in Amy's brain. She jerked and slapped her hands to her ears.

"Amy? Are you okay?"

She nodded, struggling to get herself under control. "Jake, the last person you can tell is Madame Rose. Destiny would find out and tell the whole world."

Jake took her by the shoulders. "Amy, they can help you. I know they can. You should tell Madame Rose what is going on."

He could not do this. "Jake, if you tell them, then they will tell my parents, and I'll get locked up in a loony bin. You've got to promise. Please...." *That's good,* the voice said. *You've been very convincing, Amy. Well done.*

Running his hands up and down her arms, Jake said, "Calm down. I won't tell anyone. I promise."

Amy searched his face trying to determine his level of honesty. Truthfully, she had to trust him. Pivoting on her foot, Amy entered the barn. Jake followed.

"Help me saddle Samson. I'll run him through the jumps."

"Hey, I have an idea. Sell the furniture."

Amy made a rude noise. "You know my mother loves that stuff. She's never going to sell it."

Not if I have my way....

She shivered, uncomfortable with the voice's last statement.

"No, Amy. I'm serious. Put it on eBay or something."

"Very funny. Are you going to help me with Samson or not?"

Jake grasped Amy's arm. "You shouldn't ride. You've already told me you're tired. Let me work Samson out, and you can ride him tomorrow when you feel better."

"No, I'm fine."

Jake led Samson out of his stall. The horse backed away, snorting and pawing the ground as Goliath had done when Amy approached. Neither horse had ever done that before. "What's wrong with Samson?" she asked.

Jake put a hand on the beast, and it settled down. Amy kept her distance until Jake had him saddled. She was tired but really wanted to ride. Jake led out Maggie Moo, a two-year-old mare, and joined Amy by the mounting block.

Amy approached the step, and Jake handed her the reins. Samson jerked his head, nearly pulling her off the block. He backed up, eyes rolling back in his head. He snorted and whinnied. "WTH? What is wrong with this stupid horse?" Amy yanked the reins hard, pulling at the bit in Samson's mouth.

"Easy, Amy. You'll make his mouth sore."

Fury burned through her veins. She'd show that horse who was boss. Amy pulled Samson over to the mounting block and sprung into the saddle. The mighty horse pranced and pawed like the barn was on fire. "Let's ride out to the stream and back," she said, yanking on the reins. Amy led Samson through the gate and out to the open range.

"Take it slow, Amy. No need to race." Jake mounted Maggie Moo.

Samson shook his majestic head and strained against the reins, his hooves dancing. "I think Samson wants to race. Look at him."

Samson swung his massive head around and made eye contact with Amy. Samson's eyes widened. He continued to fidget and prance in circles, fighting her hold on him. He jerked his head forward, trying to loosen Amy's hold on the reins, and she tightened her grasp.

"What is wrong with this stupid horse?" she grumbled.

"Ease up on the hold. He's going to buck if you keep that up."

Amy was going to show this horse who was in charge, whether Jake liked it or not. She kicked Samson's sides hard. Instead of bounding forward as Amy expected, he reared, front hooves slicing the air. Unprepared, she tumbled straight off his back.

Jake had taught Amy how to roll, but the jolt surprised her, and she couldn't think fast enough. She hit the ground hard. Air whooshed out of her lungs, and pain rocketed through her forearm, which took the full brunt of the weight. Bone snapped, and bile welled up in her throat, followed by her breakfast, which ended up on the grass next to her.

Jake leapt from Maggie Moo and rushed to her side. "Don't move, Amy," he said, his eyes filled with worry.

Amy couldn't move even if she wanted to. She gasped for air like a landed fish. "Why?" she wheezed.

"I don't know," Jake replied, kneeling and examining her arm. "You were yanking on him pretty hard, but he's used to that. It was like he didn't want you to ride him." He moved his hands up and down Amy legs. "Anything else broken?"

Amy rolled her head to one side, trying to get a glimpse of her arm. There was no way she'd ride in the show on Saturday. Disappointment flooded her, and the tears flowed. Why now? She cursed and tried to sit up. Where was that voice now? It certainly didn't have an answer for what she was supposed to do next.

"Hey, take it easy. Your back could be injured."

"I'm fine, except for my arm," Amy whined. "I'm not going to be able to ride on Saturday."

Jake smoothed her hair back behind her ears and picked a twig from the strands. "Don't worry about that. We need to get you home so your dad can take a look at this. Can you stand up?"

"I think so," Amy said, still breathing hard. Jake helped her establish her footing. "Stupid horse."

Jake snorted. "Yeah, he is that. I'll come back and get him after I take you home."

Amy tried walking, but it hurt too much, so Jake scooped her into his arms. Amy cried out when her arm bumped against his chest. He mumbled an apology and hoofed it back to the house.

Jake put Amy down as soon as he reached the back porch. He opened the screen door and called for Sarah. She must have observed them coming across the meadow because she reached the kitchen in record time.

"What happened?" Sarah wrapped her arm around her daughter's waist and led her to a kitchen chair.

"Something spooked Samson, and he reared. Amy wasn't prepared and fell off."

Amy glared at Jake. He told the story like she was some novice rider. "My hands couldn't grip the reins tight enough. It happened so fast," she told her mother.

Sarah inspected the arm and blew out a breath. "Even I know that arm is broken. You'll have to go to the hospital."

Amy rolled her eyes and said, "Duh."

She gave Amy a sharp glance, then twisted to call her husband. "Jeff! Come here!"

Jeff Morgan strolled into the kitchen a minute later. "What is it, Sarah?" His tone lacked pleasantness.

"Amy's broken her arm," Mom said.

Time to go, the voice said inside Amy's head. A soul-searing pain ripped through her skull, and as her eyes teared up, she observed her father's entire body jerk and go stiff. Amy held her good hand to one temple as exhaustion overwhelmed her. She sagged, and Jake wrapped his arms around her, preventing her from reaching the floor.

Amy's father, on the other hand, spun to face Jake, fury in his eyes. "How did that happen," he shouted. "I'm sure you had something to do with this!"

"Dad!"

"Jeff!"

Amy and her mother both spoke at the same time. Jeff took two threatening steps toward Jake, but Amy rose between them. She found it odd that his temper flared at almost the exact same time the voice stopped talking in her head. Could whatever that was inside her have transferred over to her father? Her body trembled at the thought.

Jake stepped around Amy and stood for himself in spite of her father's anger. "No, sir, I didn't. Something spooked Samson. He reared, and Amy fell off. I had nothing to do with it."

"Amy, you told me you were too tired to ride today," her father accused.

"We were just going for a short ride, Dad. It was no big deal. Then that stupid horse went nuts." Amy shifted in the chair. "This really hurts. Can we go to the hospital now?" She glanced back to Jake. "Will you come with me?"

"No!" Jeff shouted, startling everyone. "This was his fault, and I don't want him anywhere near you. Go get in the car, and I'll be right there."

"Dad—" Amy was mortified at her father's treatment of Jake. "He didn't have anything to do with this. He even tried to stop me. Please—"

"Shut up, Amy. I said go wait in the car."

"Dr. Morgan, I understand—" Jake started.

"I don't want to hear a word from you. If it weren't for you, none of this would have happened. I suggest you go home."

"Jeff…really," Sarah said.

Jeff smacked his hand down on the table. "Enough! Amy, get in the car."

As Amy sidled past her father, she noticed his eyes appeared very strange. His pupils were so dilated they nearly covered his irises. He looked like one of those demon-possessed people from the movies. Her heart raced. She'd seen him like this the day before, and she knew better than to argue. She waved at Jake and stepped into the garage.

CHAPTER TWENTY-SIX

Destiny paced the floor, waiting for Jake. She'd texted him over an hour ago when she'd seen him carrying Amy up to her house. Curiosity nearly overwhelmed her, plus she had an important message to deliver. He'd just texted back saying he'd be there in a few minutes. Now that he was coming, Destiny wrung her hands, trying to figure out how to deliver Andie's message. The last thing she wanted was for Jake to misunderstand.

The sound of a sharp knock reached her ears. She scuttled to the door and let Jake in. "What's going on?" she said, surprised at her calm, steady voice because her insides were like water. "You want a Coke?"

"Yeah, that would be great." He plopped into the kitchen chair.

Destiny grabbed two cans from the fridge and joined him.

"What happened to Amy? I saw you carry her home."

"God, her father really ticked me off. I've never heard him talk to me that way before. I think the man's on drugs."

Destiny scooted closer to him. "Do tell."

"Amy broke her arm today."

"How?" Her eyebrows shot up.

"Samson reared, and she fell off. Truthfully, I'm not surprised. The way Amy was yanking on those reins had to hurt his mouth. But her dad blames me."

"Wow, really?" She took a sip of her drink. "Is Amy okay?"

Jake shrugged and sighed. "Yeah, I guess. Her dad wouldn't let me go to the hospital with them."

"That's harsh," Destiny commented, reaching behind Jake for a jar of peanuts. "Here, eat a nut."

The edges of Jake's mouth quirked. "Only you would think of food as a way to solve problems."

She grinned. "Yeah, I'm good that way."

Jake took a long swallow of his Coke and then popped a handful of peanuts into his mouth. He maintained eye contact with her as he chewed. She gathered her courage. In light of what had just happened to Amy, she knew her message wouldn't be well received, but she'd promised Andie, so she plowed ahead.

"I saw Andie the other day," she began.

"Oh yeah? Why didn't you tell me sooner?" He eyed her over his Coke can.

"Because this is the first I've seen of you. She wanted me to give you a message."

Jake leaned back in his chair. "Okay, shoot."

Destiny took a deep breath...and hiccupped. Oh crap. This was hard enough without acting like a complete moron. Her cheeks reddened when Jake snickered.

"You sure that's just Coke in that can?"

She rolled her eyes, the humor breaking the tension. "Okay, here goes. Andie wants you to stay from Amy's house, *and* she wants you to stay away from Amy."

He didn't respond right away, just crossed his arms and stared. Destiny couldn't read his expression, but she was sure he thought she was using Andie as a way to come between him and Amy, which was exactly why she hadn't wanted to deliver the message. With sweaty palms, she reached for her Coke and nearly dropped it. Thanks a lot, Andie.

"Why?" Jake finally asked.

Destiny drew up a little more courage. She still wasn't completely confident Jake believed in everything she could do, and she wanted to ensure he knew the message came from his sister. "Andie thinks there is something evil going on at Amy's house, and she wants you to stay away. She's afraid something terrible might happen to you."

Jake's eyes widened, and he sat up straighter. "Wow, that is really weird."

"Why?"

"Andie's right. There really is something strange going on at Amy's."

Thank God! What a relief!

"I wanted to tell you about it." He scooted his chair closer.

"Why?" Destiny narrowed her eyes at Jake's expression. A feeling of dread settled in. She just knew he was about to ask her something she wasn't going to like.

"There's some kind of evil entity in her house, and I think you can help her. She would kill me if she knew I was telling you this, so please don't let her know I told you."

"Wait a minute," Destiny said, panic rising. "Let's back up to the part where you said I could help her. You didn't tell her about me, did you?"

"No." He lowered his head, breaking eye contact with her.

She glared at him. "Jake...."

He glanced up. "I didn't, Destiny. I swear. But you can help her. After what I've seen you can do with Andie. Maybe you can convince whatever this thing is to move on. We can ask Madame Rose to help too."

"Just what is going on?" she leaned back and picked up her Coke.

Jake told her. Some of it she'd already seen, but the parts about Amy seeing ghosts, hearing voices, and her dad acting weird were new. Destiny remembered the burned girl in the mirror and the dark entity that had tried to push into her mind and shivered. Nope. She wanted no part of this. First, Amy was the last person she wanted to know about her "gift," and second, whatever was happening in the Morgan house was uber dangerous and scared the crap out of her. She didn't even want her grandmother to have anything to do with it. That thing that tried to press through her shield held a great deal of power. She'd been singed with it. There was NO way she'd take part in anything he suggested.

Jake stared, waiting for Destiny to respond.

"I can't help her, Jake," she said. "I've seen the ghost you're talking about, and I've seen something else. Something way more powerful than me, and it's scary. I don't have enough experience to take something like this on."

Jake leaned forward and wrapped Destiny's fingers in both hands. "Don't let the fact that it's Amy keep you from stepping in. I know she's treated you like crap since you moved here, but she's really in trouble, Destiny. When her father went off on me today, he looked strange, you know? His eyes were all dark and weird looking."

"Really? Wow."

"He's never treated me that way before. Something's really wrong at their house, Destiny. I'm really worried for them."

"Well, don't you go poking around, Jake. It's way more dangerous than you could imagine. Plus, Andie will be super mad if you don't listen to her, and there are enough angry ghosts around here, trust me."

"Destiny, you can talk to ghosts or Shades, whatever you call them. Maybe you can make this thing go away. I think the entity, as you call it, came with that furniture. I told Amy to tell her mom to get rid of it, but she says her mom loves the bedroom furniture and won't part with it."

"It probably did, and it's not that I don't want to help. I just can't. The last time I practiced channeling with Grams, something very dark came after me. It tried to possess me. Grams made me promise I wouldn't channel unless I was with her."

Jake sighed, running his hands through his hair.

His defeated look tugged at her heart. She didn't want to see him hurting, and in spite of wanting to keep her grandmother safe, she said, "You need to convince Amy to talk to Grams. She's the only one who can help."

"I've already tried. Amy doesn't want anyone to know, especially you."

She cocked one eyebrow. "Oh, really?"

Jake's expression grew sheepish. "Yeah. She thinks you'll spread it around town."

Destiny pursed her lips, anger stirring. Amy had to be the stupidest girl she knew. "And what do you think?"

Jake made a rude noise. "I wouldn't be here asking for your help if I thought you would spread any rumors, now would I?"

He squeezed her hand and smiled. Warmth pooled in her belly, and her heart fluttered. Oh, how she wished that smile was just for her, and he wasn't here pleading for her to help his nasty girlfriend.

"There's nothing I can do, Jake. If Amy won't talk to Grams, then you're just going to have to see how this thing plays out. I wanted to deliver Andie's warning, and I've done that. The rest is up to you, but I agree with Andie. You better stay away from that place. It's really bad news."

"Yeah, I know." Jake punched dents in his Coke can and tapped it on the table. "There has to be something we can do."

Destiny rose and threw both cans in the trash. All of a sudden, Jake smacked both hands down on the table. Destiny yelped.

"I think I have an idea."

She flattened her palm against her heart and sat back down at the table. "You scared the crap out of me."

"Sorry," he said, leaning forward. "What if we research where the furniture came from? You know…like find its origin. Then maybe we could figure out what's going on."

"What good would that do? It's not going to make this thing move on." Destiny watched his blue eyes brighten.

"At least we might get some clue as to who had the furniture before Amy's mom got it. They might know something that can help us."

She was still skeptical on how that would help, but she could help him do some research and not get too involved. "Maybe we can do that. Do you know where Amy's mom bought the stuff?"

"No, but Amy is supposed to call me when she gets home from the hospital. I can ask her then and text you."

As if on cue, the theme to Disney's *Beauty and the Beast* rang into the room. Jake blushed, pulling out his cell phone. "Andie programmed that before she died as a joke, and I just never changed it."

"Uh-huh," Destiny smirked.

"Hello?" Jake gave her a thumbs-up sign. "Hey, Amy, how's the arm?" He listened, and then winced. "Two places, ouch. How are you feeling?" Another pause. Jake nodded. "Okay, you get some rest. Hey, listen before you go, do you know where your mom got your furniture? Who she ordered it from?" He frowned as she answered. "Because I have an idea. I want to check something out." He motioned for Destiny to give him a pen. She grabbed one from the phone desk nearby and passed it to him. He wrote a name on it. "Okay, you feel better. I'll call you tomorrow. Bye."

Destiny spun the pad around so she could read the name. Solidarity Antiques in Frosthaven, Connecticut. "How did she remember that?"

"I have no idea. Do you think you can look them up and give them a call?"

Destiny peered at the ugly cat-eyed wall clock that Grams refused to get rid of. It reminded her of Shamus, which is probably why her grandmother loved it so much. Its tail ticked off the seconds, and its googly eyes shifted back and forth. Destiny thought the thing was creepy. "It's too late to call now. We will have to try tomorrow."

"But you'll call?" Jake raised his eyebrows and stuck out his bottom lip.

Now, who could resist a look like that? Destiny nodded. "Maybe you're right. If we know the origin of the furniture, we might be able to figure out who or what is haunting it. Then I can ask Grams to make contact with the ghost girl. In the meantime, can you try to stay away from there so Andie won't drive me crazy?"

Leaning over, Jake planted a kiss on Destiny's lips. It didn't last long, but she may not have survived it otherwise. Heat lit up her system like a gas explosion. Wow. She even saw fireworks. Jealousy burned through the afterglow of the kiss. Amy better realize just how lucky she was.

Jake moved away, and Destiny sat back in her chair, blinking like an owl. Grinning, he said, "Thanks, Destiny. You're the best."

"Uh-huh," was all she could say.

Destiny...

She spun and glanced at the kitchen sink.

"What?" Jake followed her gaze. "Is Andie here?"

She nodded.

Tell him to stay away from Amy's house. It's not safe.

"Andie says to stay away from Amy's."

"So you said before. Where is she?"

Destiny pointed at the counter under the window. Jake talked directly to the sink.

"I'll try, Andie. You know she's going to want me to come by."

Destiny giggled at the spectacle, then sobered when Andie's words filtered into her mind.

Tell him that under no circumstances is he to go over there until we figure this out. I've got a really bad feeling about what's going on up there. Things are escalating, and I don't want him caught in it.

"Okay, Andie," she said and relayed the message.

"Jeez, you're still bossy even when you're dead." Jake glanced over his shoulder and grinned at Destiny, who returned the smile. "I've gotta go. I'll call you tomorrow. Bye, Andie," Jake said, patting the sink.

Destiny rolled her eyes. He'd walked right through his sister when he went out the door.

"Your brother is not the sharpest knife in the drawer, but he sure is loveable."

I know. I really hope he listens to me. I'm worried about him, Destiny.

"He'll be okay. Did you find out anything more about my parents?"

Not yet… sheesh. It's not that easy finding people over here, and with Demon Dude running around, I have to be careful. He's really scary, Destiny. I know I'm not very experienced with all this, but his power is really strong. I'm not sure what he's after, but I get the feeling he won't stop until he gets it.

"I know. I've run into him too. If Grams hadn't been with me, I don't know what would've happened." Destiny stepped from the table to stand in front of Andie. "Please find my family for me. It's very important."

I'm trying…really. Andie's expression relayed her sincerity.

"Thanks, Andie. I really appreciate it." When she'd watched her brother burn to death, her world had collapsed. She desperately needed to know what had become of them, and she needed to ask forgiveness.

Andie nodded her barely attached head and faded away.

CHAPTER TWENTY-SEVEN

After dinner, Destiny worked on her laptop, trying to find out any information on Solidarity Antiques. She googled the name, found a number, and wrote it down on a pad. Rose puttered around the kitchen, washing up the dishes and scrubbing counters. When she'd finished, she folded the dishcloth and joined her granddaughter at the table.

"What're you working on?"

"Just some research," Destiny said, lowering the lid of the computer. "How's Amy?"

"Jake talked to her after she got home from the hospital. They gave her some pretty good pain killers, so she's probably sleeping like a baby by now."

"How did she break her arm again?" Rose slid the pad over to read what she'd written down.

"Samson got spooked by something and threw her. She totally landed on her arm."

"She's lucky she didn't break her neck." Rose held her chin in one hand, rubbing her cheeks. "That horse is pretty solid. Wonder what spooked him?"

Destiny knew her Grams had a theory. She just hadn't puzzled it all out yet. She hadn't lived with her long, but Destiny knew when Grams started thinking. She got this far-off look in her eyes, and her attention drifted away. Her question didn't really expect an answer, but she said, "I don't know. Jake said it was weird that both horses were acting up this morning."

Rose's eyebrows shot up, and her hand dropped to the table. "Around Amy?"

Destiny shrugged. "I guess so."

"Now that is interesting. Sounds fishy." Rose eyed Destiny over her glasses.

"How so?"

"You remember that dark energy that tried to bully his way into your mind the other day?"

Destiny shivered. "Yeah. I'll never forget that. Do you think it has something to do with this?"

"Often evil of that magnitude will take on other forms once freed from their plane. I'm very worried that once Amy and her mom refinished that furniture, it released whatever was imprisoned there. That's why he charged at your mind the way he did. Evil likes to possess, and he's got enough energy to accomplish it." Rose tapped her chin. "Not sure what's fueling him, though."

"And you think it may have possessed Amy or something?"

She nodded.

Destiny thought about the other things Jake told her earlier, about the way Amy's dad behaved toward him when he took Amy to the house and told her grandmother about it. "And in addition to her dad acting all weird, Amy said she's seen a ghost of a burned girl. That's the same one I saw in the mirror."

Grams frowned. Worry filled her eyes. "This is escalating. You need to have Amy come and talk to me. I can help her, but I need to know all the details first-hand."

Destiny twirled a piece of hair around her finger and tapped the pen on the pad of paper. "Jake says we are the last two people that she wants help from."

Rose's jaw dropped. "You have got to be kidding me."

Destiny shrugged, but it still stung. Here, Amy was spreading all these rumors about her, which was a lie, and she had the nerve to suspect that Destiny would stoop to that level. The injustice of it burned.

Rose didn't speak for a few seconds. Her expression, brows drawn down, lips pursed, eyes narrowed, betrayed her anger. Destiny's heart warmed, knowing that her grandmother would stand for her. At last,

Rose said, "I guess Amy won't be riding in the horse show with a broken arm."

Destiny groaned. She'd forgotten about the rodeo and the horse show tomorrow. Crap. That meant Amy would be hanging around with her mother all day, and she'd be trapped with them. Awkward. She had to find a way to get out of going. "Yeah, I guess. Maybe they won't go at all. She might still be in a lot of pain." Destiny glanced at Grams Rose from under lowered lashes.

"I doubt that," she snorted. "That girl will want to see Jake ride if nothing else. That's a shame about her arm, though." Rose's icy-blue eyes brightened, and she smiled. "Hey, it would give you a good chance to talk with her. Maybe you could convince her to come to see me...let me help her."

Destiny pushed her chair back and stood up. "Did you not hear what I just said about you and I being the last people she wants to know about her troubles? Do you think for one minute that she's going to want to spend time with me?" So much for her plan to get out of going to the rodeo with the Morgans.

"Destiny, sit down, please. I didn't mean to upset you." She gestured to the chair.

Destiny plopped down, her arms crossed over her chest, huffing out a breath.

"One thing I haven't taught you about our gift is that it comes with responsibility. We can do things others can't. You and I have the power to deal with not only good energy that has passed from this Earth but the bad energy as well. With that ability comes a duty to help those in need. You can help Amy, and you should." Rose reached for her granddaughter's hand, pulling it from the crook of her arm and forcing her out of the belligerent posture. "The evil I'm sensing is only going to grow stronger with Amy's fear. The Morgans are easy targets because they aren't armed with the knowledge of what they're dealing with. We are."

Guilt poked at Destiny. Part of her knew Grams was right, but she didn't want to be anyone's savior. She was still raw and healing from her own wounds. Still trying to deal with seeing Shades and evil entities. She couldn't even build a decent shield. What help would that be? "I hear you, Grams, but I don't think Amy will care what we can do to help her. She's made up her mind that we're witches and something to be avoided at all costs."

Rose let go of her hand. "Just think about what I said, okay?" Then tapping the pad, "What's this?"

Heat flooded Destiny's cheeks…she'd been trapped. Grams was crafty. "Jake had a theory that if we could find the source of the furniture, then maybe we could learn more about what's going on."

Rose's mouth twitched. "So you are trying to help?"

Destiny's eyes narrowed. Her grandmother didn't have to look so smug. "Yes, I guess so. Amy told Jake where her mom bought the furniture, so I thought I'd call and see what I could find out. I guess they're closed now. I'll have to wait till morning."

Grams grabbed the cordless phone off the kitchen counter, not a far reach in the tiny kitchen, and handed it to Destiny. "Try now. Sometimes these store owners stay late to work on paperwork. Believe me…I do."

Rose winked at her granddaughter. It took Destiny a second to interpret the gesture, then she dialed the number.

"Solidarity Antiques, this is Margaret. May I help you?"

Rose knew someone would be there. Destiny rolled her eyes. Now she lived with a psychic too.

"Hello?" the voice said impatiently.

"Um…hi, my name is Destiny Dove, and I wanted to ask you some questions about some furniture you sold over the Internet to a friend of mine."

"Oh, okay. Did you want something similar?"

Destiny choked back a laugh. She definitely *did not* want something similar. She cleared her throat. "No, ma'am, I just need some information about where the furniture came from. My neighbor, Sarah Morgan, bought the bedroom furniture over a month ago."

"Sarah Morgan? Let me see," she said, and Destiny heard shuffling papers. "Yes, here it is. A French Roccoco set from the catalogue. What do you need to know?"

Destiny gave Rose a thumbs-up, twisted the pad around and picked up the pen. "Can you tell me where the set originally came from? Like, who owned it first?"

"I'm not too keen on giving out personal information on my clients," Margaret said.

"I understand, but it's very important. My neighbor is having some…um…trouble with the furniture, and I thought if I could learn a little about its history, I could help her."

"What kind of trouble does a person have with furniture? She bought it knowing full well there was a no refund policy on anything bought over the Internet."

The conversation grew awkward. How did Destiny explain to this woman she thought the furniture was haunted? She glanced at Rose, who whispered, "Tell her the truth."

Destiny raised her eyebrows, and Rose nodded. Drawing in a breath, she said, "We think the furniture is haunted. Strange things have been happening, and I thought if I could find out the history, I might be able to help."

Silence. Destiny pointed to the phone and shrugged at Rose and then smiled and held up a finger, signaling her to wait.

A moment passed before Margaret said, "I guess it's kind of funny that you'd call. I'd sold that furniture before to a family that wanted to do the same thing Sarah Morgan did. They wanted to refinish it and bring it back to life. They didn't keep it two days before they hauled it back in their truck. Said the furniture was making loud knocks and bangs. They told me the mirror clouded up and wouldn't come clean." She paused, and I heard the ruffle of more papers. Margaret coughed and then continued, "I gave them their money back and kept the furniture in my warehouse."

"Did anything happen in the warehouse?" Destiny asked, jotting down notes on her pad.

"I really hadn't put any thought to it, but now that you mention it, I had a few employees tell me they'd heard strange things happen when they were in the warehouse alone."

Now she had Destiny's attention. "What kind of strange things?"

"Moans, banging and whispering voices, stuff like that." Destiny heard her suck in a breath like she was smoking a cigarette. "I've never believed in that kind of thing, so I told my employees it was just the wind or something. It's a big warehouse. You'll hear lots of weird noises."

"Is that when you decided to sell it on the Internet?"

"Yes. Well, I did try selling it to one more family, but they brought it back too. I knew I needed to unload it to someone who couldn't bring it back, so I put it in my catalogue."

"So even though you say you don't believe it's haunted, you sort of do? And you sold it knowing there could be something wrong," Destiny probed, trying to get her to admit there was definitely something weird about the furniture. Her hope being Margaret would give her the information she sought.

"Aren't you a clever girl," Margaret said. "I'm still not sure I believe in all that hocus pocus, but I can't deny something was strange about it. What exactly is it you wanted to know?"

Destiny smiled at Rose. "I'd like to know the history all the way back to when the furniture was built. Who owned it first? Did anything happen to them? Was it ever in a fire? Stuff like that. Do you have any of that type of history in your records?"

"Oh, honey, I keep meticulous records on all my stock. Hold on a minute, let me see what I can find out." A crack reached Destiny's ears as Margaret smacked the phone down. Footsteps echoed over the line as she walked away.

"I think she's going to look for it," Destiny said.

"Good," Rose replied, grinning. "That was some pretty smooth talking you just did to convince her to give you the information."

Destiny winked.

Margaret came back on the line. "I pulled the file on that particular set." She rustled more papers. "Okay, here it is. That French Rococo bedroom suite was brought to me by the Frost family about five years ago. They gave it to me on consignment. They were cleaning out the old family estate and wanted it gone. I'd just never been able to unload it until I put it on the Internet."

"It was very sooty when Mrs. Morgan got it. Was it in some kind of fire?" Destiny heard the rustle of more papers as Margaret perused through the file.

"I usually ask for a family history sheet with every antique I sell. It gives the buyers some of that background they seem to think is so romantic. On this record, it says the furniture was in a fire that killed the entire family back in the 1800s. A judge by the name of Frost, a pretty prominent name in our town, was blamed for the fire. The legend says he was drunk and started the blaze that killed his family. This furniture was all that was left standing when the villagers went to clear the rubble."

Destiny's heartbeat sped up. She scooted to the edge of her chair, the pen scratching furiously on the paper. "That's really weird. You'd think the fire would've burned everything to ashes. How did this bedroom furniture survive so well?"

A tapping sound came across the phone. Destiny recognized the sound of fingers on a keyboard.

"I just found the history of the Frost family on my computer. He was said to be a mean judge and an even meaner husband. This article I'm looking at has a picture of him, and he looks mean. Anyway, that's all I have in my notes. Is that what you needed?"

Destiny wiggled in her seat. She couldn't wait to tell Jake what she'd found out. "Would you mind emailing me that link so I can see it too? My email address is ddove@tba.com."

"Sure, it's on its way. Anything else?"

The computer pinged, and Destiny lifted the lid. "I got it, thanks. No, you've been really helpful. Thanks."

"I hope that helps your friend."

"It will. Thanks again. Bye." Destiny handed Rose the phone, and she placed it back in its charger. She tapped her pen on the pad. "Do you think this judge has something to do with the evil we've witnessed?"

"Maybe he was possessed by the same demon, and that's why he was so mean. A dark entity can hang around a long time if it has plenty of energy and motivation."

"I'll take a look at that link and see what I can find out."

Rose nodded and stood. "You're doing good work there, Destiny."

She bloomed with pride. It warmed her heart to know her grandmother was proud of her.

Rose snapped her fingers and said, "I've got an idea,"

"What?"

"Tomorrow, let's try to channel the burned girl in the mirror."

Destiny cocked her head to one side. "Do you really think that's a good idea? What about Judge Evil?"

"We can hold him off with my shield. What do you say?" Rose raised one eyebrow.

Destiny had her doubts. She really didn't want to channel anything ever again, but her grandmother did have a good point. "I've only ever seen the girl in the mirror. Do you think she can travel outside the house or even outside the glass?"

Rose puzzled over that for a second. "You could be right. We might need to be close to the mirror to make contact."

"Well, that's not going to happen," Destiny said, knowing Amy wouldn't just let them into her bedroom when she didn't even want them to know. Then an idea popped into her head. "Grams, what about Andie or Patch? Do you think they could get to her?"

Rose's features wrinkled in thought. "Maybe…." She smiled and held up a finger. "You know, that's really not a half-bad idea. That way, we wouldn't even need to open a direct channel. I could ask my spirit guide to find Patch or Andie and see if either would be willing to check it out for us."

Relief flooded Destiny. She really hadn't wanted to channel that burned girl and was thrilled to pass that chore on to someone more equipped. "Patch is probably your best bet since he still haunts the farm. Andie is pretty scared of the evil judge."

Rose nodded. "That's what I'll do then. You get some rest. You've got a big day at the rodeo tomorrow."

CHAPTER TWENTY-EIGHT

Fear gripped Destiny, tensing every muscle. She stood on the wet blackened road staring at the evil goat-headed demon who'd tried to enter her mind. In his arms, he held a squirming Elijah. Destiny gasped as her baby brother, alive and screaming, reached out for her. As she charged across the street, a hand grabbed her elbow from behind, spinning her around. It was Andie, only this time she was whole, the way she'd looked in life.

"Don't go, Destiny. It's a trick."

"Let me go! That's my brother. I didn't save him once, and I won't let him go again."

"Destiny, wait! Look again. Look really close." Andie's grip tightened on Destiny's arm.

Destiny struggled to free herself then she froze. The demon approached.

"I've got something you want," it said in a deep gravelly voice. "And you've got something I want. I'll give him back to you if you agree to my terms."

"Destiny, don't do it...he's trying to trick you. Look...look at Elijah. He's not what you think."

Destiny stared at Andie. She nodded, her pink hair bobbing around her face.

"Trust me, Destiny." Andie reached up and grasped Destiny's chin in her hand and turned her to face the demon.

What he now held in his arms was the charred body of a toddler, black skin with bloody pink showing through, not the fat chubby cherub she'd seen a moment ago.

"I'm sorry, Destiny, but you have to know the truth."

The demon roared at Andie.

"You'll pay for this...dead one." He tossed the charred little body at Destiny.

She screamed.

Jerking awake, Destiny panted and clawed at her bed sheets. Had she screamed aloud? She lay waiting for her grandmother to come to her aid, but all remained quiet. Oh God that had been the worst dream yet. Poor little Elijah.

"It wasn't real," she told herself. "It wasn't real." She swiped at the tears streaming down her face. If she'd only been able to get that car seat loose. If that cop had only given her more time. If...if...if....

Stop it, Destiny.

Andie appeared at the foot of her bed.

Quit torturing yourself this way. You couldn't have saved him. It just wasn't meant to be.

"I wish I believed that. Any luck finding my parents?"

Andie shook her head. *I'm still looking. I'll find them, though. I promise. Please, try to forgive yourself, though. I know your parents don't hold all of this against you. If anything, they are blaming themselves for the accident.*

Destiny stared at Andie. She'd never thought of that. Her parents could be wandering the Great Beyond, worried about how she felt about them? Crap, that made it even more critical for Andie to find them. "Please, Andie, I really need your help on this."

I know, Destiny. I will. Just be patient, okay?

Destiny wiped her eyes again and gave Andie a weak smile.

Oh, and have fun at the rodeo.

Destiny swung her head around and looked at the clock. "Crap. I forgot. I better get ready."

See ya.

"Bye, Andie."

Destiny drug her sore, tired body to the bathroom. After a hot shower, her mood improved, and she thought about all the things she wanted to tell Jake. She needed to review the link Margaret had sent her before the Morgans picked her up. That way, she could tell Jake everything she knew about Judge Frost and the furniture's history.

Destiny padded into the kitchen, her hair still wet from the shower, and found a bowl with the box of *Cheerios* on the table beside a note. Her grandmother had gone to the bookstore early, the note said. She'd left money too; twenty dollars rested by the cereal bowl. Cool. Relieved that Grams hadn't heard her screaming from her nightmare, she shoved the money in her pocket and went to retrieve her laptop. She poured a bowl of *Cheerios,* munched while she opened the email and browsed the site Margaret had sent.

The article described the "Hanging Judge," and how more criminals had died under his watch than any judge before or after. He'd been married twice, first to a woman of noble birth and the second time to his own Irish maid. Nice guy. At least he'd waited until his first wife died before boinking the maid, unlike more recent politicians. She took another bite of *Cheerios* and read on.

The paper said Judge Frost had two children, a daughter named Enya and a son, Shane. There was some speculation that abuse occurred in the household because the children and their mother were often seen with black eyes and bruises. What a charmer. The rest of the historical account bragged about his convictions and the strict punishment he'd dolled out until that fateful day in 1815 when the entire family had been killed in the fire that burned their home to the ground. No survivors, the article said. There were no photos as the camera had not been perfected by that time, and Destiny found that really disappointing. She wanted to know what the judge looked like.

The phone rang. Destiny threw her spoon in the empty cereal bowl and reached for the cordless. Caller ID identified the caller as Jeffery Morgan. *Welcome to the day from hell.* "Hello?"

"Hi, Destiny, this is Sarah Morgan. Are you still planning on going to the rodeo with us today?"

Destiny wanted to say she was sick but didn't want to face the wrath of her grandmother, so in her most amiable tone, she said, "Yes, I'm ready to go when you are."

"Great. We'll pick you up in a few minutes. Just step outside, and we'll get you on the way down the drive."

Destiny hung up, sighed and went to the bathroom to brush her teeth. She grabbed her sneakers and had just stepped onto the porch when the Morgans arrived.

"Good morning," Mrs. Morgan said, opening her car door.

"Hi," Destiny replied.

"Hop in, and we'll be on our way," she said.

She opened the back door and climbed in. Amy sat on the other side and glared at her as she buckled in. Great. Off to a wonderful start. Determined to make the best of it, Destiny said, "Hi, Amy. I'm sorry about your arm."

"Hmph," Amy grunted and glanced out the window.

"Amy, don't be rude to our guest," Mrs. Morgan chimed in. "We are very sorry not to see Amy ride today, but there will be other times, right sweetheart?"

Amy's scowl turned to Sarah Morgan. Destiny studied Amy as she held her mother in a stare-down. Something wasn't right. Her eyes, a cornflower blue from what she remembered, were darker, almost black. The angry expression on her face marred her beauty to near ugliness. She appeared strange and distant. Destiny controlled a shiver, wondering who she sat beside. Amy? Or something else. Her pulse raced, and she struggled to slow her breathing. Amy rotated her head and bestowed a look upon Destiny that sent chills racing down her spine. She hoped that Grams would be able to get more information from Patch today because these people were in trouble.

They arrived at the rodeo grounds early. Dr. Morgan parked behind the tents, where the riders prepared their horses. Jake and his father were already there and had unloaded Goliath. Amy dashed over to Jake, making sure Destiny observed her kisses and arm pats. Destiny followed, rolling her eyes.

Glancing around the tent, she'd never seen so many beautiful animals, riders and horses alike, all dressed in bright colors. Destiny giggled when she saw Goliath, all braids and bows. He looked ridiculous, but what did she know? Maybe that came with the territory. She patted his neck and gave the horse a sympathetic smile.

"He's all dressed up for the show, isn't he?" Destiny said, rubbing

Goliath's velvet nose.

Jake laughed. "I know it. He's probably embarrassed. I'll make it up to him if he clears all his jumps."

"An apple, right?"

"Right. You remembered." Jake rewarded Destiny with one of his glorious smiles.

"Remembered what?" Amy snapped, squeezing Jake's arm. He winced and delicately tried to extricate his arm from her talons.

Goliath reared. Screams issued throughout the tent, one of them belonging to Destiny. Jake grabbed Goliath by the bridle.

"Step back, girls," Jake's father said.

"Whoa, Goliath. Easy boy," Jake wrestled with the horse until he settled down.

Jake caught Destiny's eye, and they exchanged grim expressions.

Amy snarled, the expression vicious. "That stupid horse."

Jake led Goliath away to the ring to prepare for the show, and the rest of the group went to their seats. There were several riders before Jake, and Amy had something derogatory to say about each one. Finally, Jake rode into the ring. Destiny listened to all the comments around her about how Goliath was too large for steeplechase and how Jake had to be crazy to enter that horse. In a few moments, they ate their words. Jake performed magnificently.

"Not one single error," the man next to Destiny said.

Amy leaned over, pressing her elbow hard on Destiny's thigh. "That's my boyfriend."

"Ow," Destiny said, shoving Amy away.

Instead of glaring, this time, she grinned. Her lips twisted way up at the corners, showing a mouthful of teeth. That smile reminded Destiny of the Joker on Batman. Totally creepy. "You tell him for me that he's an exceptional rider," the man said, standing to go. "I believe he's won."

Amy cheered. "I'll tell him." She leaned over to her mother. "I'm going to find Jessica and Trudy. I'll see you at the bronco event." Destiny grimaced but held her tongue as Amy came over and deliberately stomped on her foot. No need to start a brawl in the bleachers. She kept repeating that Amy wasn't herself and needed help, but somehow that didn't make her feel any better. The girl exhibited rudeness down to her very core, and whatever was inside her just magnified it. Destiny prayed her grandmother would get some answers.

"Aren't you going to take Destiny with you?" Amy's mom shouted after her.

"It's okay, Mrs. Morgan. I'll just go down to the tents and tell Jake what a good job he did."

She craned her neck to find Amy. "Are you sure? She's never been this rude before. I'm sorry, Destiny."

Destiny shrugged. "It's fine. Please don't worry about it. We just have different interests, that's all." She stood to leave.

"Meet us back here in about an hour for the awards ceremony, okay?"

"I will," she said, hopping from bleacher to bleacher. Destiny waved when she got to the bottom and headed off to the tents.

She found Jake rubbing down Goliath and freeing his mane from all the sissy bows. Sneaking up behind him, she put her hands over his eyes. "Guess who?"

He spun around and gave her a big hug. "Hey, Destiny. Did you see Goliath?"

She grinned and nodded. "I did. You did such a great job. He was amazing, weren't you, boy?" She patted the horse's neck. "I think you won."

"I know, right?" Jake hugged Goliath. "I was worried about the chestnut mare, but when she didn't clear that last jump, I knew I had her."

"I'm happy for you, Jake."

"Thanks. Hey, you want a Coke? We've got some in the cooler."

"Okay." Destiny followed him to the other side of the tent. He grabbed two sodas, and they sat at one of the plastic tables set up for the riders. Jake popped the top on his drink and took a long swallow. Destiny took the unobserved moment to admire him head to toe. He had to be the best looking guy she'd ever seen. Amy didn't deserve him.

"Did you get a chance to call that antique store yet?"

Destiny told him what Margaret had said about the furniture and that she'd sent a link on Judge Frost's biography.

Jake's eyes sparkled. "What did you find on the link?"

"Judge Frost was nicknamed "the Hanging Judge" and rumored to be really cruel. His house burned down in a fire that killed the entire family. The only thing left standing when the smoke cleared was—"

"The furniture," Jake said.

"Yep." Destiny stood to throw her Coke can away.

"Do you think this judge is our problem?" Jake rose to stand next to her.

"I do. Grams is trying to get another Shade she knows to go in and find the burned girl in the mirror to see if we can get any more information about him. But…." Destiny held up a finger. "Grams also said we can't do anything until Amy comes to us. You need to convince her to do that, Jake. I think things are getting worse."

"Thank you. I can't tell you how much I appreciate you doing all of this." In one fast swoop, Jake had a surprised Destiny in his arms. He planted a kiss on her lips, and she wished it could go on forever.

"WTH, Jake. What's going on here?" Amy shouted from across the tent.

Jake let Destiny go so fast that she nearly tumbled to the ground. Destiny winced. They were in big trouble. She could feel the hatred pulsing from Jake's girlfriend. Now might be a good time to focus on that shield Grams Rose had taught her.

Amy stomped across the tent in long strides. She covered the distance in seconds. "What do you think you're doing kissing my boyfriend?" She pressed up against Destiny's chest, her face inches away.

"Amy, it's not what you think. Destiny did me a favor, and I was just thanking her. That's all."

Her head swung from her enemy to Jake. "Oh, I just bet she did you a favor."

"Amy, calm down." Jake reached for her arm, but she jerked away and faced Destiny.

"You've wanted to get your claws into him since we first met, you skank."

"Hey," Destiny said. "Watch your mouth."

"Amy, really…." Jake started, but Amy wasn't listening. Her eyes, locked on her foe, changed color from blue to solid black. A flush crept up her neck and into her cheeks. Before Destiny could duck, Amy swung her casted arm and cracked her across the cheekbone.

Pain bolted through Destiny's head, stars appearing before her eyes. She staggered back but didn't go down. Amy leapt on her, pummeling Destiny's head and shoulders. She held her arms up to ward off the worst of the blows, but Amy managed to get in a few well-aimed punches before someone yanked her off.

Destiny stood, her eye already bruising and swollen, her nose dripping blood. She used the corner of her t-shirt to try and stop the flow. Destiny opened her one good eye and saw that Jake held Amy around the waist. She was clawing at the air, still trying to get to her.

"Amy, calm down!"

"I will not calm down. I'm going to kill her." Wild-eyed and spitting, Amy fought to break Jake's hold.

"I'll let you go if you calm down. She's just trying to help. Let me explain." Jake shook her like a rag doll. His strength surprised Destiny. She winced as she tenderly touched her cheek. That girl packed a wallop. Whatever controlled her had intensified not only her anger but her physical strength as well. Destiny reached her equally tender nose and felt it swelling as well. Great. Just great. She'd known coming to this rodeo was a bad idea, but would anyone listen to her? No.

Amy's two friends had backed away when the violence started, and now they glared at Destiny. "Why don't you go find your own boyfriend," the one named Jessica said.

"I don't want Amy's boyfriend," Destiny replied, the sound muffled through the t-shirt.

"That's not what it looked like to us, did it, Amy?"

"Jessica, shut up," Jake said. "You're only making the situation worse."

Jessica huffed out a breath and crossed her arms, hip cocked to one side.

"Amy, I'm going to let you go now. Will you leave Destiny alone?"

"Yes," Amy growled and stopped struggling.

Destiny took a step back, preferring Jake kept his hold on her. That girl had murder in her eyes, and her gaze was aimed straight at Destiny.

Jake spun Amy around to face him. "Amy, listen to me. Destiny hasn't been trying to take me away from you. She's been helping me deal with Andie's death. She can also help you with the problems at your house."

"Jake…." Destiny warned. Where was he going with this?

"Yeah, I just bet she can since she's the cause of them." She spun around. "You want me out of the way so you can have Jake all to yourself."

"You're crazy," Destiny said.

"I'll tear your eyes out, you witch," Amy lunged for Destiny, but Jake was faster. He grabbed her around the waist again.

"Amy!" He planted her feet on the ground and held her in place. "Listen to me," he shouted, moving his hands to her shoulders. He shook her to get her attention. When she turned her head to face him, he said, "Destiny can help you like she's helping me. She can see and talk to ghosts. She's going to be able to help you get rid of that ghost in your room."

Destiny's breath caught in her throat, and she dropped the shirt tail, blood still streaming from her nose. He did not just go there. Jessica and Trudy stared for exactly one moment before they burst into laughter. Tears pricked Destiny's eyes. He'd just blurted out her secret. The one thing she'd asked him to promise he would never do. A massive pressure crushed her chest. The beating she'd received from Amy didn't hurt half as much as Jake's betrayal.

Amy stood still, her eyes wide. "Did you just say she can talk to ghosts?"

Jessica giggled and whispered something to Trudy.

"Amy, it's a gift," Jake blathered on. "Destiny has been great about listening to me about Andie."

Amy's voice was venomous. "Oh, I just bet she has. She's a witch, just like her grandmother."

"Amy," Jake said. "She can talk to that ghost in your mirror—"

"Shut up! Just shut your mouth." Amy had tears in her eyes. At that point, it occurred to Destiny that Jake had betrayed two secrets—her's and Amy's. What an idiot.

"Amy!" Mrs. Morgan stepped into the tent. "What has gotten into you?"

Amy spun to glare at her mother. Mrs. Morgan took one look at

Destiny and tilted on her high heels. "Jeff," she called over her shoulder. "Get in here."

Dr. Morgan stepped in. "What's going on in here? We can hear the shouting from the stands."

"See to Destiny, would you?" Sarah said.

"What happened?" he asked.

"Amy attacked me," Destiny said simply. What good would it do to cover for her?

"Wha—" Mrs. Morgan spun to her daughter. "Oh my God. Why?"

Jake stepped between Sarah Morgan and Amy. "It's my fault. I—"

Destiny interrupted him. "Jake, Amy's right. Just shut up." She turned to Dr. Morgan. "Would you please give me a ride to my grandmother's bookstore?"

"You really should have your face seen to," he said, tilting her chin toward the sunlight leaking into the tent. "Your nose might be broken."

"It's not," Destiny said, miserable. "Can we just go now, please?"

Dr. Morgan nodded, took her elbow, and guided her out of the tent. He glanced back over his shoulder. "We'll talk about this when I get back, Amy."

Tears of humiliation burned her eyes, and Destiny didn't look back to see Amy's expression.

CHAPTER TWENTY-NINE

Destiny jumped out of the Land Rover almost before it stopped. She ran to the bookstore, pulled the door open and ran straight through the red door up to the Reading Room.

Rose, eyes wide, called after her, "Destiny? Where are you going? Destiny...." She stopped when she saw Jeff Morgan come into the store.

"Hi, Rose."

"What happened? What's wrong with my granddaughter? Is she hurt?"

"We aren't one hundred percent sure what happened, but Destiny and Amy got into a fight at the rodeo." Jeff held up his hand when alarm spread across Rose's face. "I didn't get a good look at her, but her nose got pretty banged up, and it looks like Amy got in a good right cross. I'd like to pay for all her medical bills and see her at the hospital tomorrow." Jeff Morgan hung his head and sank onto a stool near the counter. "I'm really sorry about this, Rose. Amy hasn't been herself lately. In fact, none of us have."

Rose glanced at the red door where Destiny disappeared and then back at Jeff. Deciding he needed her attention more at the moment, she perched on the stool next to him. "I'm sorry to hear you are having trouble, Dr. Morgan. It's very hard when the household is in turmoil."

"What do you think Amy and Destiny were fighting about?"

"I have a pretty good idea they were fighting about Jake. I've overheard Amy tell Sarah that Destiny is after her boyfriend, but I'm sure that's just jealousy talking. I've never witnessed Destiny do anything out of line. I have no idea what sparked the brawl at the rodeo, but I promise you I'll find out, and Destiny will receive a sincere apology from Amy."

Rose's lips curved in a sympathetic smile. "Boys and girls have been staking their claims over one another since the beginning of time. Reckon, our girls are no different. I'm sure Destiny will be fine, and they'll work this out. She's had a few bumps in the road as of late."

"I know, and I'm so sorry for your loss."

Rose inclined her head. "Thank you." She glanced at the door again. "I'd best get up there and see to her. Thanks for bringing her to me."

Jeff rose and backed toward the door. "I'm very sorry, Rose. I'll see to it she gets great medical care."

"I'll see. Thanks for the offer." Rose walked him to the door. She held his gaze for a moment, then said, "Jeff, if you need anything… anything at all, just call."

Jeff's brow furrowed. "Uh…okay. Thank you."

"In fact," Rose continued, "if you and Sarah need some time away, I'd love to keep an eye on Amy for you. A special weekend maybe?"

Jeff raised one eyebrow. "Really?" he thought for a moment. "You know, Rose…that might not be a bad idea. That's a very generous offer. We may just take you up on that."

Rose inclined her head, smiled and held open the door. As soon as the Land Rover pulled away, Rose hustled up the stairs, "I just need to get all of you away from that house," she muttered as she climbed the stairs.

"Destiny?"

Destiny was lying face down on one of the love seats, shoulders shaking from the heart-wrenching sobs that poured from her. Rose gathered her granddaughter up in her arms and held the girl while she cried. It broke Rose's heart to see Destiny so upset.

Eventually, Destiny calmed down and sat back against the loveseat. "You okay, baby?"

Destiny raised her tear and blood-stained face and shook her head. "It was horrible, Grams. I don't ever want to see any of them ever again."

Rose reached out and lifted her chin with a finger. "That's some shiner you got there. Looks like your nose might be broken too. What happened?"

Destiny relayed the events to her grandmother, leaving nothing out.

Shock filled Rose's expression. She knew Amy wasn't the nicest girl around, but she'd never heard of her being physically violent. "Have you given Amy reason to be so jealous?"

"No, Grams. I—"

Rose cocked her head to one side. "Destiny?"

Destiny sighed. "Okay, I kind of like him, but I know he's her boyfriend, so I would never go after him. I'm not that type of girl, Grams. We've just been talking to Andie, that's all. His kiss today was out of happiness for what I'd found out about the furniture. We're trying to help Amy, for God's sake, and...." Destiny rose and pointed to her face. "this is what I get."

"Okay, okay, calm down," Rose soothed.

Destiny flopped back to the love seat, tears pouring down her swollen face. "If all that wasn't bad enough, then Jake had to go and blab my secret to the whole freakin' world. God, Grams, can't anything go right for me?"

Rose put her arm around the distraught girl. "I know, honey. I know. I think there's more to this than just jealousy."

Destiny's head popped up. "So do I!"

"I don't believe that was Amy you were fighting with."

"I don't either. She was really strong." Destiny gingerly touched her nose.

"We'll get some ice for that in just a minute," Rose said, distracted. "I think that demon who tried to push his way into your mind the other day is definitely influencing what's going on with that family."

A soft pop sounded, and both Rose and Destiny looked around to see Andie seated in one of the easy chairs.

My brother is an idiot and a jerk.

Rose smiled at Andie's frustration and said, "Yes, he is, but I doubt he did it deliberately, Destiny. I know Jake would never intentionally hurt you. Maybe he got caught up in his desire to help both you and Amy. He bungled it terribly, but his heart was in the right place."

"Whose side are you on?" Destiny wiped at her eyes again. "I was totally humiliated. I will never be able to hold my head up in this town again. I don't even want to leave this room."

"Destiny, I'm on your side, honey. I know how much that must have hurt and how embarrassed you are, but you have to know that what you have is a gift. You can use it for the greater good, and right now, we need to use it for Amy."

"Screw the greater good. I am never going to use this 'gift,'" Destiny made quotes in the air, "as you call it again."

Destiny, I hope you don't mean that. You've been more help to me than you can even realize. It's completely terrifying to find out you're dead and lost and don't know which way to go. But appearing to you and knowing that you can see and hear me makes me feel safe. I can talk to Jake through you, and that makes me happy. Until I figure out what it is that I'm meant to do here, I have you for a friend.

Saying you won't use your gift anymore means I've lost that friend.

Destiny looked at Andie. She didn't want to hurt Andie's feelings, but she didn't know how it felt to have everyone laughing and thinking she was a freak. It was better if she just turned this whole thing off, ignored it, and maybe, eventually, she would grow out of it.

You're not going to grow out of this. Andie held her gaze. *It's your destiny. You've got this gift for a reason, and you need to use it to help people. It's going to be especially important soon.*

Rose spoke up, "Destiny, your mother was the same way. She allowed what her friends thought to rule her way of thinking. She didn't want to be embarrassed, so she turned her back on me and all that she knew to be true." Rose patted Destiny's hand. "She chose to hide and not use her gift, and look what it did to our family. I had to watch you and your brother grow from a distance. I couldn't be a part of your life and that hurt. I'm overjoyed that you're with me now. Please think about this. Don't just shut down because you're afraid of what people will think. This work we do is important."

"Grams, half the people in this town think you are either a loon or a witch. How is that going to help me?"

Andie winced, but Rose didn't take offense at her granddaughter's words. She knew Destiny was hurting, and she wanted to help her understand. "I know what they say, but you've forgotten something."

"What's that?"

"The other half of the people. They do believe what I do is important, and they support me and my bookstore. Even the local preacher comes in here from time to time to seek advice from his own father. He tells me it gives him great satisfaction to talk to his dad when he's having trouble with a parishioner or a sermon."

Your grandmother's right, Destiny. You can help a lot of people. I know what Jake did was stupid, but it will pass. By the time school starts, you'll have a ton of friends. That's the way it goes. Things might be rough for a couple of weeks, but lay low, and it will all blow over.

Destiny's expression clouded over with doubt, and fresh tears sprang to her eyes. "Can we just go home now, Grams? My face is killing me."

"Sure, kiddo. Let's close up and go home. Andie, you'll be sure and touch base with Patch on that little assignment I gave you two, right?"

Andie paled. *I've talked to Patch. We'll do our best, but it's going to be tricky. I hope you know what you're doing, Madame Rose.*

Destiny stared at her grandmother. "What's going on?"

"Let's go home for now. We'll talk about it later. You've had enough excitement for one day. Let's go and put some ice on that face of yours."

"Yeah, that sounds good. See ya, Andie."

Night Destiny. I'm sorry about what happened today. I promise it will be okay.

Destiny rolled her eyes.

CHAPTER THIRTY

Are you ever going to forgive him? Andie spoke telepathically to Destiny while sitting on the bed. She'd learned to control her appearance, which made it easier for Destiny to look at her. Since Destiny had given Andie the assignment of searching for her parents, Andie appeared more often. In fact, Destiny had grown used to having her around, even if she was a Shade.

Destiny sighed. "No, I'm not. He promised me, Andie."

Jake feels terrible about what he did. He didn't mean to tell your secret. He was just trying to help, and he screwed it up something terrible.

"I'll say."

Please give him another chance. It's killing him that you won't take his phone calls.

Destiny stared at Andie—or through her. "Would you forgive someone who betrayed you that badly? Honest answer."

Andie shrugged, her head wobbling only a little. *Probably not.*

"Okay then."

But Destiny, he's miserable. You should at least let him say he's sorry, even if you don't want to be his friend.

"I know he's your brother, and you're doing this to try to help him, but I just can't talk to him right now. Besides, you have a job to do. Go find my parents."

Andie sighed and faded away.

Grams knocked on the door. "Can I come in?"

"Sure," Destiny said. She hadn't left her room for days. Rose brought her soup to sip through a straw. Her bruises had turned a kaleidoscope of greens, yellows and purples. After a visit to Dr. Morgan, she'd discovered her nose wasn't broken, just badly bruised. That had been extremely awkward, and she just wanted to forget it all happened and stay in her room.

Rose pushed open the door. "Are you going into the store with me today? You can't hide in here forever."

"I know." Destiny sighed. "I just don't think I can face anyone."

"Jake called my cell phone. He wanted to know if you were okay since you weren't answering any of his texts." Rose leaned against the door jam. Her expression radiated sympathy.

"He's lucky I don't hire a hit man."

Rose laughed. "I guess he is at that. I'm sure he got caught up in the heat of the moment."

"Yeah, right. That's what Andie said, but isn't that the time when you're supposed to keep your wits about you?" She smacked the pillow on her lap. "Of all people, too. It just had to be Amy and her stuck-up group of friends."

Rose sat on the bed and took Destiny's hand. "Honey, I know this is tough, but the worst thing you can do is hide. It makes people think you're ashamed of who you are."

Tears stung her eyes. "Duh…I am ashamed."

Rose sucked in a tiny breath.

"I didn't mean it that way, Grams."

"I know you didn't, but the truth is, Destiny, you've got to learn to be proud of who you are. Our gift, while not easily understood, is very special and can bring a lot of good to a lot of people."

"I guess."

"Come on," Rose said, patting her leg. "Take your shower, get dressed and come have some breakfast. I've contacted your ghost girl."

Destiny's mouth dropped, and she winced with the pain. Her hand flew up to her chin. Her grandmother had dropped that bomb like it was a tennis ball. "What? Why didn't you tell me?"

"Well, you were…preoccupied." She smiled.

Even though Destiny no longer wanted to help Amy, her curiosity peaked. "So tell me. What's the poop?"

Rose grimaced. "Nice expression. Get ready, and I'll let her tell you herself when we get to the bookstore."

Destiny sighed, allowing her head to fall back against the wall. Her grandmother was right. She'd wallowed enough. There was nothing she could do about having her ability. Destiny just wished the Fates had dealt all these events in tiny doses instead of all at once. She was still having nightmares, she missed her family, and now her secret was all over town. Her life just sucked. But she wasn't doing herself any good by hiding away. As her mother used to always say, "That which does not kill us makes us stronger."

Destiny got ready and joined Rose in the kitchen. Rose handed her a Pop-tart and a white envelope. "This came for you a few days ago."

Destiny took a bite of her breakfast and tore open the flap. It was an invitation to a party at Amy's. There was a handwritten note inside. "I'm sorry. Please come."

She dropped the card.

Rose picked it up. "Well, that's a surprise," she said.

"It sure is. I won't be going, so you can just tear it up and throw it away."

"Aw, Destiny. Maybe this is her way of making amends."

She rolled her eyes. "A phone call would be more appropriate, don't you think? You just don't invite someone to a party. How random is that? I mean, look at me, for cripes sake. She almost broke my nose."

Rose hugged her. "I think you should go. It will give you a chance to show everyone what Destiny Dove is made of."

"I'll pass." She finished her Pop-tart and downed a glass of milk. "You ready to go?"

They arrived at the bookstore and were met by a line of people. The steady stream of customers kept them busy most of the day. At six o'clock, Rose closed the door and flipped the sign to Closed. She took Destiny's hand and pulled her through the red door and up the stairs.

"I've been dying to do this all day," she said, excited.

Still not comfortable with channeling, Destiny didn't have the same amount of enthusiasm, but she was curious about that Shade. "Let's get this over with," she said.

Rose rolled her eyes, and they took their places on the comfy chairs. Shamus wound around Destiny's legs, turning his cat eyes on her. He yowled. She wondered when she'd ever get used to that cat.

"Shamus, go bother someone else," Rose said. "We've got work to do."

The cat gazed at Destiny's grandmother and yowled again. Instead of leaving, he leapt onto the back of Rose's chair and settled in to watch the show.

"Ready?" Rose asked.

Destiny nodded, closed her eyes and cleared her mind. A loud pop prompted her to open her eyes, and shimmering at the center of the room was the burned girl she'd seen in the mirror standing next to Patch and Andie.

We don't have a lot of time," Andie said, speaking to both their minds. *This is Enya, and she wants to tell you her story. We've distracted the demon, but he won't stay that way for long.*

Destiny gasped. It was Judge Frost's daughter. She appeared the same as Destiny had seen her in the mirror, singed stringy hair, skin peeling from her face and eyeless sockets. A shock for sure, but one she'd grown accustomed to. In spite of her appearance, Enya's face still exhibited emotion. Destiny witnessed sadness, fear and perhaps even some hope drift across her severely marred complexion.

"Hello, Enya," Rose said. "How old were you when you died?"

She rotated her head, so her sightless eyes faced Rose. "Sixteen," she said, her voice raspy.

"How did you die, sweetheart?" Rose's voice was kind and gentle.

"A fire," Enya said.

Destiny saw Andie, and then Patch look over their shoulders.

Patch said, "Hurry, Rose, there's not much time."

"Tell me what happened, Enya," Rose said.

Her voice trembled. "I know now that my father wasn't evil. What was in him was." She pointed behind her. "That's a devil. He held me, kept me here. He killed my family, and there is no escape. Please help me. I just want to be free. " She swiveled her head. Her charred mouth twisted into a grimace of fear. "He's coming. He wants another soul. Yours in particular." Enya pointed a charred boney finger at Destiny.

"Don't believe anything he says. He lies."

Before Rose and Destiny could respond to her request, Patch said, "We've got to go!" With a loud pop, all three disappeared.

The atmosphere in the room grew dense and oppressive. Destiny found it hard to breathe. She trembled from Enya's words. Terror gripped her heart, squeezed her chest.

"Destiny, strengthen your shield. Hurry!" Rose grabbed her hand.

Destiny blinked, staring at her grandmother, too terrified to move.

"Destiny, damn it, NOW!"

Rose's harsh words got through. Destiny closed her eyes and concentrated on the white light. Warmth flowed over her, and the pressure began to ease as the extended protection Rose cast covered her.

A growl filled the room, followed by a booming deep voice. "So you want to set her free, do you? How about a trade? Enya's soul for yours, Destiny? I could use someone with your power."

"Shut him out, Destiny," Rose shouted. "Slam the door."

She pushed all her energy at the shield.

"Good," Rose whispered. "He's backing away."

The sound of demonic laughter rang through the room. "We'll meet again," the evil voice stated, then slithered from the room.

Destiny shuddered. Rose held tight to her hand. "Don't relax yet, Destiny. He's still close by. Give him time to go away."

"Did you hear what he said?" Her voice was unsteady.

"I heard. We're going to have to be careful around him. Enya's right. He's very powerful."

Fear crawled up Destiny's spine on little spider legs. "How can we get rid of him?"

"I'll need to do some research. Demons with his strength aren't easy to banish, but it can be done with the correct exorcism."

Disbelief radiated through her. Not more than a few months ago, she was a normal teen with nothing to worry about except what outfit to wear for the day. Now she was demon bait. That was wrong on so many levels.

"He's gone now. You can relax." Rose released her, and Destiny wiggled stiff fingers, the nerves tingling as blood returned to her hand.

"I'm scared, Grams. Let's go home," Destiny said, shivering.

***

Several minutes later, Rose drove into the driveway. Destiny shouted in frustration when she saw Jake's car. He sat on the front porch, an anxious expression on his face.

"Looks like you've got company," Rose said.

"Crap, I don't feel like dealing with this right now."

"Hear him out, Destiny. The boy had the chutzpah to come over here and wait for you. The least you can do is listen to what he has to say."

Destiny sighed. There really was nothing he could say she'd be interested in hearing, but she didn't have much of a choice.

Jake stood as they came up the steps. Rose slipped by him, unlocked the door and went into the house, leaving them alone without uttering any comment about what the neighbors would say.

Destiny sat down in the plastic chair with the crack in it. It pinched her butt, and she swore. Jake sat on the steps. "Here, take mine," he said.

"You're wasting your time, Jake. Just go home."

"Destiny, I know you're upset," he started. "If you'd just answered my calls or responded to my texts, I could've explained."

"I don't want your explanations. Do you have any idea what that felt like?" Destiny paused, lowered her voice and took a deep breath. "Having the one person you trust most in the world blurt your deepest secret out to the one person you didn't want to hear it?" She scrubbed her face with both hands. "You hurt me, Jake."

He glanced at his shoes. "I know I hurt you. And I'm so sorry. It just slipped out. I guess I just got caught up in the excitement. I wanted to help Amy, and in doing that, I hurt you. I'm not proud of that." He lifted his head and held her gaze.

"That kind of secret can't just slip out," she told him. "The entire town will now think I'm a freak. You've ruined my life here in Arcadia. Mothers will sweep their babies out of my way when I walk down the street. 'Here comes the witch,' they'll say."

"Oh, now you're just being melodramatic," Jake said.

A tear slipped down her cheek, and Destiny swiped at it. "Go home, Jake."

"Aw, now don't cry. I feel bad enough as it is. Won't you please accept my apology?"

"Maybe someday, but not now. You were the best friend I had."

"Had? You mean we're not friends anymore?"

Destiny sighed. "Just give me some space for a while. I'm really tired, and I'm going to bed." She stood and put her hand on the screen door.

Jake stood and covered her hand with his. "I'm really sorry, Destiny. I'll try to make it up to you."

"You can't," she said and opened the screen door. The massive pressure in her chest was back, and her head hurt. She wanted to go to bed.

"Are you coming to Amy's party?"

Destiny pivoted and gawked at him. "Are you kidding me?"

Jake stepped back a step. "I guess that's a no?"

"It's a no. Bye, Jake."

Destiny slammed the door in his face.

CHAPTER THIRTY-ONE

Amy studied her reflection in what she'd come to call the Haunted Mirror. She'd applied eye makeup with a heavier hand than normal because tonight was special. Azazul, her new friend from the mirror, encouraged *the* look. Amy wore tight jean shorts and a bikini top enhancing her breasts. Look out, Jake. Tonight she was queen, and everyone at the party would do her bidding. Her laugh echoed through the room with a metallic ring.

The party had been Azazul's idea. Amy's parents had decided on a last-minute trip for the weekend and gave permission for a *small* get-together. Ha! This would be the party of the century. Madam Rose, who'd volunteered to watch over things, couldn't keep up with this one. Amy just wished Destiny was coming. Disappointed, she gazed in the mirror, thinking of a strategy to encourage her attendance. Azazul was right…Destiny must pay for her witchery against Jake. But how to get her to the party…?

In the reflection of the mirror, Amy saw her new mentor standing behind her, his hands on her shoulders, smiling proudly. He wore a white powdered wig and black robe.

"Tonight, you rule, Amy. We will break down the minds of your friends and enlighten them as to your true power. You will soar to heights unimagined with their adoration. Your time to reign has come. You will captivate them, and I will take their souls."

Amy smiled, her reflection filled with admiration. This guy was cool.

"What about Destiny? If she doesn't show up, what do I do?"

"Ah, I'll take care of that," Azazul promised. "She is the ultimate prize, my sweet."

Amy sought his black eyes in the mirror, fighting the stab of jealousy. "What about me?"

His long boney hand squeezed her shoulder. "Patience, little one. You are my queen, remember? She'll fall at your feet and beg your forgiveness for all her transgressions before we're done."

Amy returned the wicked grin from the man in the mirror. "I'm ready."

Azazul patted her shoulder, and Amy's heart swelled with pride. She patted her hair and checked her makeup one last time. Amy observed the whites of her eyes melt into solid obsidian. With a sharp intake of breath, the entity filled Amy's total being. Let the party begin....

***

Destiny stretched out on the sofa and put the book face down on the coffee table. Rose was in her room watching T.V, giving Destiny some much-needed alone time. True to her word, she'd said nothing more about Amy's party. Rose planned to walk up to the house in a few hours to ensure everything remained under control but hadn't mentioned taking Destiny with her. That was just as well. Wild horses couldn't have dragged her there.

Swinging her legs off the couch, she strolled to the kitchen for a snack. Tossing the popcorn bag into the microwave, Destiny pressed the buttons and then turned to the fridge. She grabbed two Cokes, thinking her grandmother would want one, and spun around at the sound of a loud pop. Andie, along with Patch, appeared in the room. Startled, Destiny dropped one of the cans, and it rolled under the kitchen table.

"God, I wish you two had warning bells or something. You scare the crap out of me each time you pop in like that."

Neither one said anything, and Destiny caught Andie's expression, a huge grin splitting her face, eyes shining bright—well, as bright as a Shade's could shine.

"What?" Destiny asked, her heart picking up speed.

Destiny, I have someone who wants to see you, Andie said. Patch, standing next to Andie, stepped aside. The air shimmered, and three glowing forms appeared between Destiny's two Shade friends.

"Oh my God," she breathed. Her parents, along with baby Elijah, stood before her.

"Grams," she shouted. "Get out here quick."

Rose's bedroom door opened, and she shuffled into the room. "What is it, Des—?" She stopped, wide-eyed. "Oh my God!"

"Hello, baby," Destiny's mother said and then turned to Rose. "Mother."

Destiny's stomach clenched, and her eyes filled with tears. She'd wanted this for so long, but now fear of her mother's wrath held her frozen.

"Teresa," Rose said, stepping forward and wiping tears from her face. "You found us."

"Actually, Andie brought us to you. I've been trying to find my way, but I was blocked. Andie showed us the path."

Destiny couldn't hold it in any longer. She blurted, "Mom, I'm so sorry I couldn't get Elijah out of the car. I tried so hard, but I—"

She held up a shimmery hand. "It's okay, baby. I know you tried. As you can see, he's with us, and he's fine." Elijah grinned and waved his pudgy little hand. Destiny waved back.

"But in my nightmares, you were so angry—"

"That was your own guilt attacking you, Destiny. I would never be angry with you for something like that. It's a shame you wasted all that energy blaming yourself. Be free of that now. Move forward in your life, help those who need it, and be happy."

A fresh flood of tears streamed down Destiny's face as that terrible burden of guilt melted away. Her soul flew with the freedom of it.

"Mom," Teresa said to Rose. "I'm carrying my own guilt. I need to apologize to you for keeping your precious grandchildren away from you. After all that's happened, I see how wrong I was. Forgive me?"

"Always," Rose said. "Things could have been so different, but the Fates have a way of working it out. I'll take good care of Destiny. I'll raise her well. She's coming into her power with true style and grace."

Destiny's mother laughed. "Something I refused to do."

Rose just smiled.

Destiny's father, always a man of few words, spoke, "Destiny, we love you and will always be watching over you. Find comfort in that and live your life to its fullest potential. Kick some butt out there, baby."

Destiny laughed through her tears. "I love you, Daddy. I love you too, Baby Bro'."

Elijah stood on his wobbly toddler legs. "Wub you, De ne ne."

Swiping at her eyes with the tail of her shirt, Destiny hiccupped. She would miss them, but at least now she knew they were safe, and her guilt had been eased. She could move on.

A pounding on the door interrupted the reunion. Jake's desperate voice called from outside, "Destiny! Madame Rose! I need your help. Please."

Rose hustled to the door, letting Jake in.

"Something bad's happening at Amy's. You need to come. She's gone completely whacko. It's like…like…something's possessing her. I don't know what to do. Some kids have already been hurt." He gasped for breath and pivoted toward me. "Please come. Destiny, she's asking for you specifically."

Andie cursed, and Destiny flinched.

I told him not to go over there.

She swung around and mouthed, "Not now."

Rose faced her granddaughter, "Destiny, you may not feel ready for this, but it's time we sent this demon back to Hell. He's targeting you, so you'll need to be strong. Can you do this?"

Fear froze the blood in Destiny's veins. She wasn't ready.

Teresa spoke up, "I'll come with you. I can help."

Destiny whipped around and stared at the apparition of her mother.

"Whoa," Jake said from the door. "What's that?"

"Not now, Jake," Rose said.

Teresa tilted her head at her daughter. "You ready?"

Destiny nodded and turned to Rose. "Let's do this."

They ran to Amy's as fast as Rose could go. When they entered the foyer, shock bolted through Destiny's system. Two teens were face down on the floor, blood seeping from gashes too numerous to count. Furniture hung suspended in mid-air while other objects flew of their own accord, smashing against the wall. Broken glass swirled through the air, and there, in the center of it all, floated Amy. She resembled a comic book heroine in her black shorts and bikini top, blonde hair whipping about her face, arms outstretched. Her eyes were terrifying, solid black orbs. Anger twisted her features.

Her head rotated toward Destiny, and when she spoke, her voice was dark and deep. "Ah, Destiny…nice of you to join us. I see you've come to pay your debt."

Rose grabbed her hand. "Don't confront him…block your fear."

Destiny swallowed. Easy for her to say…she was scared brainless.

"Cast your shield, Destiny," Rose shouted above the din. "It's time to send this devil back to Hell."

A demonic laugh vibrated the room. "And you old woman," Amy said. "What do you think you can do? What power do you even suspect you hold over me?"

"Jake, get these kids out of here and call 911. We'll take care of the rest."

Jake hustled the kids crouched on the floor toward the door, but just as they reached it, Amy thrust her hand, slamming it shut.

"No one leaves," she commanded.

"It's time, Destiny," Rose said.

Destiny closed her eyes and pushed her energy forth. She felt the surge of Rose's power, plus something else…another crackling of power settled in with hers. Rose held Destiny's right hand, and something cool slipped into her left.

"I'm with you, Destiny," her mother said. "We'll fight this evil together."

"But Mom…."

"I've always had the power; I just chose to turn my back on it. I see how wrong that was now. Concentrate, do everything your grandmother tells you."

"Destiny, extend your shield over Jake. Block Amy's power so they can escape."

"I don't know how," she shouted.

"Think about tossing a blanket over him."

Destiny imagined the picture of a huge blanket floating over the kids near the door and watched it settle over them in her mind's eye. It worked. The sound of the door creaking open confirmed her success.

"Go, Jake, get them out," Destiny called to him.

"NO!" Amy shouted. "You can't do this!"

"Who are you?" Rose asked the demon. "What is your name?"

Destiny opened her eyes but kept her thoughts one hundred percent focused on her energy. At that moment, she wished fervently that she had kept them closed. Amy's face distorted and became the face of a many-horned demon with wickedly sharp teeth. Her voice grew deeper and more menacing. "You need not know my name, woman."

"I command you, in the name of Jesus Christ, tell me your name," Rose shouted.

"What's the big deal about the name?" Destiny hissed. "Let's just zap the dude."

Rose rolled her eyes. "When you know a demon's name, you have power over him. Now hush and let me work."

"Your name, Demon," Rose commanded.

Amy jerked, and her head rolled toward Rose. "I am Azazul. This is my domain. I control all who enter here."

"You don't control crap," Rose shouted.

Destiny was impressed. She had never heard her grandmother sound so tough.

"In the name of Christ Jesus, I command you to leave this home and go back to hell where you belong."

A surge of power rushed against the combined shield of the three women. Azazul pushed hard at Destiny's mind. Closing her eyes, she slammed her will against him. With her energy drained, Destiny realized she hadn't been prepared for the strain of demon-fighting.

"Hold fast, Destiny," her grandmother encouraged. "I feel him weakening."

A roar that rattled the windows issued forth from Amy's mouth. Intense, angry energy pounded the three women. A loud crack sounded above Destiny, and she opened her eyes, raising her face to the ceiling. The chandelier ripped from its mounting bolts and fell. Destiny dove to get out of the way, breaking the hold with her mother and Rose. She hit the floor, and before she could scramble to safety, Azazul struck. An orange bolt of power blasted Destiny into the foyer, where she collided with the wall. Pain sizzled through every nerve, ending like she'd been zapped with an intense tazer.

"Destiny, come back," Rose called. "We can't do this without you."

A mocking voice repeated Rose's words and then laughed. Destiny watched as a swirl of black smoke left Amy's body, dropping her to the table with a solid thud. The ebony tornado swirled straight for her.

"Destiny, move! Now!" her mother screamed. "Grab our hands."

They moved closer, but the demon blocked her path. Destiny's head pounded with pain as Azazul attempted to force possession. Fortifying her shield, Destiny forced herself to her feet, legs wobbling.

"Destiny," Jake shouted, returning from outside. He rushed to her side.

"Get out of here," she said. "That thing will kill you."

"Jake, push Destiny toward me, then get whatever you need from the garage to burn that furniture." Rose reached out with her hand. "It's the only way. Now that the demon and Enya are both free of the furniture, we can destroy the only haven they have. Hurry."

Destiny noticed a gathering of darker mist at the center of the tornado, and instinct told her Jake was in danger. Drawing from an inner strength she didn't know she possessed, Destiny shoved the white light forth and blasted Azazul out of the way. Jake shoved Destiny toward Rose's outstretched palm. The three women clasped hands, and immediately, Destiny's energy surged.

"By the power of three, and in the name of Jesus Christ, I command you to leave this realm." Rose surged her power, and Destiny soared with her. Her hair stood on end, strength filling her body. She cast a shield over Jake as he scuttled to the garage. He returned seconds later with a gas can and a grill lighter. He dashed up the stairs taking them two at a time. The mist trapped in the bright light morphed into a hideous demonic form, with horns and hooves, savage teeth and burning scarlet eyes. It screamed and writhed. "No! No!"

The odor of gasoline and smoke filled the room. Jake had succeeded. He rushed out the front door.

"It's time to end this," Rose shouted. "On the count of three, give me everything you've got! One...Two... Three!"

The power rushed forth from the three women, and the explosion rocked the house. Destiny landed on her butt next to her grandmother, who was unconscious. Destiny screamed for Jake even as she hauled Rose to the front door. Flames now licked the ceiling as the furniture in Amy's room burned.

Jake rushed through the door.

"Get Amy," Destiny shouted as she maneuvered her grandmother out the door and down the porch steps. She was heavy for such a small woman. Panting, Destiny glanced up and saw Jake carrying Amy in his arms.

They'd just moved a safe distance from the house when a second explosion sent flaming debris blazing into the yard. Fortunately, everyone was out of range. Destiny held Rose's head in her lap and watched the house burn.

Through the flames, a golden light drifted upward and out of the house. Destiny recognized the apparition of Enya, looking nothing like the charred girl she'd seen before. Her beautiful ethereal face now had crystal blue eyes, clear skin and a head full of brown locks. Her gaze captured Destiny's, filling her with warmth and happiness.

She mouthed, "Thank you."

Grinning, Destiny inclined her head. Enya disappeared in the soft afterglow of the Great Beyond.

CHAPTER THIRTY-TWO

After a few days in the local hospital, Destiny's life returned somewhat to normal. Her parents and Elijah had crossed over to the Great Beyond, the nightmares were gone, and Rose was safely recovering in her room. That beautiful farmhouse Destiny had admired so much did not fare so well. The firefighters were unable to save it, and the place burned to the ground. But Destiny, her grandmother, and her mom had kicked some serious demon butt.

Destiny lay on the couch recovering from the burns she'd received, courtesy of Azazul, on her chest and arms. The hospital had treated and released her, and now she watched Jake search for the new puppy he'd brought over in apology for his recent snafu.

He squeezed beneath the coffee table, reaching for the dog. The tiny Yorkshire Terrier, named Angel, yipped and scrambled under the sofa. "Crap. Where'd she go?"

Destiny laughed, gripping her chest. "Stop it, Jake. You're making my chest hurt. She's under the couch."

Wow, what a couple of wild days, Andie commented in Destiny's mind, grinning at her brother from her perch on the coffee table.

Destiny nodded. "I never did get to thank you for finding my parents."

"What?" Jake said, not realizing Destiny had spoken to Andie. His head popped up on the other side of the sofa, the squirming pup in his arms. He handed Angel to Destiny, where the dog circled her lap and promptly settled down for a nap.

Destiny rubbed the little ears. "I can't wait to see what Shamus thinks of you."

Jake snorted. "Yeah, I'd keep them separated till the squirt there has gained some poundage."

Destiny laughed again, then winced, pressing her hand to her chest.

"Who were you—?" Jake's head whipped around. "Hey, is Andie here?"

"Yep," Destiny confirmed. "Hey, I owe you a thank you too. You were a true hero."

"Aw." Jake actually blushed. "It was nothing. I'm just glad Amy's going to be okay, and it's all over."

"How is she?" Destiny smoothed the light afghan over her legs.

"Very shaken up, as you might imagine. I found out today that Dr. Morgan got a job offer up in Pennsylvania to start a new trauma center up there. I think he's going to take it. With all that's happened, I think he feels they need a new start."

Destiny watched his expression. He lowered his lids and frowned.

"You'll miss Amy, won't you?"

Jake nodded. "I will, but the more I've thought about it, the more I feel she wasn't right for me."

Thank God.

"Andie," Destiny chided.

"What did she say? I told you so?"

She chuckled. "In so many words."

"This will sure be one summer we don't forget for a long time. Let's hope the school year is completely uneventful." Jake stretched his long legs out in front of him.

A knock rattled the door, and Jake rose to answer it. "Hi, Dr. Morgan. Come on in."

"Hi, Jake. I just stopped by to check on Rose and Destiny."

Dr. Morgan stepped into the small mobile home. Rose, hearing the knock, came shuffling slowly down the hall.

"Hi, Jeff," she said. "What brings you by?"

"Hi, Rose. Come sit. I'd like to see how you're doing."

Rose smiled at Destiny, lowering into her rocker. Dr. Morgan balanced his butt on the coffee table right on top of Andie. Destiny stifled a giggle as Andie rolled her eyes and faded away.

"Rose," Jeff Morgan started, leaning toward her. "I need to talk to you about something."

"Okay. What's up?"

He sighed. "I've been offered a job in Pennsylvania to head up a new trauma center. I think the move will do Amy and Sarah good. That gas fire and Amy's sudden illness really gave us a lot to think about, and I think we need to be in a more urban environment where we have access to more of what Amy needs as she recovers."

Never mentioning the true events of the past months, Dr. Morgan preferred to put his own spin on what happened. He never referred to the event as a possession or a haunting. The Morgans chose a more practical approach to the truth—Amy's mental illness. Jake told Destiny that Amy had seen a counselor for the trauma. He wasn't sure she'd ever be the same. In a way, Destiny felt sorry for the girl. Amy had never been nice, but she hadn't deserved what happened either.

Rose took Jeff's hand in sympathy. "We'll miss you and your family."

"I'll miss you too. I want to say I'm really sorry about the house. We'll do our best to make it up to you."

Destiny sat up, wincing from the tug of the bandages on the burns. What had he said?

"No need. It was insured. I'll just build another one. Probably not so big as that one."

"Grams, what is he talking about?"

Jeff Morgan turned to Destiny. "I just feel terrible about what happened to the house we were renting from your grandmother. It was the family estate. Now…."

Family estate? Confusion bounced around Destiny's head. What was he talking about?

"Destiny, I'll explain it all later, but the short version is I own this entire estate. The house, the barn, the horses, all of it."

Destiny's mouth dropped open. If her grandmother owned the entire farm, then why had they lived in this cracker box trailer like paupers? She glanced over at Jake. He seemed as surprised as she was.

"Well, if you're sure, Rose?" Dr. Morgan raised his eyebrows.

Rose nodded. "I'm sure. You go take care of your family."

"Thank you. Jake, you need a ride back into town?"

"No, sir, I have my car, but I'd like to come by and talk to Amy. When are you leaving for Pennsylvania?"

"Probably tomorrow. No sense waiting around here. I'm sure she'd like to see you and say goodbye."

Dr. Morgan and Jake went to the door. Jake winked at Destiny. "I'll see ya later," he said.

She smiled and nodded.

When they closed the door, and the sound of car tires on the gravel receded, Destiny said to her grandmother, "Were you ever planning on telling me?"

Rose rocked a little, and then eyed her granddaughter. "Eventually. You see, Destiny, it's not all about money. It's about what you do with the gifts in life that you've been given."

Destiny understood.

Life was full of surprises, some good, some bad. And with her gift…who knew?

About the Author

Kelly is an international bestselling author. She writes in multiple genres, including thrillers, romance, young adult and action-adventure, and promising characters with Passion, Power, and Purpose. She also spends a great deal of time helping other writers through teaching workshops and with her Writing Tips on her website. She is also a Florida Writer's Association member and has served as a judge for their statewide contests. She is available to book for appearances and workshops. Just contact her through her webpage.

When not writing, Kelly enjoys spending time with her husband of 30+ years and her two college-age children when they find the time. She lives in Florida and enjoys all that living in the Sunshine State brings - boating, fishing, beaches, theme parks, and more. Her favorite pass time is reading (what a surprise!) She likes Thrillers, Romantic Suspense, and Romantic Comedy.

Stop by and visit her website for current events
www.kellyabell.com

Made in the USA
Middletown, DE
11 August 2022

71122285R00139